# A PRAYER FOR THE DEVIL

✝

## DALE ALLAN

EMERALD
BOOK CO.

This book is a work of fiction. Names, characters, businesses, organizations, places, events, and incidents are either a product of the author's imagination or are used fictitiously. Any resemblance to actual persons, living or dead, events, or locales is entirely coincidental.

Published by Emerald Book Company
Austin, TX
www.emeraldbookcompany.com

Distributed by Emerald Book Company

For ordering information or special discounts for bulk purchases, please contact Emerald Book Company at PO Box 91869, Austin, TX 78709, 512.891.6100.

Design and composition by Greenleaf Book Group LLC
Cover design by Greenleaf Book Group LLC
Cover Photo © iStockphoto/franckreporter

Publisher's Cataloging-In-Publication Data
(Prepared by The Donohue Group, Inc.)
Allan, Dale.
    A prayer for the devil / Dale Allan. -- 1st ed.
    p. ; cm.
    ISBN: 978-1-937110-34-5
    1. Twin brothers--United States--Fiction. 2. Priests--United States--Fiction. 3. Faith--Fiction. 4. Murder--Investigation--Fiction. 5. Presidents--United States--Elections--Fiction. 6. Revenge--Fiction. 7. Political fiction. 8. Mystery fiction. I. Title.
PS3601.L52 P72 2012
813.6                              2012935750

Part of the Tree Neutral® program, which offsets the number of trees consumed in the production and printing of this book by taking proactive steps, such as planting trees in direct proportion to the number of trees used: www.treeneutral.com

Printed in the United States of America on acid-free paper

12 13 14 15 16 17   10 9 8 7 6 5 4 3 2 1

First Edition

*For Dad*

# PROLOGUE

*"No one can confidently say that he will still be living tomorrow."*
—Euripides

**A HUGE CROWD OF EXCITED BOSTONIANS** applauds wildly in anticipation of seeing the hometown hero. The spectators stand shoulder to shoulder for as far as the eye can see, despite the heavy rain. Mayor Steven Westfield stands at the podium in the center of windswept Boston Common and waves his arms, trying to quiet the audience. After several fruitless attempts, he decides to speak over the roar of the people.

"I'm so proud to be part of this historic event!" he shouts. The crowd silences. "After the November elections, Massachusetts will have produced another president of the United States!"

*(Standing applause.)*

"Although our state is forty-fourth in size, we are third when it comes to producing presidents: John Adams, John Quincy Adams, John Kennedy, and George Bush Sr." He turns and points behind him. "And now, Brad Thompson!"

*(Standing ovation)*

Brad Thompson walks confidently to the podium and shakes the mayor's hand. His infectious smile and good looks captivate the cheering onlookers. A Secret Service agent flanks him, holding an umbrella. Thompson whispers something in his ear, and the agent walks to the back of the stage and sits down, leaving Thompson in the rain. This excites the crowd even more. He cries out, "If all of you are willing to stand in the rain to see me, why shouldn't I do the same?"

He then continues, "The biggest problem with our government is that today's political figures live under an umbrella of secret deals, corruption, entitlements, and special-interest giveaways. It's a sad day for America when our children no longer say the Pledge of Allegiance in our schools, but the chairman of the Ways and Means Committee, who oversees our tax laws, gets away without paying taxes!"

*(Deafening applause)*

"It's a sad day for America when a second-grader from New Jersey can be suspended from school for drawing a picture of a stick figure shooting a gun, but illegal immigrants with real guns can't be asked for proof of citizenship.

"It's a sad day in America when your hard-earned tax dollars are sent to faraway countries only to be squandered by corrupt leaders while children right here in the U.S. go to bed hungry.

"It's a sad day for America when senators take bribes and hide cash in their freezers while our elderly citizens go to bed freezing cold because they can't afford heating fuel."

*(Unrelenting applause)*

Thompson whips back his thick, black, rain-soaked hair and continues to speak over the noise of the crowd. "Many of the congressmen and senators serving today would be petrified to stand where I am." He points to the sky. "Based on their unscrupulous behavior and abandonment of God's values, they would probably be struck by lightning!"

*(Screaming, whistles, and applause)*

Thompson waves his arms and the crowd quiets. "I would be remiss if I didn't acknowledge several key individuals here with me today. First of all, my lovely wife, Jordan, whose undying support means so much to me." She stands and waves to the adoring crowd. "Next, my dedicated lawyer and campaign manager, Aaron Miller. Aaron's commitment and unparalleled work ethic inspires me every single day." Miller stands, smiles, and waves. "My pastor, Frank Fatone, who baptized me right here in Boston." With the crowd now standing and applauding, Thompson turns around and motions to a woman dressed in traditional Muslim attire. As Ablaa Raboud stands in anticipation of being introduced to the large crowd, there's a powerful, ground-shaking explosion. The entire stage erupts in a ball of fire as bodies are propelled high into the air. While most of the news reporters run for cover, a few battle-hardened veterans run toward the blast to get a closer look. The sight of carnage fills the television airwaves as the smell of death lingers in the wet Boston air.

A cold shiver interrupts the solitude of Luke Miller's prayer session in the empty, candlelit chapel of Saint Leonard's Church. As Luke tries to refocus, his attention is drawn to the squeaking of the large wooden door at the back of the room as it begins to open. Light pours into the small, dimly lit chamber, causing him to cover his unadjusted eyes in an attempt to see. Monsignor Swiger appears out of the blinding light and walks slowly to the front of the room as the door closes behind him. Still kneeling, with his arms extended out to his sides, Luke looks up as the monsignor kneels down in front of him and places his hand on his shoulder. "Father Luke, I'm so sorry to tell you this, but I have terrible news." Luke looks up, but he doesn't respond. "There's been a horrific explosion at the Common; all indications are that your brother Aaron and Father Fatone have been killed." Luke's deep blue eyes fill with tears, but he remains speechless. Swiger places his other hand on Luke's empty shoulder as he recites Psalm 23: *Even though I walk through the valley of the shadow of death, I fear no evil, for You are with me; Your rod and Your staff, they comfort me ...*

# PART I

*"God didn't promise days without pain, laughter without sorrow, or sun without rain, but He did promise strength for the day, comfort for the tears, and light for the way. If God brings you to it, He will bring you through it."*
—Unknown

**1**

**LUKE MILLER GAZED THROUGH** the dirty window as he drove his outdated pickup truck past the police officer stationed in front of his parents' house. As he searched the crowded Boston street for a place to park, he noticed his mother pacing in the front yard as she awaited his arrival. He parked the truck and took out his cell phone to dial his brother's number. In the past twenty-four hours he had called this number more than fifteen times just to hear his deceased brother's voice. Whenever he felt that he needed strength, he listened to Aaron's voice mail message. Putting the phone down on the seat, he took a deep breath and got out of the truck.

They met on the lawn. She hugged him as tears flowed down their heartbroken faces. "Mom, I'm so sorry." That was all he could say before his voice cracked and he began to sob. She held him tight and tried to comfort him, just as she had so many times in this modest house when he was growing up. Releasing her grasp, she placed her soft hands on either side of his unshaven face. "Try to be patient with your father. Please, Luke, understand that he is in a great deal of pain." He nodded as she reached up and removed the white linen Roman collar from his shirt while pulling him down to place a black kippah on his head. "Luke, just for today, don't be a Catholic, be a Jew. Please, just for today."

Luke's mother was a lifelong Catholic. When her boys were born, however, their father insisted that they be raised in the Jewish faith. She never fully agreed with this decision, but like many women of her generation, she reluctantly surrendered to his demand. When the children were born, she insisted that she pick one of the names. She chose Luke, a person that many theologians believe was the only Gentile to write portions of the New Testament. She was secretly happy and proud when, to his father's chagrin, Luke converted to Christianity in high school. Even more surprising was his decision to enter the priesthood. Family members often wondered if this was a true religious conversion or just a way to embarrass his overbearing father.

When his father realized that Luke was going to give up a University of Massachusetts baseball scholarship in order to enter the seminary, he disowned him. To many in Boston, baseball is the only religion. As much as Luke tried to make him understand, their relationship would never recover. Over the past several years they had become somewhat civil to each other, but unspoken tension still existed.

Luke entered the small, well-maintained house and immediately saw his father sitting in the dark at the kitchen table. As Luke walked across the familiar wooden floors, his dad stood and raised his arms to greet his only living child. This affectionate welcome completely surprised Luke, who quickened his pace to embrace his heartbroken father. For the first time in his life, Luke saw, heard, and felt his father cry as he wept in his strong arms. After a few undisturbed moments, he felt his mother's embrace as she joined them.

Several heart-wrenching minutes later, Luke heard a soft knock on the screen door as the limousine driver discreetly tried to get their attention. "I'm sorry for interrupting, Mr. Miller, but there's a lot of traffic and I wouldn't want you to be late for the service." Within minutes, they were sitting in the back of a black limo, on their way to the funeral with only one stop to make along the way. Not a word was said until they pulled up to Aaron's house in the exclusive suburb of Newton. "Wait here. I'll go get her," Luke mumbled dolefully, as the limo pulled through the open metal gates. As he exited the car and began walking up the long stone path toward the imposing house, the front door opened and Deborah appeared. Before leaving, she turned to say a few words to the live-in housekeeper, who held Alessa in one arm and Abel by the hand. As Luke walked to meet her, he heard Alessa yell out, "There's Daddy!" and he watched as Deborah crumbled to her knees in agony on the hard walkway.

**2**

**AS A PRIEST, LUKE** had attended and presided over many funerals, doing his best to comfort the grieving families. For the first time in his life, he finally realized the depth of their distress. Now he was the one wracked with despair, and he wondered how he could ever recover. As he watched his elderly father struggle to pick up the shovel and stumble as he threw dirt into the burial hole, Luke questioned his faith. How could God allow these innocent people to die? How could someone exist who was depraved enough to not only want to kill innocent people but also to kill them in such a horrific way? The more he kept envisioning Aaron's body being blown apart, the more he felt anger and rage well up inside of him. These were unfamiliar feelings for a priest.

On the third day of Shiva, Luke had to excuse himself to go back to his parish. At the request of the Diocese of Boston and the Thompson family, he had reluctantly agreed to preside over the funeral of Brad Thompson and his wife, Jordan. His mother understood, while his father just shook his head.

As Luke donned his vestments, he could hear the sounds of police cars and the crowds lining the streets. This event had captivated the nation and was newsworthy throughout the world. Nearly every priest from the diocese would attend this funeral, along with the country's most powerful politicians, businesspeople, and community leaders, with one notable exception: the president of the United States, who was traveling abroad. Over the past two days, the parish had been besieged by requests for interviews, most of the reporters wanting to talk with Luke.

Earlier in the day, Luke had called Brad Thompson's mother to express his condolences and to see if she had anything specific that she wanted him to say about her son. She spent most of the conversation telling Luke how sorry she was that his brother was murdered, while deflecting the attention away from her own grief. After hanging up the phone, Luke thought that she would have been a great person to meet under different circumstances. Maybe he should have tried to get to know Aaron's friends and business partners before passing judgment on them.

It had been more than a year ago when Aaron's law firm was contracted to represent a wealthy investor who wanted to redevelop part of the waterfront in suburban Boston. Unfortunately, this project would require that several elderly citizens be ousted from their homes, and it would destroy the neighborhood homeless shelter where Luke volunteered. Local politicians got involved and created an ad campaign promoting the development, touting the benefits of increased tax revenue and tourism. When Luke saw the news reports, he led the vocal opposition to their plan. Soon, the press figured out that Luke's brother's firm was involved in the project, and the unwanted publicity caused by the hometown priest destroyed the deal. After a heated argument regarding the virtues of eminent domain, the brothers stopped talking to each other. Luke would regret that day for the rest of his life.

Walking to the altar in the overcrowded church, Luke looked out at the sea of mourners. He recognized many famous faces sitting beside some everyday parishioners. Noticing the commotion when the audience saw his face for the first time, Luke addressed the confused crowd, saying, "For those of you who may not know me, I'm Luke Miller, Aaron Miller's identical twin brother."

---

Even though Luke had only met Brad and Jordan Thompson on a few occasions, he did an honorable job describing their love for each other and their lifelong commitment to helping the less fortunate. Luke's crystal clear voice, exceptional looks, and the unique way he prayed, with his hands fully extended out to his sides, made him a compelling figure on the altar. By the time the service ended, everyone was in tears. Just as he did each time he celebrated mass, Luke stood at the back of the church and shook everyone's hand as they left. His smile widened as Rebecca Bruno and her husband, Sal, the very last people in the church, approached.

Rebecca, an elegant Italian woman in her sixties, attended mass almost every day. Ever since Luke had arrived at the parish three years before, she made sure to attend all of the masses that he presided over. When the church wouldn't release the priests' schedules in advance, Sal got involved. Rumored to be a tough businessman with ties to the mob, Sal was a man of few words. After a meeting with Monsignor Swiger to "discuss the issue," the mass schedule was published in the church bulletin the following week.

Luke kissed Rebecca on both cheeks. She took his hand in hers. "Luke, I can't tell you how sorry I am to hear about your brother."

She turned and looked at Sal. "We are both heartbroken for your loss." Sal extended his calloused hand and shook Luke's firmly without saying a word. She continued, "We know you have to get to the cemetery, so we won't hold you, but if you need anything, please call." Luke thanked both of them sincerely and headed toward the door. Before he could exit, Luke was startled to hear Sal's words echo in the empty sanctuary. "Hey, Father Miller, if you need anything, call me. I've got connections."

**3**

**LUKE STAYED AT HIS** parents' house for the next four days. His presence seemed to help his father cope with the loss of Aaron. Luke wondered if his physical appearance was helping his dad forget the fact that his brother was gone. He worried that once they returned to their normal routines, his dad would really begin the grieving process. Over the past several days, many people who saw Luke had called him Aaron. This was not surprising, since it had happened to him his entire life, but now it took on an entirely different meaning. Aaron's small children hadn't yet reached the age where they could distinguish the twin brothers, making encounters with Alessa and Abel especially heartbreaking.

The longer Luke watched his parents grieve, the angrier he became. During Shiva, he heard several well-intentioned relatives say, "I would like to kill the SOB responsible for this," or "That Muslim lady is to blame for all of this." Luke had studied the grieving process as part of his vocation, so he understood that when the death was a homicide, many of the traditional grieving stages were bypassed as people close to the victim often focused on revenge. He was beginning to think that he was no different. As much as he tried to fight it, he felt himself relating more to the Old Testament than to the New. For the first time since high school, he felt more like a Jew than a Christian.

With Shiva ending, there were important decisions to be made. The local police department would be ending their surveillance at Luke's parents' house. The press and paparazzi were waiting to pounce. There had already been several front-page articles published in the *Boston Globe* detailing the troubles between the now-famous twin brothers. The media began calling Luke the "Movie Star Priest," based on his undeniable good looks, and reporters interviewed old girlfriends and teammates from high school and anyone else who would give them something controversial to print.

At a family meeting it was decided that everyone should temporarily move into Aaron's house because of the excellent security the gated property offered, and because Deborah had already hired a private armed guard service to patrol the grounds. The enormity of the house would ensure that everyone still had their privacy. Luke was surprised when it became apparent that they expected him to stay with them too. Again, he felt that his physical appearance was only delaying the reality of the situation not only for his parents but for Deb and the children as well. Yet, as much as he didn't want to move in with them, he felt that Aaron would want him there, so he reluctantly agreed to see if he would be permitted to take a leave of absence from his parish duties.

Knowing how busy most priests' daily schedules were, Luke called ahead to arrange an appointment with his boss, Monsignor Swiger. After a few minutes on hold with the church secretary, he was surprised when told that the monsignor would meet with him in an hour. Luke showered, shaved, and dressed hurriedly in his black clerical garb.

As Luke was leaving, his father insisted that he promise to meet them at Aaron's house for dinner. Luke said good-bye, kissed his mother and father, and headed out the door. After several attempts, his old truck finally started and he was on his way to Saint Leonard's parish in Boston's North End. Pulling into the parking lot, he dialed Aaron's cell number, listened, sighed heavily, and made his way toward the rectory office. Before he could reach the front door, he saw a reporter jump out of a car and hurry to intercept him. Luke put his head down and ignored the man's questions. When Luke reached the rectory door, the man gave up and walked back to his parked car.

What most people didn't understand was that running a parish was similar to running any successful business. In today's churches, there are schedules to meet, bills to pay, and paychecks to issue. Luke understood that his request for an extended leave would place a burden on the other priests and employees of the church. Before entering the building, he hoped that God would understand if he needed to be selfish at this critical time in his life.

Luke peered around the partially opened door of the simple office. Looking up from his notes, Monsignor Swiger immediately stood and waved him inside. They met halfway, and Luke collapsed in the kind old man's arms. "Luke, I'm so sorry for what you've been going through," the monsignor murmured. Once Luke composed himself, they separated and sat at opposite ends of a small antiquated table.

"Thank you so much for taking the time to see me today," Luke said.

Seeing Luke's pain, the monsignor asked softly, "How's your family?"

Luke described their difficulty in dealing with the loss of Aaron but never mentioned the inner turmoil he himself was feeling. The monsignor pulled a stack of newspapers from his desk and placed them on the table in front of Luke, pointing at them. "I'm worried about you."

Luke didn't have to look down to see what the headlines said. Not knowing how to respond, he replied wearily, "With God's help I'll work my way through this. I just need a little time away."

Swiger agreed to a leave of absence, though he felt compelled to gently remind Luke of his responsibilities before he left. "OK, take some time, but please remember that we are shorthanded and we need you here with us. The community needs you, the parish needs you, and I need you. Luke, you know that this life we've chosen is not an easy one, and God asks us to make very difficult sacrifices every day. Some of our brothers have even given their lives in the service of God. We have been given an easy path compared to others; remember this and please return as soon as possible."

Luke thought carefully for several long seconds before answering respectfully. "I've also suffered while serving God. Please don't forget that before being assigned to your parish, I spent almost four years in Johannesburg where three of my fellow priests, all close friends, were murdered in one week. One of them, Father James, died in my arms."

"Luke, I know that you have suffered a tremendous amount for your faith, especially for a man of your young age. But there is so much more you can do. Even though your tragedy has affected all of our lives and broken our hearts, it can be used to bring people to God. Since you've been at our parish, attendance has risen by over thirty percent. People want to see you preach, God wants you to preach, and I want you to preach. You have done, and can continue to do, great things for God. Just promise me that you'll pray on this and return as soon as you can."

Standing, Luke looked at his superior and said firmly, "Believe me, I've already prayed on it, and I'm doing what's best for my family. I'll check in with you every few weeks, and I promise that I'll return as soon as my family can accept my absence." Luke turned and walked out the door. As he reached the lobby and began to exit, the parish secretary yelled, "Wait, Father." Thinking that the monsignor wanted to see him again, Luke turned impatiently, trying to think of what more he could say. She stood and handed him a small note.

"A man from an insurance company who says he was friends with your brother stopped by to see you. He asked me to give you his number and said it's important. You might want to call him when you have a few minutes. He seemed sincere."

Luke thanked her and put the note in his pocket. As he opened the door to leave, a horde of paparazzi ambushed him and began yelling questions while taking pictures. Lightbulbs flashed in his face, but again, Luke put his head down and quickly ran to his truck. When they blocked the front of his truck and pounded on the hood so he couldn't leave, he rolled down his window and yelled, "Please, leave me alone." He yanked the gearshift into reverse and quickly backed up, then violently gunned it forward, swerving to avoid hitting them. Emotionally drained, he picked up his cell phone and called his brother's voice mail.

## 4

**REALIZING THAT HE WAS** being followed, Luke quickly headed toward the sanctuary of Aaron's mansion. Once the press saw the gates open and the private security guard wave Luke in, they knew they had no chance of getting to him, but they were content to sit in their cars on the quiet street and wait for the next opportunity. Before Luke could get out of his truck, his dad opened the front door and walked to the driveway to meet him. Again, he hugged Luke tight, saying, "Thank you for coming back." As they walked toward the house, Luke noticed Deborah and the children waiting at the front door. Luke knew that Deb was trying, with little success, to make them understand that he wasn't their father.

While they ate dinner, the house phone rang continuously. Deborah had stopped answering it days ago because she was sick of reliving the incident. But when her cell phone rang, she rushed to see who was calling. She answered cautiously, "Is something wrong?" Luke stood and walked over to her. She handed him the phone. He listened for a minute before saying, "I'll meet you in the driveway."

He walked out the front door and saw a tall, heavyset, imposing figure heading toward him. As he approached, Luke extended his hand. "Luke Miller. Nice to meet you, Detective."

Shaking his hand firmly, Robert Romo said, "I wish we were meeting under different circumstances, Father Miller."

Luke forced a smile. "Me too."

"I'm sorry to bother you, but it's been several days since the tragedy and we really need to ask you and your family some questions."

Looking him directly in the eyes, Luke responded sharply. "Not here. You can talk to me and Deborah but not my parents or the children."

"I understand, Father." Romo handed Luke a business card. "Why don't you come to police headquarters tomorrow morning at ten o'clock? The address is on the card. I'll do my best to ensure that your parents and the children are left alone."

Luke thanked him, placed the card in his wallet, and walked back into the house just as the cook was serving the main course. He sat, said grace to himself, and tried to eat his meal, but he merely pushed the food around on his plate, while eating just enough to sustain himself. After dinner, he pulled Deborah aside to let her know that they needed to talk to the detective tomorrow. She agreed to be questioned as long as Luke stayed with her, and he willingly concurred.

Luke woke to the sound of the in-ground sprinkler hitting the gutter downspout outside his window. Looking at the clock on the nightstand, he saw that it was 6:20 a.m. His surroundings were unfamiliar, not because he hadn't been in Aaron's house many times before, but because he wasn't used to living such a luxurious lifestyle. The king-size bed was twice as big as anything he had ever slept in. The private bath attached to his room was larger than his entire bedroom at the rectory. The fireplace, ornate columns, coffered ceiling, hardwood floors, and Persian rugs would have impressed most people, but for Luke, they just added to the discomfort of an already uncomfortable situation.

Trying to relieve some stress, Luke quietly made his way toward the gym in the basement. As he passed Deborah's bedroom, he looked through the half-open door and noticed Alessa and Abel in bed with her. Continuing down the long hallway to the stairway and into the workout area, he thought about the time he and Aaron had spent together in high school. They were both outstanding athletes. Luke was the pitcher on the baseball team and Aaron was the catcher. Both all-stars, they were highly recruited by colleges during their senior year. Luke turned down a full-ride scholarship to UMass, while Aaron attended Boston College and went on to law school at Harvard. During construction of the Newton mansion, Luke and Aaron would often meet at the property to discuss progress with the architectural teams, but what they looked forward to most was playing catch in the expansive yard. It was during one of these meetings that they decided to build the gym.

This was no ordinary gym; it rivaled any college gymnasium. The footprint of the house was tremendous, and the gym encompassed the entire lower level, with a full wall of glass doors that opened to the backyard. Looking around the room, Luke was touched to see that Aaron hadn't removed any of the baseball pictures or newspaper articles from their high school days. Aaron had surprised Luke by having many of their action shots blown up to full size and then covering the walls with them after construction.

As Luke walked around the immense area examining each photo, he realized that his anger toward the people who had killed his brother was getting more intense with every passing day. He thought about many of the funerals he had presided over and his distant words of advice that were intended to comfort the grieving families and make them feel better, while now understanding that at the time he had no idea what those people were feeling. He now knew exactly what they were feeling, and he had never imagined it would be this hard. Thinking back to his days in Africa, he wondered why the inner rage he felt now was so different. He had experienced murder up close and personal in Johannesburg, and it felt terrible, but not like this. Maybe the fact that Aaron was identical to him in almost every way meant that the murderers not only killed his brother, but they killed a piece of Luke also. Even in the pictures, it was difficult for Luke to tell the two of them apart. If it wasn't for a small, almost unnoticeable scar on Luke's chin, only God would know the difference.

Luke sat down on the shoulder press machine and started the circuit-training routine that he and Aaron had done so many times together. He worked hard and fast, finishing in about half the time it normally took to do this workout. Drenched in sweat, he moved on to one of six treadmills and began running at a seven-minute-mile pace. He was in great shape from a physical standpoint, but emotionally he was a wreck. No matter what he did, Aaron's murder was on his mind. Looking around the gym, the full-length pictures that he once loved had now become a constant reminder of his brother's death. Every time Luke looked in the mirror, he saw Aaron. His nights continued to be filled with nightmares of death, anger, and revenge.

After running three miles, he decided to move on to the heavy bag, feeling that this would be a better outlet for the suppressed rage he was feeling. The punching bag was strategically fastened to a steel beam underneath the garage floor, making it virtually soundless to the people upstairs. Starting slowly, he hit the canvas and waited, then hit it again. The more he thought about his brother, the harder and faster his punches became. After several minutes, he was grunting loudly while hitting it with both hands as fast as he could. Seeing something move in the mirror's reflection, he turned his head quickly and noticed Abel standing on the last step, watching him. Luke stopped abruptly and quickly draped a towel over his wet shirt while walking over to pick up the fragile child. Silently, he carried the boy upstairs and into the family room. Several minutes later, Abel was sound asleep in his arms as silent tears fell down Luke's flushed cheeks and blood dripped from his bruised and swollen knuckles.

**5**

**LUKE WALKED OUT TO** the backyard and took the piece of paper out of his pocket that the church secretary had given him. He dialed the number and asked for Jim Hathaway. After a few minutes, Jim picked up the phone. "Hi, Luke, and thank you for calling. Please accept my sincere condolences. I am, I mean, was, a business associate of your brother's and also a friend."

Trying to ease the awkward silence that followed, Luke replied, "Thank you, Jim. Have we ever met?"

"No, I went to law school with Aaron while you were in the seminary. About a year ago, we were reacquainted when I began working with Aaron on estate planning, but I've heard a lot about you."

Confused, Luke asked, "From who?"

"Luke, even though you and Aaron had some disagreements, he always spoke highly of you and admired your passion and conviction. My firm specializes in financial planning, so I spent a substantial amount of time with him discussing his investments and his will. We talked for hours, and in great detail, about your family so that he could decide the best way to take care of everyone if something ever happened to him. You should know that as recently as three weeks ago, he asked me to include a provision in his will that gave you sole custody of his children if he and Deborah both died before the kids were of legal age."

Luke struggled to speak, as his bottom lip quivered and his eyes filled with tears. When he didn't respond, Jim continued talking. "That's why I asked you to call me. Aaron had taken out a separate life insurance policy for two million dollars, with you as the beneficiary." Luke heard what the lawyer said, but it didn't fully register. Hearing silence again, Jim kept talking. "If his death is considered an accident, or something Aaron couldn't predict or prevent, the policy contains a double indemnity clause. This means that the payout amount could be doubled. Also, insurance payments are not subject to income tax."

Luke didn't respond but paced back and forth in the manicured yard. This prompted Jim to ask, "Luke, are you there?"

"Yes, I'm sorry, there's just so much to think about."

"I can only imagine. I wanted you to have this information as soon as possible."

Luke stated softly, "Please, just give the money to Deborah."

Jim hesitated. "Luke, I can assure you that Deborah and the children will never have to worry about money. And there's another policy for your parents."

After talking for a few more minutes, Luke thanked Jim, who asked that he call to make an appointment to sign the required paperwork. He promised to apprise his parents about the other policy.

Knowing that he needed to be at police headquarters at ten o'clock, Luke headed back into the house. Deborah had already asked Luke's parents to watch the kids while they were away. After another uneaten meal, Luke showered and shaved in preparation for the meeting. He decided that he wasn't going to wear his clerical garb because it only seemed to attract attention. Realizing that when he rushed out of the rectory he never stopped to collect any of his casual clothing, he searched the workout bag from his truck for something else to wear. Finding an old pair of sweatpants and an unwashed blue T-shirt, he hand-ironed the wrinkled shirt, dressed, and went into the family room to wait for Deb.

Deborah entered the room looking incredible. Her full-figured profile, dark olive complexion, and silky black hair were complemented by a beautiful tailored pantsuit. As Luke stood to greet her, he saw the surprise in her eyes as she looked him over. "I didn't want to wear my priest stuff because it only draws attention." She nodded, pretending that it was OK. He continued, "Maybe on the way back from police headquarters we can stop at the rectory so I can pick up some clothes."

Deb motioned for him to follow her. Leading him into her bedroom, she opened a door at the far end of the room and said, "Luke, take anything you want." He peered into the huge closet and was amazed. Hundreds of suits, pants, shoes, and shirts were arranged meticulously on cedar hangers and shelves. He felt like he had walked into the men's department at an exclusive clothing store. "Deb, I'm fine, really. After the meeting we can stop by the rectory," he said, although the rectory was the last place he wanted to be right now.

"If you're not going to wear any of these clothes, then who else deserves to have them? Please, just think about what Aaron would want. I know this is hard to hear right now, but he loved you very much, and we often talked about the need for you two to reconcile your differences. Luke, he would want you to have his things." Luke nodded as Deborah walked out of the room and closed the door behind her.

A few minutes later, Luke reentered the family room wearing navy blue lightweight wool slacks, a crisp white shirt with cuffed sleeves, and beautiful soft black leather shoes. Deborah looked up from the couch and did a double take. Luke realized that now he looked more like Aaron than before. Feeling uncomfortable, he said, "Let's just take my truck." She shrugged, and they walked out the front door. Luke rushed ahead of her and opened the passenger door of the old truck, moving some newspapers off the seat. Deborah hesitated, then climbed in while Luke held the door. Jumping into the driver's seat, he attempted to start the truck. After several futile tries, Luke saw Deb glance at her watch. "Luke, let's take one of the other cars. I don't want to be late." He tried the ignition a few more times and then surrendered to her request.

They went back into the house and down the hallway toward the garage. She opened the door and Luke followed her inside, where four cars were parked side by side on the black-and-white tiled floor. Deb pressed a button and one of the arched doors opened. She reached up to a small metal box affixed to the wall and handed Luke a set of keys. He followed her down the steps toward a sleek black Mercedes. After opening her door, he proceeded to the driver's side. Looking at the back of the beautiful car, he noticed the model number: CL550. He made a mental note to look it up on the Internet when he had time. As he backed out of the garage, he saw two other Mercedes and a car that looked like a Ferrari or Lamborghini. He was amazed at the amount of wealth his brother had amassed.

Even though Aaron was a well-respected lawyer with a thriving business, what most people didn't know was that he was also a silent partner in a hedge fund. Aaron and two classmates from Harvard had developed the idea for this business while attending school. Once Aaron's law practice became successful, he convinced several wealthy clients to invest in the startup, and the company became more successful than anyone had ever imagined.

Luke drove down the driveway and out through the security gates to the street. Reporters jumped from their cars and attempted to take pictures, but the dark tinted side windows shielded the passengers safely inside. As Luke drove, Deborah noticed him squinting in the bright sunlight that entered through the clear windshield, the only window in the car that wasn't tinted. Luke watched as she opened the glove box and handed him a pair of Aaron's designer sunglasses.

When they turned into Schroeder Plaza, Luke was relieved to see a parking spot not far from the front of the old brick building. After parking the car, he pulled on the pair of Aaron's leather gloves that were lying on the console in order to hide his swollen hands. They quickly headed into the building unnoticed. Once inside, one of the duty officers recognized them and quickly shuffled them into a conference room on the first floor. A few minutes later, Detective Romo entered. "I'm sorry to keep you waiting." Looking at Deborah while extending his hand, he continued, "I'm so sorry for your loss, Mrs. Miller." She acknowledged him by shaking his hand but said nothing. Turning to Luke, he said, "Thank you for agreeing to see me, Father."

"Thank you for agreeing to leave my parents and the children out of this," Luke replied.

Romo sat at the head of the table, with Luke next to him and Deborah next to Luke. The detective had a long list of prepared questions, general questions that anyone would have expected. "Did your husband have any enemies?" "Did your husband seem upset or uneasy that morning?" "Did you or your husband receive any strange phone calls over the past few weeks?" As far as Luke was concerned, he could have saved everyone a lot of time and done this over the phone. Once Romo finished with Deborah, he began questioning Luke. After he realized that the brothers hadn't talked for more than a year, he limited his interrogation to just a few questions. Luke assumed that the detective didn't consider him a suspect. Forty-five minutes later, Romo thanked both of them, and they were escorted to the front door.

Before leaving, Luke and Deborah donned their sunglasses. Luke walked out first and held the door for her. As they reached the curb, he extended his hand and helped her over a large pothole in the old road. At that moment, several paparazzi pounced, yelling questions and taking pictures. Taken by surprise, Luke and Deborah paused a few seconds before realizing what was happening. Finally reacting, he took her by the arm and rushed her toward the car, while fumbling for the keys in his pocket. He opened her door, and she jumped in as he ran around the car and did the same. The reporters moved to the front, in an attempt to get more shots through the clear glass windshield. Luke started the car and tried to pull out as Deb crouched down in her seat, attempting to hide her face. As Luke inched the car forward, the paparazzi finally had to relent and move to the side as the car accelerated. To ensure he wasn't followed, he gunned the powerful Mercedes and took several quick turns before heading back toward the house. An unusual day for a priest, he thought.

On the way home, Deborah pointed to a road sign leading toward the North End of downtown Boston. Surprised, Luke questioned, "Do you want to go that way?" She nodded in confirmation. A few minutes later, she pointed at another sign, and Luke continued following her nonverbal directions. They parked on the street near Christopher Columbus Waterfront Park, and she finally broke her silence. "Walk with me." Luke climbed out of the car, but before he could open Deborah's door, she was already out and walking down a path toward the water. When Luke caught up, she moved close and slowed her pace. Several minutes passed before she spoke again. "Before the children were born, Aaron and I would often come here to walk. Our life was so much simpler back then—before all the money, houses, cars, and politics; I wish we could turn back time." Luke noticed that she was so close to him that their shoulders rubbed as they walked. "I want to tell you something before you hear it in the press. I think Aaron was seeing someone." Luke didn't respond. "I'm not positive, but one of my friends saw him with a beautiful blonde woman at lunch one day a few weeks ago. When I asked him about it, he said he didn't know what I was talking about. And I've heard him on the phone late at night."

Luke stopped walking and turned to face her. "I don't think Aaron would do that. I knew him better than anyone, and he wouldn't do that."

She looked down and continued. "After Alessa was born, I couldn't lose all the weight I gained during pregnancy, and I think it bothered him. He never said anything to my face, but I would see him looking at other women." As she looked up, Luke could see tears welling in her eyes. Forcing a smile, she continued, "Do you know what women shop for when they gain weight?"

Luke smiled back. "No, what?"

"Shoes."

"Shoes?"

"Yes, shoes. When you gain weight, shopping for clothes is upsetting. It's a constant reminder that you are fatter than you want to be. But shoes, they still fit. When we get back to the house, take a look in my closet. You'll be amazed."

They shared a much-needed laugh. Getting serious, Luke held her hand. "I'm going to tell you something about Aaron that you might not know."

She squeezed his hand.

"He never liked skinny women. When we were in high school we shared a room. Sometimes late at night we would talk when the lights were out. Do you remember Jennifer Dubrowsky?"

"Yes, she was your girlfriend."

"Do you remember what she looked like?"

She smiled.

Before she could speak, he continued. "One night during one of our chats, I asked Aaron if he thought she was overweight. I know it was shallow and superficial; I liked the way she looked, but some of my friends would comment that she could lose a few pounds. Aaron didn't respond right away, but I'll never forget what he said."

Anxious to hear his response, she whispered, "Tell me."

"He said that he thought she was perfect. He didn't like malnourished women and always thought full-figured women were more attractive. For years, whenever we would see a super-skinny woman we would look at each other and smile. I'm sure he loved the way you look."

"Luke, you didn't know him for the past year; he had changed. He made new powerful friends. They attended late-night parties and political fund-raiser meetings with lobbyists. I don't know if he did this in an attempt to fill the void that was left after you two quit talking, but believe me, Luke, he had changed."

She stopped and pointed at the back of a huge yacht docked at the marina. Luke was astonished. Deborah put her arm though his and looked out at the water. "He told me that as soon as the presidential election was over, he was going to take whatever measures were necessary to mend his relationship with you. He was so excited to show you this boat." As she began to sob, Luke held her while trying to fight back his own stinging tears. The name on the back of the yacht was *Blood Brothers*.

# 6

**PULLING THROUGH THE OPEN** gates and into the garage, Luke exited the car and quickly walked over to help Deborah out. As they reached the door to the house, he handed her the car keys, but she pushed his hand away. "Luke, I want you to keep the car."

He was flustered. "Deborah, I can't."

She interrupted, saying once again, "Luke, Aaron would want you to have it. As you can see, I have plenty of cars. Please, just take the car."

Reluctantly, he nodded. "I'll just use it until I get my truck fixed." Then he took her by the hands and turned her to face him. As she looked him directly in the eyes, he brought up the subject that was on everyone's mind but no one wanted to discuss. "Deb, I don't know if my presence here is helping or hurting. I feel like I'm pretending to be Aaron and everyone is very willing to accept that. I don't know what to do, but you and everyone else need to know that I'm not Aaron. I think it's time for me to go back to the rectory."

She shook her head and pleaded, "Luke, for the sake of the children and your parents, please don't leave us. We need you now. I need you now. I promise that I'll work harder to help everyone understand, but please just give it some time. I'm so thankful that you're here, and I'm sure Aaron is too. Please, Luke, I'm begging you, stay with us a little while longer."

What could he do? He reluctantly agreed.

---

Luke played with the kids in the backyard as Deborah watched, and he tried to ignore it when they called him "Daddy." It broke his heart. He needed to spend some time alone. Excusing himself, he went to his bedroom, closed the door, and knelt down to pray. He asked for healing, for peace, and for direction, but mostly he asked for the power to forgive, the one thing he couldn't seem to do. Even as he prayed, he continued to think about justice. He wanted someone to pay for his loss and the pain it had caused his family. After about an hour, he decided to do something that none of his family had done since the explosion. He lay down on the bed and reached over to open the drawer of the nightstand, where he found the television control.

It had been ten days since Aaron's death, and the news of the explosion still filled the airwaves. Many of the so-called experts believed that the bombing had something to do with Ablaa Raboud, but government officials had downplayed these theories, noting that she belonged to a reformed Muslim movement that believed in peace, not jihad. Although relatively small in size and destruction, with "only" eight people killed and eleven injured, this event captivated the nation due to the murder of Brad Thompson, an immensely popular candidate. News trucks and reporters from around the globe continued to infiltrate the city to unearth details of what the press now termed the "Bombing in Boston."

From the White House to the local police, officials were focused on preventing another attack. National alerts were updated hourly, and security was heightened at airports, stadiums, and other public venues, leading most Americans to believe that another bombing was imminent. Luke understood the need for national security and preventing another incident, but he wondered if anyone was focused on finding out who killed his brother. It seemed to him that the country was in a defensive mode rather than taking the offensive.

Over the next few days, Luke noticed that life became more normal for his immediate family. The constant crying had subsided, and his parents were settling back in to their old routines. Deborah and the children were making the best of a horrible situation. Luke had created his own daily routine that included a morning workout before anyone else was awake, a shower and prayers, then playing with the children and reading the local papers. He had more free time on his hands than ever before, and he was becoming restless. The constant boredom wasn't helping; he was impatient for the police to solve the case. Luke finally decided that he had waited long enough for someone else to figure out what happened to Aaron. Tomorrow he would abandon his passive priest persona and go on the offensive to find the murderer himself.

# 7

**LUKE OPENED HIS EYES** and saw that the clock on his nightstand read 5:35 a.m. The sun hadn't risen yet, but he was already relieved to know that today he would recapture a small piece of his freedom. He quickly dressed, quietly opened his bedroom door, and crept down the hallway into the garage. He sat in the Mercedes and pressed the garage door opener on the visor. As the door opened, Luke started the car, hoping that he didn't wake anyone in the house. He backed out quickly and pressed the button again, closing the door. Easing down the driveway, he was surprised to see that there was no sign of anyone. He used the keychain remote to open the electric gate and drove through, startling a security guard who must have fallen asleep in his car. Waving, Luke put his foot to the floor, and the car sped down the deserted street.

He checked his rearview mirror several times to ensure that he wasn't being followed. After a few blocks, Luke turned onto a neighborhood street and then turned again, heading in the direction from which he had come. He slowed the car and pulled over to the side of the road. He waited a few minutes, looked in his mirrors one last time, and turned the wheel while pressing on the gas. The powerful sedan jumped the curb with little effort, and he steered it into a narrow clearing in the woods. He slowly inched it forward until the car was unnoticeable from the road, then he turned off the engine. He stepped out and walked over to an old stone wall, where he had strategically placed an aluminum ladder several days before, after he had cleared a pathway. Reassured that he could now escape the confines of the house without the paparazzi or reporters knowing, he climbed over the wall, strolled across the familiar backyard, and entered the house through the back door.

After breakfast with the family, Luke asked Deborah if he could talk to her in private for a few minutes. They went into the library, where she questioned, "Is everything all right?"

"Yes, everything is fine. I wanted to ask you for a few favors." Relieved, she smiled.

"Can you please call the Verizon store and ask them for a new phone for Aaron?"

Startled, she asked, "Why?"

"Knowing Aaron, there's a good chance that he had the names and numbers of his contacts stored. This way, since his phone was destroyed, his contact list can be reloaded by the phone company."

"Why do you want that information?"

"I need to know who he was talking with the morning of the bombing, and I want to reconstruct the last few days of his life. It's something that I have to do."

She nodded, understanding.

"And can you request a detailed report of all of his calls for the last three months?" Before she could answer, he continued, "I need one more favor."

"Yes, anything."

"Please make sure they don't ever turn off Aaron's number."

When she asked why, he confided that he called Aaron's phone number every day, just to hear his voice. She cried, then quickly retrieved her phone and dialed his number herself.

---

Luke spent part of the afternoon in the backyard playing with Alessa and Abel. When they came in, Deborah was standing by the back door. She bent down, and the children released Luke's hands and ran to her. Deborah smiled at Luke. "The phone store called to say the new phone is ready, and I had one of the security guards pick it up."

"Thank you so much. And the phone records?"

"They said that they would be e-mailed sometime today."

She went to get the phone as Luke headed to his room. Seeing the bedroom closet door ajar, he opened it and noticed that it was now full of Aaron's clothes. Then he saw the note on his nightstand: "Luke, please remember this is what Aaron would want. Also, here's the ID and password for our e-mail account. The computer is in the library." He showered and shaved, then knelt at his bedside and prayed. Deep in thought, he was startled when there was a knock and the door slowly opened. He stood quickly and Deborah walked in, holding the new cell phone. When she handed it to Luke, he noticed the awkward look on her face before she turned to leave. It was then that he realized he was shirtless. Quickly pulling on a sweatshirt, he examined the phone and headed to the library.

Being somewhat computer savvy, Luke quickly logged on to his brother's e-mail account. Seeing the phone company message, he opened it and began analyzing the data. Working backward from the day of Aaron's death, he documented each call while attempting to match them to the contact names on Aaron's phone. Four hours later, Luke had a spreadsheet containing the names and phone numbers of everyone that Aaron had talked to in the last few weeks before his death. There were six numbers with no matches on Aaron's contact list. Realizing that these numbers might be important, he knew who to call for help.

Carlos Sanchez answered on the second ring. "Luke, I'm so sorry for your loss." The longtime friends spent several minutes discussing the recent events and reminiscing about the time they spent in the seminary together. Carlos was in charge of the archdiocese computer systems and networks, and Luke finally got to the point. "Carlos, I need help with some phone numbers."

"What?"

"I'm trying to determine who my brother was calling in the past few months. I have his phone records, but there are a few numbers that I can't match back to the contact list on his phone, and I want to find these people."

"Luke, are you sure you know what you're getting into? Think about Washington, DC. Do you remember?"

Luke stood and walked over to the ornate mirror hanging on the wall. Looking at his reflection, he gently ran his index finger up and down the small scar on the underside of his chin, the only distinguishable difference between the twin brothers.

Not hearing a response, Carlos asked, "Luke, are you still there?"

"Yes."

"Do you remember? You can't lose your temper, for God's sake, you're a priest now."

Luke thought about that winter day—January 22, to be precise. As much as he tried, he could never forget it. While in the seminary, he and Carlos took a trip to DC on the anniversary of Roe versus Wade to join the antiabortion protesters. Shortly after getting off the bus, they were confronted by an arrogant pro-choicer who took exception to their presence. After calling them insulting names, he moved so close to Luke that when he started screaming, "Damn your God, damn your God," a mist of his saliva covered Luke's face. Then he pushed a poor, defenseless old woman out of his way, causing her to fall as he laughed and ran away.

Before leaving on the bus back to New York, Luke insisted that Carlos come with him on a walk through the downtown club area. Finding the jerk outside one of the local bars, Luke handed Carlos his collar and verbally confronted the man. When Luke turned to walk away, the coward hit him with an uppercut that he never saw coming, causing the scar on his chin. Something in Luke snapped, and he started punching the man uncontrollably, not stopping until Carlos pulled him off.

Although Carlos was horrified, he agreed to keep the events of that day a secret as long as Luke went to confession and promised to pray for strength to control his rage. Luke met Carlos in the confessional the next morning, and Luke's problem with anger in response to injustice had remained suppressed since then. But now Carlos worried that the murder of Aaron would unleash it once again.

Realizing that Carlos was waiting, Luke finally responded, "I want to understand who he was talking to and why. I really need to know."

After a few moments of silence, Carlos reluctantly asked, "What's your e-mail address? I know there are several websites that offer this as a free service. Give me fifteen minutes, and I'll send you an e-mail with a web link."

Luke thanked him and promised to keep in touch.

Using the reverse-lookup website, Luke located the missing names and was surprised that the site also listed their addresses. His list was complete except for two numbers, which must have been unlisted. Unfortunately, they were the two numbers called most often. One was the number Aaron had called right before he walked onto the stage on the morning of his death. Luke knew he had no choice but to call each one.

# 8

**THE FIRST NUMBER HE** called was disconnected. Luke assumed that whoever it belonged to was probably dead. While carefully dialing the second number, he now panicked that he hadn't rehearsed what he would say if someone answered. However, after several rings, the phone went silent. Hesitant about redialing, he lay on his bed and reviewed the other numbers on the list. Another one suddenly caught his attention. On the morning of the bombing, Aaron had spoken to Ablaa Raboud, the Muslim reformist, for more than twenty minutes. There were also several other calls to her number on prior days. Knowing that it was useless to call her because she, too, was dead, Luke decided to take a ride by her house first thing in the morning to see if anyone else lived at that address.

After dinner, Luke returned to his room while the rest of his family moved to the den to watch the nightly game shows. His parents were getting stronger day by day, but he worried about Deborah. He sensed that she could fall apart at any moment. The responsibility of raising two small children alone and making all the day-to-day household decisions, while trying to figure out what to do with Aaron's law firm and clients, was noticeably wearing on her. Luke was doing all he could to help, but Deborah tried to ignore everything except the children, causing important decisions to be made in crisis mode, further adding stress to her now complicated life.

The next morning, Luke told Deborah that he had some errands to run. Before she could ask how, he explained his new clandestine escape route from the backyard. Already having too many things to worry about, she didn't question him, but she agreed to keep the children and his parents occupied until he returned. Aware that his clerical clothes could actually help in some situations, Luke put them on and quickly headed out the back door and over the wall. As he entered the address into the Mercedes' GPS, he saw that Ablaa Raboud's residence was located on Malcolm X Boulevard in the heart of Roxbury. This didn't surprise him, since the Islamic Society of Boston Cultural Center was located on the same block. The ISBCC was the largest Islamic center in New England and the second-largest on the East Coast. Noticing that his destination was only twenty minutes away, he backed out of the woods onto the empty street.

When the GPS announced, "You have arrived at your destination," Luke waited patiently as an elderly couple slowly maneuvered out of a parking space directly in front. Pulling in, he called Aaron's cell number for encouragement once again before he left the car. He found the address numbers on a brick apartment building, and he entered and looked for apartment 1C. He quickly determined that the arrangement of the mailboxes in the lobby corresponded to the floor plan of the building. Relieved that 1C was located on the first floor, he walked back outside and looked at the structure again. It appeared that each apartment contained two large side windows, so he walked on the grass to the rear of the building and approached. Holding his hands up to shield the sun's reflection on the glass, he peered through the blinds to see inside. Hearing something behind him, he turned quickly but saw nothing unusual. Turning back to look in the window again, he was startled as he saw a figure staring back at him. He backed up quickly and stumbled over his own feet, falling hard on the uneven ground.

As he struggled to get up, he tripped several more times. Finally regaining his composure, he got to his feet and started to run toward his car until he heard, "Stop right there! Don't move and place your hands were I can see them!"

Luke froze and slowly lifted his hands above his head. Out of the corner of his eye he saw a man dressed in a dark suit moving into his line of sight. His attention was immediately drawn to the gun that was pointed directly at his chest. The man was talking on a radio with one hand, while the other held the unwavering weapon. The gunman quickly placed the radio in his coat pocket and pulled out a badge. Addressing Luke, he said, "Boston police. What are you doing here?" As Luke came into full view, the detective saw Luke's collar and immediately recognized him. Luke finally spoke. "I'm sorry, Detective; I just stopped by to see the Raboud family. I wanted to express my condolences."

As the officer holstered his weapon, Luke saw his gaze drawn to something behind him. Turning his body without moving his feet, Luke recognized the person from the window walking toward them. The female figure approaching was wearing a full burqa that covered her entire body except for an open slit for her eyes. She stopped while a few feet away and addressed the officer. "Detective, who is this man?"

Feeling like a criminal, Luke turned completely around and said sincerely, "I'm so sorry that I frightened you. I'm Luke Miller. My brother Aaron was also killed in the bombing. I came here to extend my condolences to Ablaa Raboud's family." As she moved closer, Luke could see the compassion and hurt in her eyes, her only visible feature.

Extending her hand, she said in perfect English, but with a Middle Eastern accent, "I am Jamilah. Ablaa was my sister."

Shaking her hand, Luke replied with the trite response he had heard every day for the past few weeks. "I'm sorry for your loss."

Sensing that there was no immediate danger, the detective excused himself and returned to his lookout post. Luke walked to the front of the building with Jamilah. She explained, "The police have had Ablaa's apartment under surveillance since her death. They worry about retaliation because many Americans think that she had something to do with the bombing." Before Luke could speak, she continued, "My sister was only interested in peace. She would never condone violence of any kind."

Luke saw her eyes squint as if she was smiling. "My outfit frightened you?" she asked.

He laughed. "Frightened me? It scared the heck out of me!" He could tell she was laughing. "I was nervous to be looking in the window to start with. When I saw your covered face, my heart just about stopped!"

"I apologize. Today is the holy day of Eid al-Adha, the festival of sacrifice. For Muslims, it signifies the willingness of Abraham to sacrifice his son Ishmael as an act of obedience to God."

Understanding that people of the Islamic faith believe in specific sections of the Old Testament and revere Jesus as a great prophet, he smiled. "Yes, the book of Genesis; Abraham and Isaac on Mount Moriah."

Luke saw her looking at the street, where many Muslims, dressed in traditional clothing, were making their way toward the Islamic center for the midday prayer. Seeing that some were staring at her, she whispered, "Perhaps we can talk tomorrow? I really have to get to the center."

Luke replied, "What time is best for you?"

"How about ten in the morning?"

Feeling embarrassed about getting into the Mercedes, Luke said good-bye and walked down the street in the other direction until she was out of sight, then he backtracked and hurried to the car.

Before turning the key in the ignition, he clenched the steering wheel with exasperation and moaned, "What the hell am I doing?" Luke reluctantly conceded that it was probably a longshot that his meeting with Jamilah the next morning would provide any clues, but he decided that a longshot was better than no shot at all.

# 9

LUKE WAS ANXIOUS TO investigate another number on the phone list, one that Aaron had called many times over his last several weeks. Knowing that Mark Aldridge was still alive, because his name wasn't on the bombing death list, he took out his cell phone and dialed.

"Aldridge residence; how can I help you?" a female voice answered.

"Can I please speak to Mr. Mark Aldridge?"

"May I ask who is calling?"

"This is Luke Miller."

Luke heard muffled voices but couldn't decipher what was being said. What felt like minutes passed before an elderly, deep voice responded, "This is Mark Aldridge."

"Mr. Aldridge, this is Luke Miller, Aaron's brother."

The elderly man hesitated, then spoke softly, obviously overcome with emotion. "You sound just like him. I miss hearing his voice."

"Me too, Mr. Aldridge." Getting to the point, Luke continued, "I've been trying to investigate my brother's death and am attempting to piece together the last few weeks of his life. I would really like to talk to you; do you have a few minutes?"

Aldridge replied abruptly, with a sharp voice, "Not on the phone. You're welcome to come to my house to talk, but not on the phone."

They agreed to meet in forty-five minutes at Aldridge's house. Realizing that he had time to kill because he was only a few minutes away, Luke decided that he was finally brave enough to drive past Boston Common to get his first look at the bomb site where his brother was murdered. Yellow police tape surrounded the entire area. Luke noticed that the homeless people had moved back into the park and were preparing for the winter months; park benches were popular locations during the harsh weather. Luke made a mental note to return with warm clothing to help them cope with the upcoming frigid temperatures.

He cruised along the quaint streets of Beacon Hill, where Luke's Mercedes fit right in. The exclusive residential neighborhood was known for its distinctive architecture: nineteenth-century brick buildings and sidewalks, decorative ironwork, and perpetually burning gaslights lining the narrow streets. These sought-after town homes were exquisite, but many lacked one important characteristic—a garage, making parking extremely challenging. Driving slowly, Luke continued to circle the block, praying that someone would pull out of a spot. It reminded him of an old priest joke: *"A man circles the crowded parking lot looking for a place to park during the Christmas rush. After making several passes and not finding a spot, he starts to pray. Seconds later, a car pulls out of one of the best spots in the lot. Looking up to God, he says, 'Never mind, I found it myself.'"*

Luke smiled to himself when, sure enough, a car began to pull out of a spot. While parallel parking, he felt his cell phone begin to vibrate in his coat pocket. He pulled it out and saw that it was Robert Romo. Luke answered quickly. "Good morning, Detective."

"Good morning, Father. I just heard that you were confronted by one of my colleagues at the home of Ablaa Raboud this morning."

"Yes, that was me. I never had a gun pointed at me before."

"I'm sorry; you should have let me know that you were going there."

"I didn't realize that she had a sister. I just wanted to see where she lived. My brother had spoken to her several times in the days before his death."

After a few seconds of silence, the officer asked, "How exactly do you know that?"

Luke answered awkwardly, "I was able to get my brother's cell phone records from his last few weeks, and I've been reviewing who he called."

"Why?"

"Detective, put yourself in my position and please tell me what you would be doing."

Chastised, he reluctantly replied, "I guess I'd be doing the same thing."

"Have you heard anything on the case? Any suspects yet?"

"The feds have completely shut us out of the investigation. They're considering the incident a threat to national security, so they revoked all our jurisdiction and authority."

Hoping the detective's annoyance at being excluded would make him more cooperative, Luke asked the question he'd been waiting to ask since his phone rang: "Do you have a way to get information on unlisted phone numbers?"

There was a hesitation on the line, then a simple answer. "Yes."

Acting nonchalantly, Luke continued, "So, if I give you a few numbers, you could tell me who they belonged to?"

He wasn't fooling the detective. "I could, but that doesn't mean I will." Luke held his breath as Romo continued, "Why don't we meet? How about this afternoon?"

Thrilled to have his help, Luke quickly agreed. "No problem. Where?"

The detective immediately responded, "It has to be someplace where we won't be recognized."

"OK, four o'clock at the old cemetery on Tremont Street. I'll see you there."

# 10

**LUKE WALKED TO THE** door of the impressive row house and lifted the massive knocker. When he released it, the sound echoed throughout the three-story mansion, and he heard footsteps approach. He looked up and noticed a security camera as the heavy door swung open. A petite young girl smiled and invited him inside, obviously expecting him. She locked the door behind him and motioned for Luke to follow her into an elegant wood-paneled library. She offered him something to drink and, when he declined, she excused herself to get Mr. Aldridge.

Luke stood as the young girl pushed Mark Aldridge's wheelchair through the open door. Mark extended his hand and Luke gently shook it. Although they had never met, there was no need for introductions. "Please, sit down. I was very close friends with your brother. I know that this is awkward because we've never met, but I know a lot about you. Aaron was very proud of his younger brother."

Luke smiled. Aldridge's comment confirmed that he really must have been close to Aaron, since not many people knew that Aaron was born a few minutes before Luke.

"Thank you for taking the time to see me, Mr. Aldridge."

"Please, call me Mark."

Not wanting to waste any time, Luke took a deep breath and began. "I've been going through my brother's phone records, and I'm trying to retrace the last few days of his life. I noticed that he talked to you many times in the days before the bombing."

"Do you know anything about me?"

Luke grinned. "Only your name, phone number, and address."

The old man smiled back and then quickly became serious. "I'm a political consultant who has worked for five presidents and dozens of congressmen and senators. I first met your brother a few years ago at a fund-raiser for Brad Thompson. His good looks and impressive background made him the perfect candidate."

Bewildered, Luke interrupted, "Candidate?"

Squinting, Mark looked directly at Luke and asked, "When was the last time you talked to Aaron?"

"Over a year ago."

"Yes, I remember now. He often talked about the need to patch things up with you. Luke, he loved you very much, and we talked about you so often that I'd forgotten that you two hadn't spoken in a long time."

Tears filled Luke's eyes, but he didn't reply.

"Most political insiders knew that once Brad Thompson became president, Aaron would run for senator in the next election two years from now. Being a longtime Boston resident, a graduate of Boston College and Harvard, and a well-respected lawyer, he was someone we felt couldn't lose. He even had a Catholic priest as a brother! He was the perfect candidate. Did you know that Massachusetts has the second-highest percentage of Catholics in the country?"

Luke shook his head no.

"Well, then, I bet you didn't know that Massachusetts has the fourth-highest percentage of Jews."

"How do you know all these statistics?"

Mark smiled. "Luke, it's my job to know these things. No candidate that I've represented as a client has ever lost a race." He hesitated as tears filled his tired eyes. "Except for Brad Thompson."

Luke stood and walked over to a nearby table to get a tissue, which he handed to the distraught man. Kneeling down next to his wheelchair, Luke put his hand on Mark's and looked him square in the eyes. "I need to know who killed Aaron and why."

Looking back at Luke, tears rolled down the old man's face. "I was supposed to be there that day. I didn't feel well that morning and called your brother to get some advice. He told me that I should stay home and get better, and he promised to come and see me as soon as the speech was over."

Luke squeezed Mark's hand.

"He was like a son to me. He was the only one who came to see me just to talk. He was a good man."

Luke asked more directly, "Do you have any idea of who would have wanted Brad Thompson dead?"

Mark dried his eyes and answered, "I don't know, but I wouldn't rule out anything."

Puzzled, Luke asked, "What does that mean?"

Mark pushed himself up in his chair. "It means that I wouldn't assume that it had anything to do with that Muslim lady. Hell, it might not even be directly related to Brad Thompson. Luke, politics is a dirty game. If Brad Thompson was elected president, there's a good chance that he would have been responsible for nominating the next three Supreme Court justices."

Luke said softly, "But you just said it might not be about Brad."

"I just don't want you to focus all of your energy in one place. If your brother was elected to the Senate, it's likely that he would have been the fifty-first vote, the deciding one. With a Republican Congress and president, his vote could have had a dramatic impact on laws like Roe versus Wade, English as an official language, offshore oil drilling, and securing our border with Mexico. The elections of Brad and Aaron would have drastically changed the balance of power and the direction of our nation. Anyone from special-interest groups concerned with those issues would have greatly benefited from their deaths and could be responsible."

Luke sighed. "It's just so frustrating, since it feels like the police are getting nowhere with this case. That's why I'm starting my own investigation."

Aldridge replied gravely, "OK, I understand, and I'll do anything I can to help. But let me give you some strong words of advice: Don't discuss any of this on the phone, and be extremely careful. You can't trust anyone."

# 11

LUKE PULLED BACK INTO his hidden parking spot in the woods, climbed the ladder, and did a quick visual sweep of the backyard. With none of his family in sight, he quickly traversed the manicured sod and entered the house through the rear door. When the children heard Luke in the kitchen, they ran to see him, and he bent down and hugged them tight. Looking up, he saw Deborah standing in the doorway watching. "They've been asking for you all morning." He smiled and stood up with Abel and Alessa in his arms. She continued, "Your father has been asking for you also. He wants to talk to you about something."

Still holding the children, Luke walked into the family room, where he knew his parents would be watching television. He sat the children on a small love seat and walked over to greet his parents. While kissing his mom on the cheek, he extended his hand toward his dad. He could tell that his mother was upset. As Luke stood, his father said to the children, "I think your mother needs you in the kitchen." They quickly ran to find her. His dad pointed for Luke to sit down. Luke moved an ornate chair from the other side of the room so it was in front of the couch, directly facing them.

Glancing at his mom, Luke's dad spoke. "We've decided that after Thanksgiving, we're going to move back home. We want to be in our own house." He quickly added, "But we want you to stay with Deborah and the children. We won't leave unless you promise to stay." Surprised at this turn of events, Luke looked down and noticed the newspaper on the coffee table. It was open to the gossip page. There was a half-page picture that must have been taken outside police headquarters a few days ago. It showed Luke extending his hand to help Deborah over a pothole in the street. Of course, there was no sign of the pothole in the picture, leading the reader to believe that they were holding hands. They looked like a Hollywood couple, complete with designer clothes and sunglasses. The sleek black Mercedes was in the background. But what really caught his eye was the headline, "Thou Shalt Not Covet Thy Brother's Wife!" He couldn't believe that this headline had planted a seed of doubt in his parents' minds. "Dad, you can't possibly think that there's something going on between me and Deborah?"

"Of course not, we know that," his father answered nervously. "But think of how nice it would be if you stayed here with Deb and the children. Your brother would be so happy."

Ready to angrily argue back, Luke bit his lip, knowing that his parents were just thinking of what would be best for the children. Instead, he said, "Listen, we have a few days before Thanksgiving. Let's just take it slow and see what happens." Content that he didn't reject the idea, they nodded at him and smiled at each other.

Luke excused himself from his family and, after another unde-tected getaway, he made his way to the cemetery for his meeting with Romo. Before leaving the car, he pulled on a hooded sweatshirt, then he stepped out and began walking quickly in the brisk fall air. He hoped that the cold weather would be keeping crowds of visitors and tourists to a minimum.

The Granary Burying Ground was a Boston landmark, established in the mid-sixteen hundreds. It was the final resting place of some of America's most prominent historical figures, including three signers of the Declaration of Independence: Samuel Adams, John Hancock, and Robert Treat Paine. Paul Revere and five Boston Massacre victims were also buried here.

Walking down the old sidewalk that ran alongside the wrought iron fence surrounding the cemetery, Luke was relieved to see that the grounds were practically empty. He stepped through the massive stone entryway and scanned the graveyard for Detective Romo. Not finding him, he waited next to the twenty-five-foot-tall obelisk that marked the tomb of Benjamin Franklin's parents.

A few minutes later, he was relieved to see a tall figure approaching wearing a wool stocking cap and sunglasses. He sat down next to Luke without looking directly at him.

"Nice to see you, Father."

Luke mischievously responded, "Is that you, Detective?"

He smiled back. "So Father, tell me, how's your investigation going?"

Luke laughed. "I wouldn't really call it an investigation."

The detective glanced around to see if anyone was watching. "Luke, I was a freshman in high school when you were a senior. I watched just about every baseball game you played. I even went to Boston College a few times to watch your brother play. My mother is a longtime parishioner at Saint Leonard's, so I feel like I've known you for a long time despite the fact that we met just days ago. What I'm trying to say is that you need to be very careful. I've been given strict orders to stay out of this investigation. If I try to help you in any way, I'll be fired immediately and will have to forfeit my pension. If anyone followed me here today, there's a good chance I'll lose my job. I borrowed my sister's car to try to conceal my identity because I felt obligated to meet you, but I can't assist in any official way."

Shocked, Luke quickly replied, "I completely understand your predicament. Please forgive me, I never meant to compromise your career. I won't bother you again. Please accept my sincerest apology."

With that, the detective stood and whispered, "Talk to you soon," before walking away. Confused, Luke now wondered why the detective agreed to meet him to begin with. Dejected, he tried to figure out what to do next. He heard something buzzing and looked around, noticing a brown paper bag on the bench. He picked it up and opened it, finding a vibrating cell phone inside. Unsure of what to expect, Luke opened it and listened. "Luke, I'll help you any way that I can. Just remember that we have to be careful. The phone I left for you is a pre-paid cell phone that can't be traced to me. You can use it to call or text me at the number saved in the contact list, but don't call from inside Aaron's house, since it might be bugged. If I can't answer, I'll call you back as soon as I can."

Relieved that the detective hadn't abandoned him after all, Luke responded, "Thank you so much and God bless you, Detective." Thinking quickly, he asked, "Hey, one more thing, where do you buy prepaid cell phones?"

# 12

**DURING DINNER, LUKE WAS** disappointed to notice that once again Deborah had consumed several glasses of wine. This was now becoming a recurring activity, happening nightly for the past week. He knew that his parents would never mention it, so he decided to talk to her himself.

Searching the house, he found her sitting on her bed, looking out the window. Knocking softly on the open door, Luke asked, "Can I come in?" She didn't answer but waved him inside and motioned for him to sit down on the bed next to her. Looking straight ahead with his hands on his thighs, Luke asked, "How are you doing?"

"I just want this sick feeling in my stomach to go away. Sometimes at night I dream of Aaron and I feel so good, then I wake up and the sick feeling immediately returns."

"Does the wine help?"

She turned to face him, understanding the implication of his question. "I know, I need to stop, but it sometimes dulls the hurt."

Smiling, he replied, "Until the next morning."

Not wanting to dwell on the topic, and now certain that she knew he had noticed, he moved to another subject. "Have you heard from the financial planner?"

"Oh, Luke, I'm so sorry, I forgot to tell you. He wants to meet with us. We need to sign some papers and let him know where the money should be deposited. I'm forgetting everything lately."

Perhaps the wine has something to do with that, he thought wryly, but he didn't bring it up again. "I'll call him tomorrow and set up an appointment."

She put her hand on his. "Thank you for being so good to me and the children. I don't know what we would do without you."

Luke smiled weakly and quickly changed the subject. "Do you know if Aaron has any old clothes, especially winter coats, that I could bring to the homeless people in the park?"

Pondering for a moment, she replied, "I think there's an entire closet full of old clothes in the basement. Take anything you want."

Realizing that he was still sitting next to her on the bed, and feeling uncomfortable, Luke quickly stood and replied, "Great, thanks. I'll see you in the morning."

She forced a smile as he walked out the door.

Luke quickly located the closet in the basement. When he opened the door and peered in, he was surprised to see how big it was. True to form, it was neat and organized, containing several long shelves stacked with boxes and another section with hanging items. Turning on the overhead light, he entered and began exploring. The boxes were labeled: "trophies," "college books," "Hanukkah," "wedding pictures," and so forth. Focusing on the hanging clothes, Luke moved deeper inside. There was a section with double rods that contained two rows for shirts and short jackets, and another full-length area for long coats. As he shuffled through the garments, he remembered Aaron wearing several of the items. Looking specifically for winter coats, he began pulling each one off the hanger and piling them in the center of the room. After gathering several short jackets, he moved on to the longer items. As he tossed each coat to the pile on the floor, he couldn't help but notice the tags on the inside: Burberry, Polo, Billy Reid, Boss. He smiled, thinking to himself that there were going to be some well-dressed people in the park that evening. Any hesitation he felt about giving these beautiful clothes away was quickly overcome by knowing the good it would do.

As he carried an armful from the closet, he noticed that one of the full-length coats felt heavy. Assuming it was the quilted lining, he didn't pay much attention to it until he dropped it on the floor and heard a clunk. Puzzled, he picked up the coat, put it on, and began searching the pockets. As he reached into the inside lapel pocket, he felt something. Realizing what it was before he saw it, he slowly pulled out the semiautomatic pistol. Horrified, he looked up and saw his shocking reflection in the mirrored walls. A priest holding a gun; what a blasphemy. Hearing footsteps coming down the stairs, he quickly jammed the gun back into the pocket.

Deborah appeared, with Luke's mother. "We came down to see if you needed any help," she announced. Knowing Luke better than anyone, his mother immediately sensed something was wrong. "Are you all right, Lukey?" She hadn't called him that since he was a child. Forcing a smile, while trying to compose himself, he responded, "I'm fine, just trying to find some clothes for the homeless." Looking at Deborah as if trying to impress her, his mother said, "He's always had a great big heart and an unbelievable amount of compassion for the less fortunate. When he was a small child, he would give away his lunch money to his classmates who didn't have any." She walked over and hugged him.

Embarrassed, Luke returned her embrace while turning his body to the right to make sure she didn't feel the handgun in his pocket.

Deborah smiled. "Lukey. That's so cute! I'm going to call you that from now on too!"

Grimacing at his mom, Luke replied, "I'll get you for this!" and they all smiled.

As she helped him gather the coats, Deborah asked, "Was the coat you're wearing in this closet?"

Luke was taken aback at the question. "Yes, why?"

"Oh, it's nothing. I'm just surprised, because Aaron wore that coat often."

Thinking quickly and not wanting to take it off, Luke asked, "Would you mind if I kept this one?"

"Of course you can, Lukey!"

They laughed, and each of them took an armful of coats and headed upstairs. Rummaging through the garage for several empty boxes, they started packing the coats for Luke to take to the park. But he found himself thinking the whole time, *Why in the world would Aaron be hiding a gun?*

# 13

**AFTER SAYING GOOD NIGHT** to his parents and Deb, Luke left the house through the kitchen door and carried three boxes of coats to the back of the property. Hoisting each box to the top of the wall, he gently pushed them over and loaded the car. With the backseat full, he headed to Boston Common.

"The Common," as it was commonly referred to by Boston locals, was a national historic landmark. Used as a cow pasture in the early sixteen hundreds, the park has played an important part in Boston's history. Mary Dyer was hanged from a large oak tree for preaching Quakerism in 1660, and British soldiers occupied the grounds before the Revolutionary War. Protesters filled the park to denounce the Vietnam War in the 1960s, and many famous people, including Martin Luther King Jr. and Pope John Paul II, have given important speeches there.

In August of 2007, two teenagers were shot on the Common, causing a strict curfew to be instituted for visitors. This restriction was protested by the homeless population who inhabited the park grounds after dark. Weeks after the shooting, the local police turned a blind eye, and the homeless returned.

Walking past Brewer Fountain, Luke thought that to today's generation, the park would forever be known for one thing: the bombing in Boston. He had been to this park many times to encourage the homeless to go to the local shelters during the cold winter months. He and his fellow priests often brought clothing and food to those who refused.

Luke sat down on a bench and started to open the first box of coats when someone yelled, "Stop right there!" Startled, he saw a police officer walking toward him, with his right hand inside his coat pocket, obviously holding a gun. "Stand up slowly and move away from the box," the officer commanded. Doing exactly as instructed, Luke stood and waited for the cop to approach. Realizing that his scarf was covering his priest collar, he innocently moved his hand to expose it. "Put your hands up and leave them there!" the officer yelled. Luke quickly complied. Moving closer, the officer cautiously examined the box, pulling open the top with one hand while still holding the gun with his other. Seeing the coats, he asked, "Who are you?"

"I'm Luke Miller, a priest from Saint Leonard's parish. I've come to give some old coats to the homeless."

"Can I see identification?"

While unbuttoning his coat, Luke realized that he still had Aaron's gun in his pocket. Noticing the officer moving closer, he started to panic.

"Are you the one whose brother was killed in the bombing?"

"Yes."

Recognizing him and now seeing his collar exposed in the bright moonlight, the officer pulled his gun hand from his pocket and shook Luke's. "Nice to meet you; sorry for your loss."

Seeing that several of the homeless had gathered after hearing the commotion, the officer said good-bye and walked away into the darkness.

Luke stood with his heart pounding and began giving coats to the waiting people. When he carried the third box from the car, he saw that word had spread, and a dozen or so more were standing by the bench in the frigid air. Handing the last coat to an elderly woman, he noticed that there was still one man waiting in the distance. Luke's heart was breaking as he thought about what to do. Without hesitation, Luke turned his back to the man and untucked his shirt. He quickly removed the gun from the coat pocket and placed it in his pants, covering it with his shirttail. Turning around, he saw the man still waiting. Walking slowly toward him, Luke took off the coat and handed it to him. Obviously grateful, the man quickly put it on. As Luke started to walk away, the homeless man said, "Thanks. Are you the priest whose brother was killed?"

Luke stopped and turned. "Yes, I am. How did you know that?"

"I'm sorry, Father. I read the papers when people leave them on the benches. Sometimes I'm a day or two behind on the news, but I try to stay informed."

Luke smiled and waved as he turned again to walk to the car. Then the man said something that made him stop dead. "One of the guys who lives here in the park says he knows who did it."

Luke froze. "What?"

The man looked down. "Well, he says he does. And he says the police are never going to figure it out."

"Where's this man?"

"I can't say. He's a recluse, and like most people who live here, sometimes he's full of shit." Remembering that he was talking to a priest, the man quickly apologized. "Sorry, Father, I didn't mean to curse in front of you."

"Believe me, I've heard worse. Do you think this guy would talk to me?"

"I don't know, but I can ask."

"Let's find him now. Where do we look?"

"Nah, we won't find him now. He said he wouldn't be around for a few days. But I promise I'll keep looking for him."

Luke quickly jotted down his name, address, and phone number on a piece of paper.

"Please, you have to convince this man to talk to me. It's extremely important."

Feeling a need to tell Luke his story, the gray-haired man stepped forward and introduced himself. "I'm John Daly. I've been living in the park for about a year. I was laid off from my job and lost my house. My wife was a realtor, but she hasn't sold a house for over a year, so when she and the kids went back to live with her parents, I just couldn't go with them. I'm too ashamed. So I live here now. I guess you've heard it all before, Father." When the man saw Luke reach into his pocket for some money, he said, "No, that's OK. I've been unloading crates at the docks and hope to have a full-time job soon."

Thinking quickly for a way to make sure that the man would follow up on the lead, Luke asked, "John, if I come back here in two days with another coat, could I trade with you? That one belonged to my brother, and I would like to keep it for sentimental reasons." John immediately started to remove the coat, but Luke convinced him to keep it, promising to return in two days with another one. After saying good-bye, Luke blessed him and walked away.

Returning home, Luke quietly put his key into the back-door lock, opened it, and silently made his way down the hallway. When he entered his room, he took the gun out of his waistband and once again stared at it with disbelief. Why in the world did Aaron have a gun, and why was it hidden downstairs? Unsure of what to do with it, he finally decided to hide it on a top shelf in the closet under some shirts, hoping that there was no way the kids could get to it. He washed up and climbed into bed, but instead of sleeping, he twisted and turned all night while wondering if the homeless man could really tell him what happened.

# 14

**LUKE WOKE AT FIRST** light, anxious to meet with Ablaa Raboud's sister in a few hours. Sticking to his morning routine, he started his day with prayers and a workout. After a quick shower, he joined his family in the sunroom as breakfast was being served.

Both children sat on his lap as he ate. He felt encouraged for the first time in a long time. He was finally doing something meaningful to figure out what happened to his brother, and maybe he was actually making progress.

After eating, he said good-bye and walked out the kitchen door. Before he entered the woods, he looked back and saw Deborah kneeling with the children at the full-length window, watching him walk away. When they saw Luke turn, Alessa began blowing kisses and Abel did the same.

Luke drove to Jamilah's neighborhood and parked the Mercedes a few blocks away from her apartment building. He walked through the front entry and knocked on the door for apartment 1C. He saw someone look through the peephole. The door was opened by an attractive young lady dressed in blue jeans and an MIT sweatshirt. Taken aback, he said, "I'm Luke Miller; I was supposed to meet with Jamilah

Raboud." The young lady responded with a beautiful smile, showing her perfect white teeth. "Luke, I'm Jamilah."

Flustered, Luke responded, "Sorry, Jamilah, I didn't recognize you."

They laughed and shook hands. "Please call me Jami." Noticing that Luke wasn't wearing his clerical clothing, she replied, "I almost didn't recognize you, either!"

She motioned for Luke to sit down on a small couch and offered him something to drink. He politely declined. Sitting across from him in a wooden chair, she became serious and picked up the conversation from the day before. "Luke, my sister was a very peaceful person. She loved the U.S. and its people."

Seeing tears forming in her expressive eyes, Luke quickly spoke up. "I'm not here because I think your sister had something to do with the bombing. I'm here," he began, but remembering that Mark Aldridge had warned him about not trusting anyone, he caught himself, deciding to limit the amount of details he would divulge. "Well, I'm not really sure why I'm here. I guess I wanted to see how the other victims' families were coping."

Her response surprised Luke. "Who else have you met with?"

He wondered if the question was an innocent response or an attempt to get information from him. Thinking quickly, he answered truthfully. "I've talked with Brad Thompson's mother."

"Anyone else?"

"Not yet. You were the next one on my list." As soon as the words left his mouth he regretted them, knowing what her next question would be.

"You have a list?"

"I think everyone read about the people who were killed." Wanting to take control of the situation, he quickly changed the subject. "Enough about me. How are you doing?"

She looked up and her voice cracked as she asked, "Do you know what Ablaa means?"

He shook his head. "No."

"It means 'perfectly formed.' She was perfect. I miss her terribly." She tried to continue but couldn't.

Luke gave her a few minutes to compose herself, then he said, "Let's not talk about the bombing. I didn't come here to upset you." While she dried her eyes, Luke asked, "Where are you from?"

She forced a smile. "Egypt."

"Really? I've also lived in Africa."

Surprised, she asked, "Where?"

"I worked in Johannesburg for four years."

"Southern Africa is much different from northern Africa."

Intrigued by her statement, he asked, "What do you mean?"

She seemed flustered, and Luke noticed red blotches forming on her neck. "As you must know, there are vast religious differences between the regions." At that moment her cell phone rang and she politely excused herself, walking into the bedroom to take the call.

Luke knew that part of the world very well, and the differences weren't just that people quietly believed in different religions. Yes, northern Africa was made up of mostly Muslims who practiced Islam, while southern Africa was populated mostly by Christians. However, after his fellow priests were murdered in Johannesburg, there were rumors throughout the area suggesting that the killers weren't burglars, as advertised by the local media, but Muslim extremists who hated Christians.

Sharia law was prevalent in the north, and Luke had spent countless hours researching it. The more he learned about Sharia, the more concerned he became. Defined as "the path" or "the way," Sharia law was derived from two primary sources of Islamic law: the divine revelations set forth in the Qur'an, and the example set by the Islamic prophet Muhammad. Luke's concerns had nothing to do with the law itself but with the far-reaching and extreme interpretations of the law.

The openly discussed portions had to do mostly with women's rights, including covering their faces in public, being subservient to their husbands, and not dating before marriage. These were archaic by twenty-first-century standards but not unexpected, considering the traditions of this part of the world.

The hidden side of Sharia, however, was unthinkable by Western standards. Luke had read horrifying depictions of amputations, beatings, stonings, and honor killings, yet these draconian acts were seldom discussed. The Egyptian government recently had outlawed female circumcision, only after a twelve-year-old girl had died from an anesthesia overdose while having this nine-dollar procedure to remove her clitoris. Government statistics documented that over 50 percent of girls aged ten to eighteen had been circumcised; UNICEF's research showed the actual numbers to be much higher.

When word of widespread honor killings was published in the European and American press, the Egyptian government's official response was, "Egypt has no honor killings." Yet, not by coincidence, the number of young women "reportedly" committing suicide was increasing at an alarming rate.

Stories of daughters being decapitated for having a boyfriend, or being beaten and electrocuted because they received a phone call from a boy, were common in this part of the world. One story Luke heard about from a fellow priest made the hair on the back of his neck stand on end. The priest told of a young mentally handicapped girl who was buried alive in the ground up to her neck and stoned by her father and others because she became pregnant. After they dug her up and realized that she wasn't dead, they reburied her and threw rocks at her head until she died. What most people didn't know was that her own father was the one who was responsible for impregnating her. Incest was another growing atrocity that many pretended didn't exist.

Northern Africa, including Egypt, continued to have problems with religious tolerance. The Christian Coptic community, which comprised approximately 10 percent of the population, was being persecuted by Muslim extremists. If a young Muslim man saw a Christian girl that he wanted to take as one of his four wives, she would often be kidnapped, tortured, drugged, and raped until she submitted and became a Muslim, never seeing her family again. All of this was happening while government officials looked the other way. Recent bombings of Christian houses and churches had caused an outcry by Pope Benedict, who denounced the violence while stressing religious acceptance.

Jami returned, apologizing for the interruption. Wanting to follow up on her previous statement, Luke said, "You were saying that there are vast differences between northern and southern Africa, but as you know, they're not only religious."

She smiled politely and changed the subject. They talked about general topics for the next half hour. As Luke stood and prepared to leave, he said, "Before I go, can I just ask you one question? Do you have any idea who did the bombing? And do you think your sister was a specific target or just an innocent bystander?"

Flustered, Jami just shook her head. Disappointed that she didn't want to speculate or offer any information, and losing his nerve to press her further, he thanked her for taking time to meet with him.

Then she asked unexpectedly, "Can you come back and visit me again?"

Luke was surprised but said, "Certainly." After exchanging cell numbers, Luke asked, "What does the name Jamilah mean?"

She smiled and then quickly looked down. "It means beautiful."

He waited for her to look up, then he smiled and said, "I should have known."

✝

# 15

**WHILE SITTING IN HIS** parked car, Luke decided to call Jim Hathaway, his brother's financial adviser, to follow up on the settlement of Aaron's life insurance policies. Jim had done as much as he could on his own, but now he needed to meet with the family to finalize the paperwork and money transfers.

"When's the earliest we can meet?" Luke asked, anxious to put the financial side of Aaron's death behind him.

"Hold on for just a minute."

Luke waited patiently until Jim got back on the phone. "I'm sorry to keep you; I just talked to the bank and reviewed my schedule. We can meet in about an hour if that works for you."

Luke was surprised. "So you're also going to be there?"

"Yes, I want to, in case there's a problem. It's the least I can do."

"Thanks so much. Let me check with Deborah, and if you don't hear back from me within ten minutes, I'll see you at the bank in an hour."

Luke called the house to apprise the family of the appointment. Deb was concerned about leaving the children alone with the servants at this point, so Luke said, "Let's just bring them with us." She thanked him profusely for understanding.

They arrived at the bank without incident. Entering the massive stone building, they were asked to sit in the general waiting area until Mr. McMahon, the bank president, was available. The adults sat silently while the children began exploring the unfamiliar building. Suddenly, out of the corner of his eye, Luke saw something horrifying. While standing in line for a teller, a bank patron lifted his phone to take a picture. Quickly reacting, Luke jumped up and ran to the children, grabbing each one by the hand and pulling them back to their mother. By the time he walked into the waiting area, several other customers were also taking pictures. Deborah realized what was happening before his parents did, and she told them, "Hurry, look down!" At this point, half of the people in the bank were taking photos. Not knowing what else to do, Luke stood and commanded, "Let's go!" As they started toward the exit, he saw Jim Hathaway walking up the front steps to enter the bank. Seeing the commotion, Jim asked the security guard to make sure no one got close to the family, as he ran for assistance. Seconds later he returned and said, "Follow me." With their heads down, they walked quickly across the marble floor and into an executive office at the far end of the bank.

After a multitude of apologies from Jim and Mr. McMahon, they began signing the stacks of paper that were shuffled in front of them. Deborah and Luke's parents already had accounts with the bank, so their transactions were straightforward. When McMahon asked Luke, "Where do you want your money deposited?" he replied, "Just put it in one of their accounts," as he pointed toward Deb and his parents. After objections from his family, Jim suggested that the bank open a new account for Luke. McMahon picked up his phone, and seconds later a middle-aged woman knocked on the door. He instructed her to create Luke's account and to deposit the checks from the insurance company "with no hold." Without any prompting, he also instructed her to make sure Luke was also issued an ATM card. Not wanting to make a scene, Luke didn't protest.

Fifteen minutes later, the woman appeared and handed receipts to everyone in the room. Glancing at his, Luke was shocked to see an amount of two million dollars printed on the small piece of paper. Jim whispered, so the children who were playing in the corner of the room couldn't hear, "I know this is the least of your concerns right now, but you need to know that once the accidental death investigation is completed, additional checks for the same amount will be issued to each of you." As Luke looked at the ATM card he was handed, the bank lady explained, "It has a temporary initial password; you need to walk outside with me and sign on to the system so your permanent password can be created. I must warn you, though, there's a crowd of people waiting to take pictures."

"I really don't need the card," Luke argued, but his father insisted.

"Luke, you never know when you might need it. Please, just take the card."

Not wanting to upset his father, Luke followed the lady to one of the ATM machines, where a security guard was standing. As he walked through the bank with his head down, he saw faint flashes of light from cell phone cameras. Once he arrived at the machine, the guard did a good job of making sure that no one could get close to him. Looking toward the exit, he saw a crowd forming outside. After following the ATM's instructions, he entered his new password: "temptation." Soon he was back in the office with his family, preparing to leave.

Trying to protect Abel and Alessa from the reporters, Luke thought it would be a good idea if the children left the building with his parents, since most of the onlookers had no idea who they were. What they really wanted was to see Luke and Deborah. "Mom, no matter what happens, go to the car, get into the backseat, and lock the doors. Deborah and I will leave a few seconds after you, but we're going to stay in the bank until we're sure that you are safe inside the car." His parents agreed. Deborah bent down and said to the children, "We're going to play a game. You go with Grandma and Grandpa, and walk to the car as fast as you can." Trying to lighten the mood so that the children weren't scared, she continued, "Uncle Lukey and I are going to give you a head start, then we're going to try to beat you there. Don't let anyone distract you. Whoever gets to the car first wins a prize." Abel and Alessa laughed, hearing their mom say "Lukey." "Do you understand?" They both shook their heads in agreement.

Luke opened the door, and his parents walked out quickly with the kids. A few seconds later, he and Deb walked into the lobby. To draw attention to himself, Luke said in a loud voice, "Thank you so much, Mr. McMahon, for all your help." In an instant, every person inside the bank was focused on Luke. He saw his parents exiting the building, while the customers and employees turned their attention to him. Estimating that it would take his parents twenty seconds to reach the car, he and Deb looked down and waited. After counting, he took her by the arm and they walked briskly, with Jim Hathaway leading the way. Getting to the front door was a breeze, but none of them were prepared for what happened next.

Looking outside, Luke could see that a tremendous crowd had formed. There were reporters with cameras waiting, along with a horde of spectators. Luke assumed that someone who saw them in the bank had contacted the press. It was lunchtime in downtown Boston, and also an unseasonably warm day, so many people who worked in the nearby offices joined the gathering, not even knowing who they were waiting for. Stopping near the security guard who had locked the bank doors, Luke looked at Deborah and said, "I'm not going to leave you. Just stay by my side and try not to look up." She smiled nervously and nodded.

Seeing the crowd of people pressed against the glass, the guard looked at Luke and said, "Are you sure you want me to unlock the door?"

Luke joked nervously, "We'll be OK; we have God on our side."

The man smiled and replied, "I hope you're right."

The heavy glass doors opened outward, which was the first sign that someone was watching over them. As the guard pushed the door open, the people on the other side had to back up, thus creating a temporary void for Luke and Deb. Seeing the size of the crowd, which was getting bigger by the minute, Luke quickly maneuvered Deborah so that she was directly behind him; she wrapped her hands around his waist and clasped them. Putting his head down, he walked forward as flashbulbs and shouts erupted. After the first ten feet, he had no choice but to become somewhat aggressive as he began pushing his way through the crowd. He hated doing this, but he told himself he had to protect his family. He began making headway, considering the circumstances. He realized that people were tripping and falling as he forced his way, but he told himself that he couldn't be concerned with that right now. He could hear people yelling, but he didn't listen to their words because he was focused on just getting to the car.

Luke went directly to the driver's side, opened the door, and shoved Deborah inside. While she was moving into the passenger seat, photographers pushed their cameras inside and snapped pictures blindly. Once Luke got in, he slammed the car door, not realizing that a reporter's arm was still inside. As the man screamed, Luke's first instinct was to be compassionate and get out to check the man's condition, but instead he opened the door to release the arm, slammed the door again, and locked it. Edging the car forward, it took more than ten minutes before he was able to leave the crowd behind. Only after the security guard at Aaron's house waved the Mercedes SUV through the electric gates could Luke feel his pounding heart and high blood pressure begin to normalize.

# 16

**GRATEFUL THAT HIS FAMILY** was now home and safe, Luke decided to tackle another unpleasant task that had been weighing on his mind for the last several days. Leaving once again from the woods behind the house, he drove to Roxbury and eventually pulled through the black iron gates of a small, secluded cemetery. He eased the car down the winding road leading to Aaron's grave and parked on the grass that lined the narrow lane. Mesmerized, he stared at the headstone in the distance without blinking, wishing that this was a bad dream and that he would eventually wake up.

He emerged from the car, relieved to see that there was no sign of the press. Weeks had passed since "the incident," so he figured most of them had quit stalking the cemetery and had moved on to other places in hopes of getting pictures of his family. As he knelt in the freshly excavated dirt and read the name on the headstone, he started to cry.

"I'm sorry I hurt you; I can't believe we weren't talking to each other. Aaron, I love you with all my heart. I really don't know what to do about Deborah and the children, but you have my word that I'll always stay close and watch over them. Dad and Mom are getting stronger, but they miss you so much." He smiled, tears rolling down his face. "You're not going to believe it, but Dad and I are friends again. I never wanted to hurt you or the family. If I thought that being a priest was going to drive us apart, I never would have done it. If I wasn't a priest, I wouldn't have known about the homeless shelter in the middle of your project, and we would have never stopped talking. Maybe you wouldn't have been on that stage with Brad Thompson." Burying his head in his hands, he pleaded, "God help me!"

After walking back to the car, he got in and sat, drained. He didn't know why, but he couldn't leave. Maybe he just wanted to be close to his brother, but he had no desire to be anywhere else. Nearly an hour passed before he looked at the clock on the dashboard and decided it was time to go. Putting his hand on the ignition key to start the car, he instinctively looked in his rearview mirror and saw something that made him stop.

A white Cadillac inched down the narrow road. Hoping that it was just another mourner, but wanting to be cautious, he moved his hand from the ignition to the side of his seat, pushing the recline control. The seat inched slowly backward as the white car got closer. Luke realized that the tinted windows would make it hard for anyone to see him, but he wasn't taking any chances. As the car passed, he couldn't see inside from the position he was in, but he noticed the license plate, "LS 1." The car slowed and parked about fifty feet ahead of him on the same side of the road.

Curious, Luke waited. After fifteen minutes, he returned his seat to its normal position in anticipation of starting the car, but he stopped when a tall blonde woman wearing high heels emerged from the Caddy and walked down the row where Aaron was buried. Luke was dismayed when she stopped in front of his brother's grave. Determined to find out who she was, he quietly got out of the car, not wanting to be noticed. Walking silently on the grass, he moved closer. When he was about fifteen feet away, she looked up, obviously startled, and began to cry. Luke continued walking toward her.

By the time he was standing next to her, she was hysterical. Raising her hands to hold her face, she dropped her purse. When she bent down to get it, her sunglasses fell to the ground. Luke bent down to pick them up and noticed that her heels had sunk into the loose dirt. When he stood, they were standing face to face, looking into each other's eyes for the first time.

"I'm Luke, Aaron's brother," he said, while handing her the glasses. She opened her purse, placed them inside, and fumbled for a tissue. Sobbing, she extended her hand and said, "I'm Lori Simpson." When she didn't continue talking, Luke asked, "Have we met before?"

She turned to face him. "No, I'd only known your brother for about nine months. But I know a lot about you." Realizing that she was very upset, he didn't prod further but stood silently while she attempted to compose herself. Uncomfortable after several minutes of silence, he turned to leave. She looked up and said, "Please don't go. I was a very close friend of your brother. We need to talk." She slowly began walking and Luke followed.

"As I'm sure you know by now, Aaron was planning to run for senator in the next election. I was going to be his campaign manager, press secretary, and eventually, once he was elected, his chief of staff. We met while working on Brad Thompson's presidential campaign after his first manager quit and Aaron reluctantly accepted the job. For the past several months, we spent an enormous amount of time together, working seven days a week, fifteen hours a day." She continued walking, while dabbing her eyes with a tissue. "We were very close, and I can't tell you the impact his death has had on my life."

Feeling he should say something, Luke stated the obvious. "Mine also." He wanted to ask her if they were having an affair, but he didn't want to embarrass her.

She continued, "I just keep asking myself, why? Why did this happen?"

Now Luke had his opening. He stepped in front of her and she stopped walking. He asked, "Do you have any idea who did this?"

"I don't know. There are rumors in political circles that it had something to do with Brad Thompson. I've heard allegations about everyone from pro-choice groups to Mexican drug lords. I understand that the FBI has questioned Steve Hinkley."

"Who's he?"

"A local pro-choice activist who made threats on the Internet."

Luke asked in disbelief, "How could a local guy like that have the resources to pull off a bombing of that magnitude?"

She raised her voice and said, "I don't know. I'm just telling you what I've heard."

Sensing her frustration with his questioning, Luke said softly, "Who did you hear this stuff from?"

"I have a connection in the governor's office."

"Who's that?"

"My husband is the lieutenant governor."

Without thinking, Luke said, "You're married?"

Agitated, she replied sharply, "Regardless of what you've been thinking, Aaron and I were only close friends. It wasn't my choice, since I would have left my husband in a second for him, but unfortunately he was completely committed to his wife. Everyone seemed to assume that we were having an affair. Your brother was one of the best people I've ever known. Be sure to let his wife know that he loved and admired her. He talked about her all the time. And when he wasn't talking politics, or about his wife and children, he was talking about you."

Luke remained silent and she continued. "The day Aaron was killed, I lost everything: my best friend, my career, and my future. All I have left is a loveless marriage." She began crying again.

Not knowing what to say, Luke asked gently, "Do you come here often?"

"Just about every day. I have no place else to go."

Realizing how close Lori was to his brother, he bluntly asked, "Why did Aaron have a gun?"

"There were constant threats from people who disagreed with Brad and Aaron's political views. None were specifically directed at Aaron that I know of, but just about every day we would receive an intimidating letter or voice mail message."

"How did he get the gun?"

She looked at him in disbelief. "Luke, if the bombing had never happened, Brad Thompson would be president right now. Aaron would have been the closest and most trusted confidant to the most powerful man in the world. If he wanted a military helicopter, he could have gotten one."

Turning the last bend of the circular road that led through the graveyard, they approached their cars. He opened her door and said, "I'm really glad I met you." When he extended his hand to shake hers, she moved his arm aside and hugged him tightly. Before driving away, she asked, "Will I see you again?"

He smiled. "You will if you're here tomorrow."

# 17

**AFTER DINNER, LUKE CHECKED** the cell phone detective Romo had given him and noticed a text message: "The two phone numbers you gave me to trace must belong to high-ranking government officials. I can't get any information without sign-off from the FBI. Sorry." Disappointed, Luke sent a text back, thanking him.

Seeing Deborah sitting alone in the living room, he stopped and sat on a chair across from her. "Can you take a ride with me tomorrow?"

In slurred words she asked, "Where to?"

Realizing that she was drunk, he answered, "I'll tell you in the morning."

She took a sip from her glass and nodded affirmatively.

Annoyed that she was drinking again, he sarcastically asked, "How's the wine?"

She gave him an aggravated look as she attempted to stand, but she wobbled on her high heels and landed back on the couch, red wine splashing all over her white blouse. Refusing to help, Luke forced himself to walk out of the room in silence. He realized that she was in no condition to take care of the children, so he occupied them by playing games until their bedtime. When it was time for them to go to sleep, he walked down the hall and saw Deb in her room, passed out on the bed, so he decided to let the kids sleep in his room while he spent the night on the floor.

The next morning Luke decided to skip his workout, and he opened the door to retrieve the morning paper that the security guards placed on the front steps each day. Noticing that the paper was placed with the front page down, he immediately turned it over and realized why. Under the headline "Who's Your Daddy?" was a picture taken in the bank, showing Luke walking while holding the children's hands.

Flipping to the article as he walked into the library, he was shocked again. Someone from the bank had leaked the exact amount of money that Luke, Deborah, and his parents had received from Aaron's life insurance policy. The subtitle read, "Vow of Poverty? Not for the Millionaire Priest." The reporter knew every detail, including the double indemnity payment.

Luke stared at the headline, thinking that if the reporter had spent just a few minutes researching the rules for diocesan priests, he would have known that they don't take formal vows of poverty, chastity, or obedience like religious priests do. They do, however, make promises at their ordination to lead a celibate life, to respect and obey their diocesan bishop, and to live a simple lifestyle. While in the seminary, Luke had known several priests who came from extremely wealthy families and had inherited large amounts of money. Most took the opportunity to use these funds for charitable work.

Gazing out the window, Luke thought about the unlisted phone numbers. He was almost certain that one of them belonged to Brad Thompson, but what about the other one? He had an idea. Taking out his cell phone, he looked up Rebecca Bruno's number, pressed the send button, and waited.

She answered on the third ring and said in a beautiful Italian accent, "Father Luke, it's so nice to hear from you."

Luke smiled. "Very nice to hear your beautiful voice, Rebecca."

"How're you doing? How are Aaron's wife and the children?"

Luke spent fifteen minutes updating her on everything that had been going on. Toward the end of the small talk he interjected, "I've been spending time trying to reconstruct the last few weeks of my brother's life."

There was silence for a few seconds before she responded, carefully choosing her words. "I admire your determination. If that was my brother, I would spend every penny I have and search until my last breath trying to find the SOB responsible for his death."

Luke had never seen this side of her before, but he found himself agreeing with her statement. He figured the time was right to ask his favor. "That's why I'm calling you today. I was wondering if Sal could help trace a few phone numbers that my brother called before his death."

He could hear her rummaging through some papers in the background. "Give me the numbers."

Luke repeated them twice to ensure she had them written down correctly. "Rebecca, please let him know that this can wait until after Thanksgiving."

"I'll call him right now."

Thanking her, he closed the phone and walked into his bedroom to check on the kids. Luke sat on the edge of the bed and watched the two angels as they slept. They were perfect, innocent children whose lives were turned upside down by people who probably didn't even know their names. He gently took Alessa's soft hand in his and rubbed it while thinking, "How much would Aaron have paid to do this just one last time?" Looking up, he saw his father watching from the doorway, and they exchanged smiles.

Deborah was absent from breakfast, so Luke and his parents entertained the children. When she finally shuffled into the kitchen, he immediately observed her bloodshot eyes and pale complexion. As soon as she sat down at the table, he stood, excused himself, and walked into the library. Seeing that he had two new voice mails on his cell phone, he picked it up and listened. Aaron's financial adviser and the bank president had both left messages apologizing for the leak of his personal financial data to the press. Jim Hathaway let him know that the teller responsible for the leak was fired.

Deep in thought, Luke looked up to see Deborah standing in the doorway. Knowing he was disappointed in her, she said, "Sorry," and turned to walk away.

Before she was out of earshot he asked, "Can you take a ride with me?"

She turned back. "Where to?"

"I'll tell you when we're in the car."

# 18

**ONCE LUKE TOOK THE** Roxbury exit, Deborah didn't have to ask where they were going; she knew. They followed the winding road that led to Aaron's grave in silence. Stepping out of the car, Luke walked slowly toward the grave with Deb holding his arm. When they reached the headstone, she fell to her knees and wept. Luke felt awkward but remained standing next to her with his hand on her shoulder. After a few minutes, Luke heard something and looked up. The white Caddy was pulling onto the grass. He told Deb, "Wait here for a minute," as he hurried to greet Lori.

Lori didn't have to be told the identity of the woman at the grave; she had stared at Deborah's picture on Aaron's desk many times.

When Luke approached, she asked, "Luke, do you think I should be here? Now?"

Luke helped her from the car. "She needs to meet you. She thinks that you and Aaron were having an affair and it's killing her."

Understanding, Lori took a deep breath and proceeded toward the grave. As they approached, Deborah looked up, puzzled. She quickly dried her eyes, put on her sunglasses, and stood. Luke took charge.

"Deborah, this is Lori. She worked very closely with Aaron on the campaign."

Lori wiped a tear from her eye and reached out her hand. Deborah shook it suspiciously. Luke suggested, "Let's take a walk." After a few minutes, Luke asked, "Lori, were you having lunch with Aaron downtown when one of Deb's friends saw you?" Deborah immediately looked up.

Lori looked at Deb and answered, "Yes. He was upset because he didn't want you to know."

Deborah asked sharply, "Know what?"

Lori stopped walking and grabbed Deb's hand while facing her. "He didn't want you to know that he was planning a party to celebrate your tenth wedding anniversary."

Deborah began to cry. "So you weren't having an affair with him?"

Now also crying, Lori answered, "He loved you so much. When he wasn't talking about politics, he was always talking about you and the children. He was a good man, a decent man. I admired him so much and can only imagine how you must feel. I'm so sorry. But to answer your question directly, no, we weren't having an affair. He would never do something like that. You had to see the way his eyes lit up when he talked about you."

Lori and Deborah were now walking in front of Luke with their arms interlocked, talking quietly. As they finished the loop, Luke headed toward the car so that the two women could spend time together at the grave. When Deborah noticed this, she quickly ran back and insisted he join them. Standing there with the two of them, he knew Aaron was happy. Before leaving, Luke watched as Lori and Deborah hugged each other and exchanged phone numbers.

As they drove home, Deborah thanked Luke several times for introducing her to Lori. She promised that she would control her drinking, pay more attention to the children, and be more responsible. This time he actually believed her. After they parked the car in the secret spot, Luke helped her over the wall and into the house.

They were home only for ten minutes when Luke's cell phone rang. Seeing the security guard's number, Luke asked, "Is everything OK?"

"Yes, Mr. Miller, but there's a black limo here, and the man inside says he needs to talk with you."

"Who is he?"

A new voice on the phone said, "Father Miller, I'm Anthony Amato, Mr. Bruno's driver. He sent me to pick you up. He told me to tell you that he has the info you requested and wants to see you in person."

"How did you know I was home?"

He laughed. "Father, Mr. Bruno knows everything. I don't think you should keep him waiting."

Luke quickly explained to Deborah that he had an appointment. She didn't ask any questions but told him to be careful. Approaching the car, Luke was surprised to see two people sitting in the front seat. A man quickly jumped out and opened the back door for Luke. "I'm Bobby. I work with Anthony." Luke shook his hand and sat in the backseat.

The two goons sat in front, singing along with the songs from the radio as they sped through downtown Boston. Luke wasn't surprised when they reached the North End, also referred to as Little Italy. Pulling up to Dom's Restaurant, Luke was surprised when a man appeared out of nowhere and moved two orange construction cones so that the limo could park directly in front.

✝

# 19

**THE RESTAURANT LOOKED MORE** like an old house than a place to eat. As Luke was ushered inside, he wasn't surprised to see that the inside decor matched the outside appearance. He was led into a small dining room containing five tables with white linen tablecloths and red napkins. Sal had been looking out the small front window, awaiting Luke's arrival. When he saw him, he quickly walked over and shook Luke's hand.

"Thanks for coming."

Luke thought to himself, Like I had a choice? But he said, "Thank you for inviting me." Sal cut an imposing figure: tall, big boned, tan, and completely bald. When he looked up sharply, a waiter hurried over and pulled out two chairs, inviting them to sit down. Without a word, red wine was poured. Sal took a sip, nodded, and motioned for Luke to do the same. As Sal reached into his suit pocket, Luke saw a holstered gun. Retrieving a piece of paper, he placed it on the table and pushed it toward Luke, who picked it up. Upon opening it, he was immediately disappointed, saying out loud, "I should've known."

The first name was exactly who he thought it would be: Brad Thompson. The second was his new friend from the cemetery: Lori

Simpson. Remembering that her husband was the lieutenant governor, he was irritated that he hadn't figured this out himself, especially since now Deborah even had the same number stored in her phone. Looking up, Luke said, "Thank you very much."

For the first time ever, Luke saw him smile. He took the red cloth napkin and tucked it into his shirt collar, creating a makeshift bib that protected his expensive suit and tie. Appetizers were served and little was said. Sal ate like a man who hadn't eaten for days. His mouth was so busy chewing and drinking that there was no time to talk. After he had devoured everything in sight, he looked up at Luke and grinned again. Luke motioned to let him know that he had a piece of lettuce stuck between his fake front teeth. He quickly used one of his big fingers in an attempt to remove it. When Luke shook his head to indicate that it was still there, he looked at him and said, "You're not screwing with me, are you Father?"

Luke smiled. "No, Sal, I wouldn't do that."

"Thanks. Most of these meatballs I have working for me would have let me walk around all day with that stuff stuck in my teeth and would have laughed about it behind my back."

Luke was amazed that he actually said more than two words in a row. Sal said, "Rebecca insisted that I meet you for lunch. She has a great fondness for you."

"As I do for her."

"When you called, she made me promise that I would find the information on the phone numbers immediately, telling me to cancel any appointments and make sure I took care of you first."

Luke smiled and Sal continued, "Father, God may have some issues with me, but Rebecca is an angel. She's the best person I've ever met, and I would do anything to make her happy. Now tell me, why did you want those numbers?"

Figuring that he could trust Sal, Luke answered honestly. "I need to know who killed my brother."

Sal pondered that statement for a moment. "Well, Luke, let me tell you what I know. The FBI is keeping tight wraps on all information regarding the investigation. But I have, let's say, a connection, with a few federal judges. I've asked some questions and know that they have no solid leads. They've gone as far as working with that Internet company, Google, to review satellite images from the past three years. What's it been, about a month since the bombing?"

Luke nodded.

"Well, from what I'm told, let's just say they have nothing."

Sal had probably used up a week's worth of words at this point, but Luke decided to ask a few questions anyway. "Do you think this judge is telling you the truth?"

Sal smiled. "I know he is."

Curious, Luke asked, "How do you know that?"

"Because he wouldn't be a judge if it wasn't for me."

Luke tilted his head, not understanding. Sal elaborated. "Luke, when a judge is under consideration for a federal appointment, a complete background check is done on him. Well, most of these guys have been lawyers or local judges before their selection. Many times, we know something about their past that they don't want anyone else to know. Capice?"

Seeing Luke's puzzled look, he continued. "Let's just say they owe me a favor. You never know when you're going to need information. Father, there are things you're better off not knowing, but remember, the federal courts prosecute counterfeiters, money launderers, and crimes having to do with interstate commerce."

Shocked, Luke changed the topic. "How come they've only looked at three years of satellite pictures?"

"I think that's all they store. Why, do you think they should look further back?"

"I don't know."

Sal looked at his Rolex and said, "I better get you home."

They stood and shook hands and Luke thanked him. While escorting Luke toward the door, Sal said, "If you need anything else, call."

Running out of clues, Luke decided to try a long shot. "Do you know who Steve Hinkley is?"

"No, that name doesn't sound familiar. Who is he?"

"A local pro-choice guy that the FBI questioned about the bombing."

"What did they find out?"

"I'm not sure."

Sal wrote the name down and said, "I'll have someone check it out."

Luke thanked him and left.

Still deep in thought when they pulled up to the gates of Aaron's house, Luke sat motionless until Bobby said, "You OK, Father?"

Luke looked up. "Yes."

Bobby jumped out to open the door for him. As Luke climbed out of the car, Anthony said, "You seem a little down, Padre. We're going to meet some babes at a club tonight. Maybe you want to come with us?"

Bobby laughed. "Yeah, Father, you need to live a little."

Enjoying the moment, Anthony joked, "One night out with us and you'll feel like you lived a complete life."

Smiling, but annoyed, Luke leaned down and looked in the front window. "When you two rocket scientists get home, do me a favor and spell 'live' backwards. If you figure that one out, try spelling 'lived' backwards."

As Luke walked toward the iron gates, he heard Bobby yell, "Good one, Father!"

Walking to the house, Luke felt defeated. If the feds didn't have any leads, and they'd been looking at three years of satellite imagery, what chance did he have of ever figuring anything out? Detective Romo couldn't help him. Now the unlisted phone numbers were a dead end. What the heck was he going to do? He decided he would follow up on his last lead, John Daly, the homeless man. If nothing came of it tonight, he was through.

# 20

**AFTER DINNER, LUKE PACED** back and forth in his room, waiting impatiently for the time to pass before heading to the Common to find the homeless man who said he knew who killed Aaron. When the clock on his nightstand finally read 9:45, he couldn't wait any longer. Remembering the incident with the cop the last time, he changed into his clerical outfit and purposely selected a coat that exposed his white priest collar.

Luke parked on a street near the Common. The night was frigid, and he walked quickly. Within a few minutes he was sitting on the same bench where he had distributed the coats two nights before. He saw people in the distance, but there was no sign of John Daly. After fifty minutes, he decided to get up and search for him.

Starting at the Brewer Fountain, Luke walked briskly around the outskirts of the park, oblivious to the danger of doing so. After passing Parkman Plaza and the Central Burying Ground, he remembered that the homeless often congregated with the drug dealers near the bandstand. So he changed direction, walking toward the center of the park. As he reached the bandstand, he was surprised at how dark it was. He heard a man laughing in the shadows. Feeling uneasy, he approached, and a horrible stench filled the air. When their eyes met, the bearded man looked at Luke and said, "Faddah, can you help an old altar boy? I'm a Catholic." Remembering that same line from *The Exorcist*, Luke felt involuntary chills run up his spine.

His pace quickened as he thought to himself, I should've brought the gun. Shocked at his own thoughts, he said the Our Father silently, until he said out loud, "Deliver me from evil," without regard for who might hear. As he reached the Charles Street Gate, he frantically realized that his chances of finding John Daly were diminishing by the minute. By the time he passed the Shaw Memorial, he had asked almost twenty people if they had seen John Daly. Determined not to give up on his last lead, he turned around and backtracked, then headed toward the Public Garden, another park across the street. He kept repeating the same question over and over to anyone he passed, all with the same results. Not knowing what else to do, he continued roaming the surrounding streets for hours. Finally, tired, cold, and totally dejected, he punched the car door before reluctantly heading home.

When he entered the house through the kitchen door he was distraught, not only because he had bashed his knuckles but worse, because he had just exhausted his last lead. In an uncharacteristic desire to dull the excruciating pain, he grabbed a glass and a bottle of wine from the cooler. Not wanting to disturb anyone, he padded toward the front of the house and into the library, closing the double doors behind him. As he sat in a leather chair, he filled his glass, raised it, and said, "Aaron, I'm so sorry. I tried and failed." He took huge gulps in between sobs, and it didn't take long until the bottle was empty and Luke was passed out on the floor.

When he opened his eyes, he saw Deborah kneeling next to him with tears streaming down her face. After blinking several times, he realized where he was and what had happened. Ashamed, he attempted to stand and saw the broken glass and spilled wine on the floor. She helped him to his feet, and he held his head. "What's wrong?" he asked.

She burst out crying. "When I saw how late it was, I checked to make sure you came home. I couldn't find you in your room. I didn't know if something happened to you or if you decided not to come back. I ran to the wall, climbed the ladder, and saw your car. Then I came back and began searching the house. I saw you lying on the floor." She began sobbing. "The wine looked like blood."

Realizing what she must have thought, he said, "I'm so sorry, Deb. I really am. I didn't mean to frighten you. I had no right to tell you not to drink. Look at me. Who am I to give anyone advice?"

She hugged him as tight as she could, whispering, "I thought I lost you."

He returned her embrace. Looking at the floor over her shoulder, he released his grip and began picking up the pieces of broken glass. She bent down to help.

"I hope I didn't stain the marble."

She dismissed his concern. "It doesn't matter."

As they both stood together, Luke took the broken glass from her hand and placed it in the garbage can next to Aaron's desk. She led him to the couch and said, "Stay here. I'll be right back." A few minutes later, she returned, holding a big glass of water and two Advil. "I know from experience—this is the only thing that will help you feel better." He smiled and took the pills.

When she sat down next to him, he noticed that her short satin nightgown exposed her naked thighs. As he glanced at them, he saw her look down also. Realizing what he was looking at, she surprisingly made no attempt to cover up.

"Luke, we should get to bed. Remember, tomorrow is Thanksgiving, and we have to get up early to cook."

He held his head and smiled wobbly. "Is that tomorrow already?"

She smiled. "Can we try to make it a normal day? I just want to forget for one day."

Luke said without much conviction, "OK, we can try."

# PART 2

"*If you don't know where you're going, any road will get you there.*"
—Lewis Carroll

# 21

HEARING LAUGHTER NEAR HIS bed, Luke slowly opened his eyes and felt the children tickling his feet. He pretended to be asleep, waiting until Alessa walked toward the head of the bed to look at him. Opening his eyes quickly, he grabbed her by the arms and hoisted her over his head. She erupted in laughter, and Abel did the same as he jumped into the bed on top of Luke. Sensing someone else was present, he sat up and saw Deborah laughing from the open doorway.

"OK, let's leave Uncle Lukey alone so he can get dressed."

The children protested until Luke pulled Abel close and hugged him tight. "Go with your mom, and I'll meet you in a few minutes."

After a quick shower, a shave, and a few more Advil, Luke walked into the kitchen. Most of the servants were busy preparing food for the Thanksgiving feast. Seeing Luke, the children ran to his side and each one hugged one of his legs. As he walked to the other side of the room with a child still attached to each leg, he was handed a large bowl and a mixer by Ethel, the head cook. Everyone was smiling, laughing, and having fun. Luke decided that he wasn't going to think about reality today, he was just going to enjoy the moment.

Plugging in the mixer, he strategically placed the bowl full of cake mix on the counter next to the backsplash. Propping it up so it balanced on the edge of the bowl, he turned the mixer on and watched as it began mixing without any assistance. Proud of his invention, he called across the room, "Hey, Ethel, what else do you need me to do?" Everyone in the kitchen looked as the normally grouchy cook turned and smiled. At that moment, the vibration caused the mixer to fall, still running, shooting cake mix across the room. Luke and the children got the worst of it; they were covered. Wiping the thick yellow paste from his eyes, Luke began licking it off his fingers. The children, watching him, began doing the same as the entire kitchen erupted in laughter. Hearing the commotion, Deborah opened the door and yelled, "What's going on in here?" The kitchen went silent until Luke swiped some of the mix from Alessa's hair and licked it off his finger. Then everyone howled as Deborah began laughing. Reaching into the bowl, Luke took what was left of the mix and hurled it toward Deb. She quickly closed the door as the mix splattered on it. For the next hour, Luke and the children cleaned the kitchen as the cooks cooked. The cake mix fiasco set the jovial tone for the day.

Luke cleaned up the kids the best he could, although Alessa still had sticky spots of batter stuck throughout her long, dark hair. He returned to his room to find a clean shirt, then he chose a sweater from Aaron's vast selection. When he walked back through the dining room, Deborah was setting the table. She looked up at him, and her eyes immediately filled with tears. "What's wrong?" Luke asked.

She smiled. "That's the same sweater Aaron wore every Thanksgiving Day." When he began removing it, she rushed over and stopped him. "Please leave it on." He complied. For the rest of the morning, the children stayed by Luke's side. The mood in the house was lighter than it had been in weeks.

In the early afternoon, Luke, Deb, and the children stood by the front door and welcomed the servants' families. Most of the visiting children had been at the house before, and they immediately rushed to the large playroom on the far end. Sounds of laughter filled the house for the first time in months. As the children played, Luke and Deborah prepared to serve the appetizers. The adults sat at a long antique table in the elegant dining room. The children's table was located in the adjoining room, although they had no interest in eating at the moment.

Before beginning the meal, Luke watched as the servants' families all held hands. Realizing what was about to happen, Luke's mom nudged his father, who reluctantly held the hand of the smiling lady sitting next to him. Luke and Deb rushed to sit down. Johnny, a long-time employee and one of the older men seated at the table, took out a small piece of paper and began speaking in heavily accented English. "Thank you, dear God, for the food we are about to eat and for all of those who prepared it. Thank you for the children, as we see you in their loving eyes every day. Thank you for Deborah and Luke; they are very good to us." His eyes filled with tears as he looked around the table. "And most of all, please, God, bless Aaron." His voice cracked as he added, "We miss him so much." At this point everyone was drying tears from their eyes. After gaining his composure, he continued, "With all of our troubles, we have so much to be thankful for. We give glory to God. Amen."

While everyone was preparing to eat, Luke's father spoke sharply, trying not to cry. "I have nothing to be thankful for—absolutely nothing." Seeing the surprise and shock of everyone at the table, he put his head down. Embarrassed, he stood and walked out of the room. When Luke's mother got up to follow him, Luke interceded. "Mom, let me go. You stay here and eat."

Luke headed down the long hallway to the guest room, where he knocked gently on the oversized door. When there was no answer, he turned the knob and peered inside. His father was sitting on a chair, blankly staring out the window. Luke pulled another chair close and sat next to him. When his dad didn't acknowledge him, Luke leaned over and grasped his hand. Looking straight ahead, his father finally spoke. "I'm sorry that I ruined your day."

Luke smiled and squeezed his hand. "Dad, everyone understands. Can you please do one thing for me, just one thing?"

The father turned to face Luke. "Anything."

Luke took a deep breath and sighed. "Remember how much Aaron loved Thanksgiving? It was always his favorite holiday, and it made him so happy to have his family and employees enjoying a great meal together. I know it's hard, but please think about what he would want us to do. I know he's watching us now and is happy that we're carrying on the tradition."

His dad wiped his eyes and forced a smile. Then he said something sobering. "Luke, if you honestly believe that Aaron is watching over us, please remember that when you're making decisions regarding your future. Your mother and I are moving back home tomorrow." Luke pondered that thought for a few seconds and then convinced his dad to return for dinner.

# 22

**WHILE LUKE HELPED SERVE** the main course, his cell phone began vibrating in his pocket. He placed the large platter of turkey he was carrying on the dining room table and rushed into the library to answer it. Seeing the number, he became concerned.

"Is everything all right?"

The security guard answered calmly, "Yes, Mr. Miller, but there are two people here to see you."

Luke's mind raced. Someone from the church? Sal and Rebecca? Who could it possibly be?

"Who?" he asked impatiently. He could hear the guard talking but couldn't tell what he was saying. A few seconds later, the guard spoke into the phone. "It's a Mr. John Daly and another man. He says he knows you and that you gave him this address. He insisted that I call you." Then he whispered, "They look like a couple of homeless guys to me. I can get rid of them if you want."

Luke quickly opened the door and frantically searched his pants pockets for his keys. Once he had the key fob in hand, he pressed the button and jogged down the stone driveway toward the opening gates. "Don't let them leave!" he yelled into the phone. Arriving at the gate, he saw John and a man who was sitting on an old bicycle. The rusty metal baskets were filled with old bottles, and there was a black plastic bag hanging from the handlebars. Luke immediately rushed over to John and extended his hand. "Thank you for coming."

John walked close and whispered, "I'm sorry for showing up here unannounced." He motioned toward the gray-haired, bearded man on the bike. "He wouldn't let me call on the phone. He says that if anyone knew what he knows, he would be as good as dead." As the man pushed the old bike through the gates, Luke walked over and introduced himself. "I'm Luke Miller. Very nice to meet you."

The weather-beaten man stared at the house and responded, "The church must be paying pretty good these days, Father."

Luke smiled. "This was my brother's house."

Turning to face Luke for the first time, he extended his calloused hand. As he came into full sight, Luke saw the jagged scar on the left side of his face. It ran from just above his eyebrow to his chin and looked like he had stitched it together himself. "I'm Blade. Nice to meet you, Father."

Realizing that he was staring, Luke forced himself to look away. "Thank you for coming. Please come inside and eat with us."

John spoke up. "Are you sure? Looks like you have company."

Luke smiled. "I'm sure. The people who work here are inside eating with their families. I'm inviting you."

John looked down at his old pants and shoes, then looked at Blade's ragged clothing and asked again, "You sure?"

"Absolutely."

Concerned, the security guard asked, "Do you want me to search them?"

"No, that won't be necessary."

Luke waved to the guards, and the gates began to close. He walked toward the house with the two men at his sides. As they entered, Deborah was waiting in the entry. It wasn't until they were inside that Luke could detect the rancid smell emanating from the men. Deborah was horrified. "What's going on?"

Luke smiled awkwardly, "This is John and," he hesitated, "what did you say your last name was?" he asked, looking at Blade. Understanding the sensitivity of the situation, Blade replied, "Franklyn Hennessey."

As Luke led the men past Deborah, she noticed that John was wearing Aaron's coat. Speaking softly so only Luke could hear, she said, "Nice coat." Undeterred, Luke continued walking. To get to the doorway that led to the basement, they had to pass the dining room. As they did, the entire group of visitors looked up, obviously surprised to see the homeless men. No words were said, but he could tell his parents and the guests were horrified.

They quickly descended the stairs, and Luke pointed to the gym showers. "Take all the time you want; there's towels and shaving equipment in the drawers. I'll get you some clean clothes to wear." Luke hurried back upstairs, and Deborah was waiting for him. Pulling him into the library, she whispered, "What are you doing?"

Deciding that the less she knew, the better, Luke looked directly at her while gently grabbing both of her arms and said, "I can't tell you why they're here, but you have to trust me, there's a very good reason." He could tell that she wasn't happy as she turned and walked away in silence.

Luke hurried into his room and rummaged through Aaron's clothes, grabbing underwear, socks, pants, and shirts, then he rushed back downstairs. As he passed by the dining room again, he saw everyone staring.

Back in the basement, he heard showers running. As he put the pile of clothing down on a workout bench, John appeared with a towel wrapped around his waist. Luke was saddened to see how skinny he was; all of his ribs were visible.

"How do you feel?"

John smiled. "I haven't felt this good in a long time. Thank you."

Luke gestured for him to pick out some new clothes from the pile. John walked over and picked up a pair of pants. Looking at the size, he said, "These might be a little big for us."

Smiling, Luke grabbed a belt from the bottom of the pile. "That's what this is for!"

John disappeared into the locker room. Several minutes later, Blade appeared, also wrapped in a towel. His shaven face clearly displayed the ghastly scar that traversed the entire left side. Trying to make him feel safe among friends, Luke smiled and repeated the same scene he had a few minutes earlier with John, being sure to also give him a belt.

Once they were both completely dressed, Luke led them upstairs.

# 23

WITH MANY OF THE guests already finished eating, it was easy to find three chairs at the table. Everyone who remained felt uneasy as John and Blade sat down. Luke served each of them, taking pieces of turkey from the large platter and loading their plates. When Ethel walked out of the kitchen and saw the two strangers, she quickly returned to get mashed potatoes and warm bread.

Trying to do the right thing, Deb reluctantly joined them and began talking. "I'm Deborah, Luke's sister-in-law." John looked up with his mouth half full and responded, "We know who you are. We've seen your pictures in the papers." She smiled and he continued, "Thank you for having us. You have a beautiful home."

Trying to make Blade feel at home, she said, "You're left-handed, like me." He looked up but didn't speak. Deb smiled uncomfortably and watched curiously as John turned his head, stood, and moved closer to a ceiling speaker that was playing music. "Chopin?" he said.

Deb looked at him in disbelief and asked, "You know Chopin?"

Looking at her while still standing, he replied, "Oh yes, I know Chopin very well." He put his finger to his mouth to indicate silence.

As he listened, tears filled his bloodshot eyes. After a few seconds, he announced, "Fantasie Impromptu."

Deborah was amazed. "How do you know that?"

He smiled. "My mother was Polish and she loved Chopin."

"Do you play?"

"Not in years. Why, do you?"

Deborah loved music and had played the piano since she was a child. When the house construction was completed, her antique Steinway was the first piece of furniture to enter. Intrigued, she continued the conversation. "How long have you been playing?"

"Since I was eight years old. My mother taught me how to read music."

Deborah smiled. "Just like Chopin."

He smiled back. "Yes."

After John and Blade had finished eating their first full meal in months, she asked, "Would you like to play now?"

"Oh, it's been so long, I don't know if I can."

She then did something that impressed Luke. Standing, Deborah extended her hand and helped John up out of his chair. Still holding hands, she led him into the massive formal living room toward her piano in the far corner. Seeing it, he immediately said, "I can't believe it's a Steinway."

She smiled and pulled out the bench. "Please sit."

Looking like a child on Christmas morning, he didn't protest but sat down and gently ran his fingers along the keys. Then, without any music to guide him, he began playing the Chopin piece that was on the stereo earlier. Deborah was incredulous. Not only was this piece extremely difficult to play, but to play it without any sheet music was remarkable. When John finished, Luke looked at Deborah, who had tears streaming down her face. Impressing Luke even more, she sat down on the bench next to John, nudging him over with her hip, while taking a book from a table on the side of the piano. She quickly flipped through it, finding the page she was looking for, and placed it on the piano where they both could see. They whispered a few words to each other before Deborah looked up and said to Luke and Blade, "Chopin's Minute Waltz, four hands."

Simultaneously, they began playing the beautiful music. The waltz echoed throughout the mansion. They played with passion and grace. By the time they finished, most of the adults, including Luke's parents, and several children had wandered in to watch. Seeing Abel at the edge of the room, Deb waved for him to come close. She lifted him onto her lap and asked John, "Please, play something else." When he began playing "I'm a Believer," everyone started singing. When he finished, Deborah asked, "Why did you choose that song?" He answered, "It's from the movie *Shrek*; I thought the children would like it. I used to play it for my kids on a little keyboard."

Heartbroken, she looked at him and said, "Please, play something else. You play so beautifully."

He smiled. "Thank you, but I think it's your turn."

She grabbed a book of popular songs and began playing. For the next hour, they took turns at the piano while everyone sang. Luke thought to himself, "Deb really has a kind heart."

When Luke's phone buzzed, he walked out of the room to answer it. Again, it was the security guard. "Mr. Miller, I have Lieutenant Governor Simpson and his wife Lori here."

"Please send them through."

Luke bent down and whispered in Deb's ear, "You invited Lori Simpson?"

She smiled while still playing. "Yes, for dessert."

Luke hurried to the front door and watched as the black limo approached. The driver got out, opened the rear door, and Richard Simpson appeared. Noticing that he didn't try to help Lori out of the car or wait for her, Luke thought to himself, "This guy is a real jerk." Luke walked past him without acknowledging his presence and helped Lori out of the car.

Walking toward the front door, Luke saw Richard already waiting there with an impatient look on his hardened face. Luke shook his hand. "Nice to meet you."

"Same here. I've heard a lot about you and your brother."

Luke led them inside, directly into the living room where everyone was still singing. When the song ended, Lori and her husband approached Deborah to say hello. Deborah stood, hugged her, and announced, "This is Lori Simpson and her husband, Lieutenant Governor Simpson." Luke saw Blade hunch down when he understood who was standing next to him. As Richard began to give one of his impromptu political speeches, Deborah made room for Lori and persuaded her to sit down next to her while she began playing. Her music interrupted his words, and once again singing filled the room.

When the music stopped, Ethel announced, "Luke and Deborah will be serving dessert in five minutes." Deborah stood, raised a glass of red wine, and said, "Let's have a big round of applause for Mr. John Daly, the best pianist I know." Everyone clapped except for an aggravated Lieutenant Governor Simpson.

# 24

**WHILE LUKE AND DEBORAH** were saying good-bye to the guests, the two homeless men walked outside to check on their bicycle. When Luke saw the lieutenant governor's driver taking pictures of the crowd, he hurried over to where Lori was standing. "Can you please make him stop?"

Turning around to see who Luke was talking about, she was horrified. Her high heels clicked loudly on the pavement as she ran to her husband and yelled, "This is not an effing photo op." She pointed at the driver. "Make him stop now!" Richard, who Luke was now mentally calling "Dick," strolled over while talking on his cell phone and whispered something to the man. He snapped a few more shots, then put the camera into the car and opened the door. Still talking on his phone, "Dick" waved to everyone and disappeared into the backseat. Lori apologized to Deborah and Luke. Before Lori left, Deborah said, "Please know you're always welcome here. I'll call you tonight." Luke wondered if there was a hidden message in that statement. They hugged each other, and Lori hugged Luke before getting into the car.

As the dinner guests began walking through the gates to their cars, Luke heard several of them comment that "this was the best

Thanksgiving ever." He smiled. When everyone had gone, the gates closed, and they returned to the house. Luke, John, and Blade walked into the library while Deb, Luke's parents, and the children headed for the family room.

The two men sat on the leather couch. Luke immediately dragged a chair in front of them. Getting right to the point, he said, "Blade, you told John that you have information regarding the bombing in the park. What is it?"

The man looked around the room and replied, "I do."

When he didn't continue, Luke gently prodded, "Can you tell me what you know?"

Blade looked at John, who said, "He wants to know how much money you are going to give him for the information."

Blade interjected, "I'm not being ungrateful for what you've already done for us. Most people would have never invited us in, fed us, and gave us clothing." Motioning with an open hand, he continued, "But we don't live like this, Father."

John chimed in. "Father Luke, I just want you to know, I don't want any money. You've done enough for me already."

This didn't deter Blade. "I've been living on the streets for over fifteen years. This is my one chance to help myself."

Not knowing what to expect, Luke asked, "How much do you want?"

Looking directly at Luke, he answered, "Two thousand dollars."

Relieved, Luke smiled. "How about we make it five?"

Blade frowned. "Five hundred?"

"No, five thousand."

The two homeless men looked at each other in disbelief. Luke extended his hand and Blade shook it.

"So tell me what you know."

Blade looked down and said, "I will, as soon as you pay me."

Disappointed, Luke said, "I don't have the money on me right now and the banks are closed."

"I'm sorry, but living on the street has taught me one very important lesson: Don't trust anyone."

Panicked that he might lose his opportunity, Luke asked, "Can you stay here tonight? First thing in the morning we can go to the bank and I'll get you the cash."

"Believe me, I promise to meet you in the morning at the fountain. I have someone who's waiting for me now."

John added, "He has a girlfriend."

"Well, let's go get her. She can stay here too."

"She would never do that. She's very nervous around strangers. It took over two years before she would even talk to me."

Luke wondered if Deborah had that much cash somewhere in the house, but he didn't want to involve her. What if it turned out that Blade didn't know anything? He wouldn't want to get her hopes up. "Can I at least give you a ride back to town?"

"What about my bike?"

"You can leave it here, or we can put it in the trunk."

"OK, let's put it in the car."

"Wait right here. I'll be back." Luke rushed off and returned a few minutes later with Deborah. She looked at John first. "Luke says you might consider staying with us tonight?" He nodded affirmatively. "That's great." Then she looked at Blade. Remembering his name, she said, "Franklyn, you're also welcome to stay."

He didn't look directly at her but awkwardly replied, "Thank you, but I can't." She shook both of their hands. Before she left the room, Luke asked, "Do you mind if I take your SUV to drop Franklyn off? We need to put his bicycle in the back."

Deb smiled. "Of course you can take it."

Luke pulled the SUV out of the garage and into the front drive-way. Within minutes, he and the two homeless men were driving toward the city. When they drew within a few blocks of the Com-mon, Luke had an idea. He pulled the car over and said, "I'll be right back." He walked quickly toward the ATM machine, inserted his card, and requested the maximum cash withdrawal of five hundred dol-lars. Hurrying back, he climbed in the truck and handed the cash to Blade. "Here's a down payment." Trying to seal the deal, he contin-ued, "When I see you tomorrow, I'll have forty-five hundred dollars more." For the first time, Blade smiled, exposing his decayed teeth. They unloaded the car and Luke reminded Blade, "I'll meet you at ten o'clock by the fountain."

Blade shook his hand and said, "Damn right you will."

# 25

**WAKING THE NEXT MORNING,** Luke walked into the basement gym to check on John. Even though it was still early, he had already showered and shaved, and he was sitting on an exercise bench reading the newspaper. When Luke approached, he looked up and said, "Thank you for letting me stay here."

Luke smiled. "I don't know why you wouldn't sleep in one of the spare bedrooms upstairs." He pointed to the stack of mats on the floor. "Were you comfortable?"

"That was the best night's sleep I've had in months." Changing the subject, he added, "You're in the paper again today."

Luke asked, exasperated, "For what now?"

"You should probably read it yourself."

John flipped back several pages and handed the paper to Luke, who read the article while shaking his head in disbelief.

John asked, "Do you know this guy Sal?"

"Yes, his wife is a regular parishioner at my church."

"Sounds like he's connected, if you know what I mean. Did you ask him to have that abortion guy beaten up?"

Luke looked at him in horror. "Do you think I would do something like that?"

"No, but the article kind of says you did."

Luke immediately took out his cell phone and called Sal's number, not caring if it was too early in the morning. When Sal answered, he asked sharply, "What did you do?"

Sal calmly replied, "Father Luke, please listen to me, I can explain. After we talked at the restaurant, I asked a few of my men to visit Steve Hinkley, with specific instructions that he shouldn't be harmed in any way. They were told to ask him a few questions regarding the bombing and nothing else. We never expected that he had anything to do with it but thought he might tell us what the feds said. After they arrived, he started shooting off his big mouth and became aggressive. When he poked his finger in my man's chest the first time, he was warned. When he did it again, Anthony slapped him across the face. When Hinkley spit in his face, he lost his temper and beat him, telling Hinkley, 'This is for Father Luke.' I don't know why he said it, but he did. I'm really sorry. The feds must have had him under surveillance. When they barged in and saw Hinkley bleeding on the floor, they arrested Anthony and Bobby. I don't know who talked to the press, but it probably was Hinkley."

Mortified, Luke said, "Please don't do me any more favors. You've done enough." Before Sal could respond, Luke hung up the phone.

Shaken, Luke looked at John and asked, "Want to take a ride with me?"

"Sure, where are we going?"

"To Massachusetts General."

"For what?"

"To see how Steven Hinkley is doing." Pointing to the door, Luke said, "I'll meet you in the backyard in ten minutes."

Confused, John asked, "The backyard?"

"Yes."

Dressed in his priest clothes, Luke led John across the yard and over the wall. Soon they were driving to the west side of downtown Boston. Nearing the glass-faced building, Luke found a spot and parked the Mercedes on the street.

He knew this hospital well from the time he spent there visiting sick parishioners and distributing communion. He also knew that a priest could wander around the hospital without being questioned, similar to doctors. Entering the front door, he said to John, "Stay close."

Luke walked up to an elderly volunteer at the front desk and said, "We're here to see Steven Hinkley."

The woman typed the name into her computer and said, "He's in room 204, Father. Take the elevator around the—"

Luke politely interrupted her. "I know the way, thank you."

Pausing outside the doorway of Hinkley's room, Luke took a deep breath, looked at John, and said, "This should be interesting."

Luke stepped inside and saw the patient lying in bed with his eyes closed while the television was on. He walked to the bedside as John hovered in the doorway. Watching the abortion activist breathe laboriously, Luke wondered, "What makes a person choose a life like this?" Noticing the patient's black eyes and contusions, he felt sorry for him. He never would have said anything to Sal if he had known this man was going to suffer in any way. Deep in thought, Luke was startled when Hinkley's eyes opened and he fumbled for the nurse's call button. Retrieving it from under the sheets, he pressed it frantically. Not knowing what to do, Luke did nothing. A few minutes later, the nurse arrived. Expecting to be booted out of the hospital, he was surprised that Hinkley whispered to her, "I really need to go to the bathroom." She helped him across the room, and when they returned, she got him back into bed and left without saying a word. Recognizing Luke, Hinkley said, "Why are you here?"

"I wanted you to know that I had nothing to do with what happened to you."

He smirked. "Yeah, right."

"I'm a priest, and even though we have little in common, I would never want to see you hurt in any way."

In an arrogant tone, Hinkley replied, "I had nothing to do with your brother's murder. I want to be clear. I'm not sorry that he's dead, but I had nothing to do with it."

Luke was furious. The man's blatant arrogance regarding Aaron's death made his blood boil. Uncharacteristically, he grabbed Hinkley's wrist and squeezed it as tight as he could. Realizing that he was about to lose control, just as he had with the abortion protester in Washington all those years ago, he quickly released his grip and rushed toward the door.

Laughing, Hinkley yelled, "In my book there's a big difference between performing abortions and murder."

Luke stopped and thought about the pain and regret this man had caused to so many confused young women when he turned to face him. "Not in mine."

Before following Luke out the door, John entered the room and walked over to the bed. Looking down with his face an inch away from Hinkley's, he said, "I want you to know you're a real asshole." Hinkley pressed the call button again.

# 26

**THEY LEFT THE HOSPITAL,** and Luke drove to the bank and parked in front. "I'll just be a minute," he said to John. "If anyone has a problem with the car being parked here, move it."

John looked surprised. Luke figured that there weren't many people who would leave a stranger in their hundred-thousand-dollar Mercedes with the keys. As he entered the bank, he buttoned the top of his coat in an attempt to hide his collar. The bank had just opened, and the lobby was empty except for a few elderly customers. After examining Luke's ID, the teller counted the cash and placed it in an envelope.

Luke walked back to the street without incident, and the car and John were still there. As they headed to the Common, Luke asked, "Do you think Blade really knows who's responsible for the bombing?"

"He seems to think he does. I told him not to BS you." Looking at Luke, John continued, "I just don't know if it was a good idea to give him the down payment last night; that's probably more money than he's had at one time in years."

"Yes, I've been thinking the same thing. I thought it would show that I was serious about paying him the rest, but after I gave it to him, I worried that he would buy drugs with the money."

"I don't think he's into drugs, but five hundred can buy a lot of whiskey."

"Do you know where he sleeps at night?"

"No. His girlfriend is a little crazy and suspicious of everyone. I think she has some mental problems. They keep to themselves, but he should be meeting us at the fountain in a few minutes."

Luke and John walked into the park. Not seeing any sign of Blade, they waited. At ten thirty, Luke suggested, "Let's split up and try to find him. We can meet back here." They quickly headed off in separate directions. Luke jogged as he frantically searched for the only lead he had left. Coming up empty, he was disappointed to see John sitting by the fountain alone. "Any sign of him?" John shook his head. As Luke paced, trying to figure out what to do next, his cell phone rang.

He looked at the display and saw that it was the parish secretary. Realizing that it had been weeks since he had checked in, he immediately answered it. She told Luke that Monsignor Swiger wanted to meet with him. Flustered, he asked, "When?"

She replied, "He's free now."

Wanting to be respectful to his boss and friend, Luke agreed to go to the parish. He looked at John and said, "I have to go to an appointment. I shouldn't be more than an hour or so."

Before Luke could ask, John insisted, "I'm going to stay here and search for Blade."

Luke reached into his pocket and took out the cell phone that Detective Romo had given him. After punching the numbers into both phones, he handed the prepaid one to John. "If you find him, please call me. If I don't hear from you, I'll pick you up after my meeting."

Jogging to the car, Luke knew that he should have checked in with Swiger weeks ago, but the reality of being a parish priest was fading into the distance as his new life with Deb and the children and trying to figure out who killed Aaron were becoming his new reality. Unfortunately, the children were becoming more and more dependent on him each day, as was Deborah. And even more sobering was the realization that he was beginning to enjoy being part of a family. He thought, What have I gotten myself into?

Pulling into the rectory parking lot, Luke did something that he hadn't done in weeks. He dialed Aaron's cell number and listened to his message. As he exited the Mercedes, he saw Monsignor Swiger looking out the window. He entered the reception area, and the secretary said, "Go right in, he's waiting for you." The monsignor was still standing when Luke entered his office. The older man smiled and said, "It's so good to see you," and they embraced.

As Luke sat down, he noticed that day's newspaper open on the small circular table in front of him. Getting right to the point, he said, "Did you read the paper yet?" He knew the answer before Swiger answered yes.

"Well, I'd like to explain." Luke told him everything about his meeting with Sal at the restaurant and his subsequent phone conversation earlier in the morning. He explained that he had already visited Steve Hinkley at the hospital, just minutes ago. The monsignor listened carefully without responding until Luke was finished.

"Luke, I understand. I never believed that you personally had anything to do with the violence, but your actions provoked unintended consequences." After a lengthy conversation about Rebecca and Sal Bruno, the monsignor ended the topic by saying, "Just because someone donates tremendous amounts of money to the church doesn't mean that they've earned God's favor."

Changing the subject, the monsignor asked, "How are your parents doing?"

Luke had no choice but to tell him the truth and let him know that they were moving back home. "So that means you will be back to work soon?" Swiger asked, assuming that Luke would be returning to his normal church schedule.

Luke dejectedly realized that he was at a dead end with regard to the bombing and that his one last lead, Blade, had proven to be anything but reliable, so he sighed and answered, "I won't be much longer."

The fact that Luke was discussing coming back to work seemed to satisfy Swiger. But before Luke walked out of his office, the monsignor offered some words of advice. "There is temptation everywhere. Be careful not to fall prey to it." He added, "I'm always praying for you."

As soon as Luke left the building, he checked his cell phone. No messages. Disappointed, he did something else that he hadn't done in weeks. He entered the beautiful ornate church that looked more like it belonged in Rome than in Boston, and he walked directly to a small alcove containing a statue of the blessed Mother holding Jesus after the crucifixion, where worshippers could light a candle. Kneeling, he prayed. He prayed for his family, for direction on Aaron's case, and for Blade to come through. He even said a prayer for Steve Hinkley.

He was walking back to the parking lot when his cell phone rang. Seeing the number, he answered it quickly. "Did you find him?"

John answered in a somber tone. "Yes, but I don't have good news."

# 27

THE MERCEDES' TIRES SCREECHED as Luke sped across town toward the Common. He parked illegally near a fire hydrant and ran into the park, frantically heading toward John and Blade. Turning the bend near the fountain, he saw John holding Blade under his arms as he attempted to walk. Blade's worn-out shoes dragged on the pavement as John stepped forward and then lugged the unconscious man toward Luke. Without saying a word, Luke grabbed Blade's ankles, and they rushed to the car. Crossing Tremont Street, they attracted stares from pedestrians as the two men struggled to get Blade into the backseat and out of the frigid weather.

They sped to the mansion, where Luke honked the horn and the guard stepped aside as the gates opened. Pulling up to the house, they hoisted Blade out of the car and again struggled as they carried him into the backyard and toward the downstairs gym doors. Glancing up as they rounded the corner of the house, Luke saw Deborah and the children looking out the family room windows. Abel pointed and said something. Luke didn't need to know what was said to understand Deb's reaction; it was written all over her frightened face. Undeterred, he used his key to open the door and lay Blade on the padded floor.

Luke had worked with drug-prevention organizations and was trained in CPR and basic medical procedures, so he knew what to do. After checking his vital signs, he quickly removed Blade's shoes and socks, searching his toes for needle marks. As he was rolling up his shirt-sleeves, John remarked in an agitated voice, "I already told you, he doesn't do drugs."

Luke continued searching. "We can't take any chances; his life might be at stake."

"He's just drunk. Can't you smell the alcohol?"

"I smell urine."

"He must have peed his pants. Star told me he'd been drinking."

"Star?"

"Yes, his girlfriend. She said they rented a hotel room and he's been drinking whiskey and beer all night. "I told—"

Luke interrupted, "I know, I never should have given him the money."

After undressing Blade and dragging him into the shower, Luke ran upstairs to get some dry clothes. As he searched his closet, Deborah entered the room. "What's going on?"

Luke looked up. "Just trying to find a few things."

She responded sharply. "Tell me the truth!"

Luke stood to face her. "I thought we already had this conversation. Please trust me."

"Do you know what Abel said when we were watching you out the window?" Luke didn't respond, so she continued. "He asked, 'Is that man dead like my daddy?'"

She started to cry, and he put his arms around her. Holding her, he pleaded, "Please, Deb, I just need a few more days to figure some things out. I can't tell you everything that's going on because I'm not sure myself. But trust me, I would never do anything to put you or the children in danger."

When he released his hug, she didn't, but squeezed him tighter. He rewrapped his arms around her and returned her embrace.

Luke headed back to the basement and entered the shower area. He saw that John had found a plastic chair and placed it in the shower. Blade was propped up with water cascading over his body as his head rested on the tiled wall. "Has he said anything yet?"

"Yes, he's mumbled a few things. I think he was asking about Star."

Luke looked at John. "I can't thank you enough for helping me."

John smiled. "No problem. It's nice to do something meaningful again. I should be thanking you."

Blade began sobering up once they removed him from the shower. Knowing that he needed time to sleep it off, they laid him on John's makeshift bed and covered him. After watching him breathe for a while, Luke asked, "Can you stay with him for a few minutes? I need to go upstairs, and he shouldn't be alone."

John looked up, smiled, and said sarcastically, "Let me check my calendar."

Luke grinned back at him and quickly headed upstairs.

He searched the house for Deb, finally finding her in the library. She looked up from the computer when Luke entered the room. "Deb, do you have any work that needs to be done around the house?"

Knowing that the servants did everything, she looked at him like he was crazy. "What do you mean?"

He sat down next to her. "As you know, John Daly has fallen on hard times. I wanted to see if we had any work to do around here. I would like to give him money, but I know he won't accept charity."

"Do you think he can be trusted?"

"Yes." Luke relayed everything he knew about John from their conversations. When she understood that he had a family and was living on the streets because he couldn't go and live with his wife's parents, her heart sank. Remembering her conversation with John when they were playing the piano, she asked, "Doesn't he have children?"

"Yes, two daughters."

Her expressive eyes saddened. "Well, there has to be something we can do." She thought for a few minutes, then she looked up. "I know. He can be in charge of cleaning out Aaron's office and taking care of the building. I keep putting it off and it has to be done."

Luke was excited. "That's great."

As he got up to leave, Deborah said, "I'll pay his salary; let's ensure he makes enough money to find a place where he and his family can stay." Reluctantly, she added, "I know they are good people, but I would feel better if they didn't stay here anymore."

Luke understood her concern, especially after what had happened with Blade. But he had to get the information he needed, so he asked, "If necessary, can they stay one more night?"

"Are you talking about John?"

"Does it matter?"

"Yes, the other man scares me and the children."

"I understand."

# 28

FOR THE NEXT FEW hours, Luke and John watched Blade continue to get better after throwing up several times. Not wanting to involve any of the maids, Luke carefully cleaned up after him and put his clothes in the washing machine. In the late afternoon, Blade finally was in a condition to sit up and talk.

Luke struggled with his conscience as he opened his wallet and retrieved the bank envelope. He worried that Blade would use this money to drink himself to death. If someone died because of his attempts to find his brother's killers, how would he feel? It was such a long shot anyway. Should he take the chance?

As he handed the cash to Blade, he warned, "Please don't hurt yourself with this." Blade grabbed the envelope and counted the money several times. Looking up at Luke, he put the envelope in his pocket and began talking. "OK, here's what I know. I've been sleeping in the park for over ten years. During that time, I've moved the spot where I sleep many times. Several years ago, when I was sleeping on a bench near the bomb site, I saw construction crews working late at night."

Uncharacteristically, Luke interrupted. "Did you say several years ago?"

Blade sighed. "Yes, it was several years ago."

John and Luke looked at each other in disbelief. Noticing this, Blade said in an agitated tone, "Why don't you let me finish before you judge what I'm saying?"

"I'm sorry, please continue," Luke answered.

"I'd been sleeping in that spot for a few weeks when I noticed the trucks. They arrived at about eight each night and would leave around ten."

"Ten in the morning?" asked John.

"No, ten at night."

Hearing this, Luke began to doubt the legitimacy of his story, but he waited and listened politely.

Feeling bad that he was responsible for setting up this meeting, John questioned in disbelief, "They only stayed for two hours a night?"

Undeterred, Blade continued. "That's what made me curious. Another guy named Shorty, who slept not far from me, also thought something was weird. One night when we were both awake, he began talking to me about the reason that they were working at night and why such strange hours. When he said he was going to ask them a few questions, I told him not to go. He was determined and ignored my warning. When he returned, he told me that they showed him a work permit and that one of the workers handed him a fifty. He was so excited to get the money that he didn't tell me any other details. When one of the workers looked and saw me, something didn't feel right, so I moved my sleeping spot to the other end of the park that night. That was the last night that anyone ever remembers seeing Shorty. He disappeared."

Luke found the story interesting but doubted its relevance to his brother's death. He thought to himself that Shorty probably took the fifty, got drunk, and moved to another area, and that maybe there were electrical restrictions that required the construction crews to work at that time of night. When Blade couldn't tell him Shorty's real name, he knew that he had no way of verifying the information. Aggravated, he stood and headed toward the door until Blade said something that made him stop.

"Father Luke, do you know what year it was?"

Luke turned. "No."

"It was 2004. October of 2004, to be exact." Luke's heart was pounding, but he didn't respond, so Blade asked, "Do you know what happened in October of 2004?" Luke knew very well the biggest event that happened in Boston in October of 2004. He stared at the man and said nothing until John asked, "What the hell are you talking about?"

Luke spoke up. "The Red Sox beat the Yankees in seven games."

Not understanding the big picture, John said, "So?"

Luke continued as he stared at Blade. "The Sox were down three games to none and went on to win the series four games to three. Then, after an eighty-six-year drought, they finally won the World Series."

John replied, "So what?"

"All of the games at Fenway were played at night," Luke continued. "The first home game set a record for the longest nine-inning game ever, and the next two games both went into extra innings, ending late at night." Still not understanding, John shrugged, and Luke explained, "I bet Blade is going to tell us that the construction crews only worked during home games."

Blade smiled, exposing his rotten teeth. "Very good, Father. They must have known that the local police who normally patrolled the Common would be assigned to Fenway Park for extra security. We could hear the games from their truck radios, and as soon as they ended, the workers quickly packed up their equipment and left."

Intrigued, Luke walked back, sat down, and began documenting everything that Blade had told them. When he finished writing, he asked, "What was the name of the construction firm?"

Blade thought for a few minutes. "Sorry, but I don't know."

"Please, try to remember. It's very important."

"I've been trying to remember for the past few days, but I can't."

Feeling defeated again, Luke asked, "Please think. Is there anything else you can tell me?"

"I don't know if this means anything, but I remember that the trucks had a moon painted on the side."

"A moon?" John asked

"Yes."

Luke passed a piece of paper to Blade and said, "Can you draw it for me?"

The old man scribbled on the paper for several seconds and handed it back to Luke.

Looking at it, Luke declared, "That's not a moon; it's a crescent." Standing up, he asked a critical question. "Was there a star next to it?"

"There might have been. I'm just not sure."

"Do you remember what color it was?"

"I think it was green."

Luke spent the next twenty minutes going back over everything that Blade said, while reviewing his detailed notes. No new information was uncovered, but John and Blade promised to ask some of the elderly park residents if they knew Shorty's full name. Before taking Blade back to the Common, Luke pleaded with him not to use the money for alcohol.

# 29

**WHEN LUKE PULLED UP** to the house, returning from dropping off Blade, he was anxious to log on to the computer and try to find the name of the construction company that had done the work in the park. Wanting to be alone, he asked John, "Do you know anything about cars?"

"What do you mean?"

"My truck won't start, and I was wondering if you could figure out what's wrong with it."

John laughed and pointed at it. "That's your truck?"

Luke smiled. "Yeah. What's so funny?"

"Sorry, Father, it's just that when I saw you driving the Mercedes, I figured that the truck belonged to the gardener."

"Well, do you think you can fix it?"

"I don't know, but I can try. I used to work on old cars." Looking at the truck, he added, "That thing is so old I'm sure it's not computerized."

Luke handed him both the car and truck keys. Reaching into his pocket for money, he gave him two hundred dollars, adding, "There's a toolbox in the garage. See what you can do, and if you need anything, just go get it. I'll tell the guards to open the gates for you."

John smiled and hurried over to the truck. As Luke opened the front door to the house, the other man called out, "Thanks, Father!"

Luke walked into the library and logged on to the computer. Deep in thought, he heard something and looked up to see Deborah standing in the doorway. She asked excitedly, "Did you tell him?"

Confused, Luke asked, "Tell who, what?"

"About the job?"

He smiled. "Not yet. I have one more test for him. He's going to try to fix my truck. I gave him the keys to the Mercedes and two hundred dollars."

"Do you think that was a good idea?"

Still smiling, he replied, "I guess we're going to find out."

She looked out the window. "Lori's here."

Luke looked and saw Lori's white Caddy pulling through the open gates. He was happy that the two women who knew Aaron best were becoming such close friends; they needed each other. After greeting Lori and receiving an earnest hug, he excused himself and continued his investigation. He did Internet searches on everything from homeless people killed in the park to construction company permits. Looking out the window every now and then, he saw John working on the truck.

The last time he looked, the Mercedes was gone. He wondered what John was doing. Did he take the car to his mother-in-law's house to show his family? Or was he on his way to Florida? Luke really didn't care, as long as the other man was safe. Luke had never really valued material things, and he could happily return to his room at the rectory without missing the opulent lifestyle he'd been living.

After more searching without success, Luke stood up and stretched. Seeing that the Mercedes was back in the driveway, he smiled. He walked out the front door and heard his truck running.

John was revving the engine from under the hood and didn't notice Luke until he was standing right next to him.

Slapping him on the back, Luke yelled over the roar of the engine, "Great job!" John stood up and smiled, with grease covering his face and hands. Taking a rag off the truck's fender, he wiped his hands and hurried over to the Mercedes. Carefully reaching inside, he handed Luke receipts for everything he had bought, along with the change. Luke said, "Thanks! Give me a second and we can go for a ride."

Luke ran back into the house to grab a jacket and find Deborah. Not seeing her, he walked to the hallway and called her name. "We're in here, in my room," he heard her say. Luke walked into her bedroom but still didn't see anyone. Noticing a light coming from the bathroom, he walked cautiously toward the open door, asking, "Are you dressed?" Deborah and Lori laughed, while Lori added, "Do you want us to be?" Deborah giggled and said, "Yes, you can come in." Peering into the doorway, Luke was confused. One of them was sitting in front of the expansive makeup mirror, with the other standing behind doing her hair. The confusing part was that they both had blonde hair. As Deborah stood and smiled, Luke was struck not only by her beauty but also by the fact that she and Lori now looked so much alike.

"What do you think?"

Without hesitating, he said, "You look beautiful." Catching himself, he quickly added, "You both look great."

Deb fluffed her hair and said, "You know what they say—blondes have more fun."

They all laughed. Deborah explained that Lori had bought the wig for herself after her husband suggested that she dye her hair blonde; she wanted to see what it would look like before she agreed. Lori suggested that if Deborah wore the wig and sunglasses, she could go shopping or out to lunch without being hounded by the press. Understanding that she had been confined to the house more than anyone, he replied, "That's great!" Deborah quickly added, "Would you like to join us?"

"No, thank you. John fixed my truck, so I was going to ask you for the key to Aaron's office so we could stop by and take a look."

"So he didn't steal the Mercedes?"

Luke laughed. "Not yet."

"The key should be on the same keychain as the car key." Excited, she added, "Did you tell him yet?"

"No, I was going to surprise him after we looked at the office building."

"Margaret is still working there, answering the phones and all, so you might run into her."

Luke said, "Have a great time," before he turned and walked out the door.

# 30

**JOHN DROVE THE TRUCK** along the congested roads toward downtown Boston, and Luke was gratified to see the look of satisfaction on his face as the motor hummed. Although Luke was trying to enjoy the moment, he was preoccupied with how to determine the name of the mysterious construction company. Obviously, something was not right. When all the nonconnected events relayed by Blade were linked, it created a picture that was hard to ignore. Adding in the crescent logo and its color, Luke knew it was too much to be a coincidence.

He knew that the color green had a special meaning in the Islamic faith. Some people claimed that green was the favorite color of Muhammad because he wore a green cloak and turban. Even the Qur'an said that the inhabitants of paradise wear green garments of fine silk. And during the Crusades, green was the color worn by the Islamic soldiers. Based on everything pointing back at Islam, Luke made a mental note to visit Jami and see if she could provide any insight.

They turned onto State Street in the financial district, then Luke pointed to a small side street and said, "Turn here." The impressive three-story brick building they faced was more than two hundred years old and contained ten offices. Aaron had purchased the building when the property was undervalued, so the rents from the building's inhabitants more than paid the mortgage.

"You can park in the lot in the back," said Luke.

John asked, "What are we doing here?"

Luke smiled. "John, how would you like to work for Deborah?"

John was excited and confused at the same time. "Doing what?"

"This was my brother's office building. There are nine tenants, and Aaron's office is on the third floor. When Aaron worked here, he managed the building. If a toilet broke or the air-conditioning wasn't working properly, he would call a plumber or whoever he needed to fix the problem. Now that he's gone, there's no one to take these calls. Also, Deb needs someone she can trust to pack up his office and get it ready to lease."

John was overwhelmed. "Really?"

"Hey, I figure that if you can fix this old truck, you can do anything!"

John laughed nervously. As they entered the building, he handed the truck keys to Luke. Thinking for a second, Luke handed them back, saying, "John, I want you to keep the truck."

"You're kidding me."

Luke put his hands on John's shoulders as they faced each other. "No, I'm not. Now look who's laughing at that old truck."

John smiled, not fully believing what he was hearing, and replied, "I'll pay you for it."

Still standing in front of him, Luke looked directly in his eyes and said, "No, I want you to have it. It's a gift to start your new life."

They took the elevator to the third floor and stepped out into an impressive hallway. Luke knew this building well, having visited Aaron here often. As he approached the glass doors to the law offices, he noticed Margaret sitting behind the cherry desk, talking on the phone.

When he opened the door, she looked up and began to cry. Flustered, she hung up the phone and tried to regain her composure as she stood to welcome Luke. He smiled and walked behind the desk, where they embraced. "Luke, I'm so sorry. I can't believe he's gone. I sit here every day expecting him to walk through that door. When I saw you, for a few seconds I thought you were Aaron."

Luke smiled. "I understand and I miss him also, but you know that he wouldn't want us to be sad. The best way to honor his memory is to live the way he did." She smiled and wiped the tears from her face. "He was always happy."

He apprised her of Deborah's plan to have John work in the office for the next several weeks, telling her that any tenants with problems should call John. She immediately replied, "The doctor on the first floor just called a few minutes ago and said that one of his sinks is leaking." Before Luke could speak, John said, "I'll go take a look."

Margaret asked, "Do you know where to go?"

John smiled. "Is there more than one doctor on the first floor?"

She shook her head. "No."

The phone rang and Margaret hurried to answer it as John headed out the door. Luke walked into Aaron's office. Sitting down behind the desk, he saw a picture that made him smile. He remembered the day but didn't think he'd ever seen the photo. It was a black-and-white shot of Aaron and Luke blowing out candles on their seventh birthday.

After looking through everything in Aaron's desk and file cabinets, Luke walked around the office. He noticed that a small room next to the bathroom contained a cot. As he sat back down in Aaron's chair, his hand inadvertently nudged the mouse attached to the computer. A second later, the screen illuminated, displaying a document that Aaron must have been working on before the bombing. Examining it closely, he saw what looked like an organizational chart. It displayed names, titles, and comments about each person that would be involved in his run for the Senate. The first name under Aaron's was Lori Simpson, with the title: Chief of Staff. The comments next to her name read, "A great person, great organizer, and outstanding leader." As he continued reading, he recognized many of the names from Aaron's phone contacts. Seeing Ablaa Raboud, Jami's sister's name, he stopped scanning and read the title: Special Adviser. The comments that followed were heartwarming: "The kindest and most loving person I've ever met, she's an inspiration to me."

Luke gazed toward the window, lost in thought. If Blade's theory was correct, Ablaa couldn't have been involved in the bombing because the explosives were put in the ground years ago. If she had any idea that the stage was going to blow up, she wouldn't have been there. Picking up his cell phone, he called Jami and arranged to meet with her in the morning.

# 31

JOHN DROVE HIS NEW truck through the mansion gates and Luke got out. As the motor idled, he walked to the driver's side and told John, "You're welcome to stay here tonight."

John smiled. "Thank you so much, but I think I'm going to take a ride by my mother-in-law's house to check on my wife and kids."

Luke nodded and handed him the key to Aaron's building. "There's a cot and a bathroom in the office if you need a place to stay."

"I can't thank you enough."

Before he could drive away, Luke reached into his pocket and handed him a hundred-dollar bill. John protested. Determined to give him the money, Luke said, "I would have had to pay someone more than that to fix the truck."

John laughed. "But you gave me the truck."

"That was after you fixed it."

Both men were laughing now. John finally gave in and took the money after Luke conceded that it could be a loan.

As Luke entered the house, he noticed that it was very quiet, with no sign of anyone. With his parents now living back at home, the huge house felt empty. He went to the kitchen and saw Abel and

Alessa playing outside with one of the maids. Thinking about John, he opened his phone and called Jim Hathaway, Aaron's financial adviser. Jim agreed to meet with John and get him on the payroll. While discussing the details, he asked Luke, "How much do you want to pay him?" Not knowing what would be fair, Luke explained the job responsibilities and asked Jim's opinion. "I would say about forty thousand a year."

Luke thought for a few minutes and said, "Let's make it sixty." Before hanging up, Luke asked Jim to do him a favor.

"You name it, you got it."

Luke grinned. "When you meet with John, can you try to figure out if there's any way he can get his house back? The bank foreclosed on it."

Jim agreed.

Luke headed into the library and logged on to the computer again to do more research, but he came up with no leads. Distracted by voices in the distance, he looked out the window and saw the two blondes, Deborah and Lori, laughing as they walked from the car with their arms full of shopping bags. He smiled and went to open the front door for them. Each one hugged him as they entered the foyer. Hearing the commotion, the children rushed in. But rather than running to greet their mom, they ran over to hug Luke.

Luke returned to the library, but he didn't know what to do next. He thought about calling Detective Romo, but he didn't have enough reliable information to involve him at this point. He figured that the detective would think he was crazy to believe an old drunk guy who lived in the park. As he was dialing the number for Sal Bruno, he questioned if he should really make the call. But Sal answered on the first ring. "Father Luke, so nice to hear from you." Before Luke could say a word, he continued. "I want to let you know that Anthony and Billy told the cops that you had nothing to do with the beating incident."

Luke thanked him. "I called to ask for another favor." He couldn't believe what he was saying, as he spoke.

"Just name it."

"I just need some information, but I also need your word that no one will get hurt."

Sal thought about that for a few seconds. "I'll do my best."

Realizing that this was as much of a commitment as he was going to get, Luke continued. "I need information on a construction company that had a green crescent moon on the side of their trucks. They were doing business in the city in 2004."

"OK, what's the name and what do you need to know?"

"That's my problem. I don't know the name or who owned the company."

"Is that all of the information you have? A green moon?"

"A green crescent moon, and unfortunately, yes, that's all I have."

"I'll see what I can do, but you're not giving me much to go on."

Luke thanked him and closed the phone.

He was still sitting at Aaron's desk when Deborah and Lori walked into the room with shopping bags. Deb spoke first. "We bought you a few things." Luke wanted to protest but instead decided to appreciate their thoughtfulness. He smiled and said, "Can't wait to see this."

Lori laughed and asked, "Are you being sarcastic?"

"Who, me?"

Deb handed him the first box. Opening it, he saw a handsome light blue cashmere sweater. "It matches your eyes," she said.

"Thank you very much, it's beautiful."

She continued handing him box after box. They had bought him new sweatpants and workout clothing, including a few pairs of running shoes. Luke was amazed at how easy it was for them to walk out the door and buy just about anything they wanted from any store without thinking twice. Putting things in perspective, he also thought about how Deborah treated the people who worked for her and what she was doing for John; she was an extremely generous person. He still felt guilty, but he decided that for every new item he kept, he would donate something that he already owned to the homeless shelter.

Then out of nowhere, Lori said, "Tell him what happened at the restaurant."

Embarrassed, but smiling, Deb said, "No."

Lori continued. "Luke, the waiter asked for Deborah's phone number."

Luke smiled and Deborah added, "I could have been his mother."

Having fun now, Lori kept going. "He was tall, dark, and handsome—a hunk. Can you believe it?"

Luke blurted out, "I'm not surprised," but then wished he hadn't.

Obviously feeling awkward, Deborah quickly changed the subject. "Lori is going to join us for dinner."

Luke politely excused himself and went to his room to pray. Lying on his bed, one thought kept crossing his mind: How was he going to feel when she did find someone?

# 32

**DURING DINNER, DEB AND** Lori were having a great time laughing with the children and each other. Of course, "Lukey" was the brunt of many of their jokes. Trying to be a good sport, he played along, but he was preoccupied thinking about Blade's story and frustrated that he couldn't verify it. After eating, Luke excused himself and went to his room to do something he had never done before.

Undressing, he cracked the bathroom window and waded into the whirlpool tub as it filled. Sitting back, he pressed the button, and water shot out of the jets with such force that initially it hurt his skin. After setting the water temperature on the controls, he settled in. Steam filled the room as his mind began to wander.

The more his body relaxed, the faster his mind raced. Other than meeting with Jami, what else was he going to do? Who else could he talk to? Was Blade telling the truth? Maybe he had concocted this story to get money. He wanted to go see his parents to assure himself that they were safe, now that they had moved back home. Wait, Mom's closet—the old phone books. He remembered that his mother never discarded any of the old Yellow Pages. He and Aaron used to make fun of her because she had stacks of them. Maybe the construction company had an ad that showed the crescent symbol. Even if there was an ad printed in green, he would go and look at their trucks.

Before going to bed, Luke went to the family room and said goodnight to Deborah and Lori, who were still up, sipping wine and chatting. Knowing that his parents would be up early in the morning, he set his alarm clock for 5:00 a.m. so he could work out before visiting them.

The next morning, as he was pulling out of the gates, he noticed that Lori's car was still in the driveway. Maybe she'd had too much to drink and didn't want to drive home. Over the past several days, Luke hadn't seen any reporters on the street. Maybe it was because the holidays were coming and they had other stories to cover, or maybe they finally realized that cars with tinted windows and security guards provided little opportunity for a big money shot.

It was still dark as Luke parked the car on the street in front of his parents' house. As expected, the kitchen light was on. Not wanting to alarm them, he called their home number from his cell phone. Excited to see him, his mom rushed to open the front door.

His mom kissed him on the cheek, and his dad shook his hand and embraced him. They walked into the kitchen and sat at the table that was at least as old as Luke. They talked for about half an hour before his mom pointed to the newspaper. His dad quickly flipped through several pages, then pointed at a picture with the heading: "Lieutenant Governor Simpson shares Thanksgiving with the Miller family and the homeless." The picture taken by Simpson's driver showed Luke and Deb standing next to Richard Simpson, with a clear image of Blade and his newly shaven face that displayed his jagged scar.

Luke took a few minutes to read the article. It was actually well written and flattering. It described Thanksgiving at the Millers' in detail: everything from Deb and Luke serving the help to clothing the homeless men from the Common to Deb's piano duet with John. The only issue Luke had with the article was that Lieutenant Governor "Dick" never even asked permission to publish the details of a very private day.

After eating breakfast, Luke asked his mom about the phone books. "What do you need them for?" she asked.

Not wanting to lie to her, he replied, "Just looking for a construction company that did some work in this area a few years ago."

He was relieved when she didn't ask any other questions but pointed to the closet. "You know where they are." As expected, the books were stacked in the far corner in descending order by year. With his parents watching TV in the other room, Luke placed several books on the table and began his search.

He looked up every category that had anything to do with building, from commercial construction to new home builders to every other related category. He examined each page, starting with the 2004 book and continuing for several more years. Not finding any crescents or stars, he tore out a few ads that had green lettering or symbols. Realizing that it was almost ten o'clock and that he was scheduled to meet Jami, he put the pages in his pocket and said good-bye to his parents.

Jami smiled as she answered the door and invited Luke inside. He had decided that he would share Blade's story with her because not only did he need her help but also he had no other leads. After some small talk, Jami asked him directly, "Did you have that abortion man beaten?"

Luke realized that she must have read the article in the newspaper. "No, I would never do something like that. But I think I may have inadvertently caused it." He went on to explain everything that happened with Sal. Jami seemed to understand, but he noticed a slight change in her demeanor.

"So you are investigating the bombing?"

Luke answered honestly. "I've been trying to re-create the last few weeks of my brother's life."

She looked up and said, "You didn't answer my question."

Flustered at her persistence, he replied, "Yes, I need to know why he was murdered."

"And what have you found?"

"I think someone from the Muslim community is responsible."

Before he could continue, she blurted out, "I should have expected that from you." She stood and started speaking faster and louder. "Do you think my sister was involved?" Before he could respond, she said, "Think of how many people around the world have been killed in the name of Christianity before you indict Islam. How many of your priests have admitted to abusing children?" Now Luke was getting annoyed, but she wouldn't give him a chance to respond. "My sister fought for peace and she died for peace. Don't try to tell me that she was involved. Islam doesn't condone violence!"

Luke lost his temper as he tried to explain. "I don't believe that your sister had anything to do with the bombing. As a matter of fact, I know she's innocent. And as far as Islam goes, you and your sister may not condone violence, but don't tell me Islam doesn't. Muslims danced in the streets after 9/11, and I've had a priest die in my arms in the name of Islam. There are big differences between Christianity and Islam. My God forgave the adulteress; your prophet had her stoned to death. When a Christian commits an act of violence, the pope condemns it; when it's a Muslim, there is silence." Upset at himself for losing control, Luke stood and walked out the door.

✝

# 33

AS LUKE HASTILY OPENED his car door, he heard Jami calling his name. Looking up, he saw her running across the frozen ground in her socks. He closed the door and waited for her to approach. "Luke, I would like to apologize. I'm sorry; I should have let you finish. I thought you were saying that Ablaa had something to do with the bombing. Please forgive me."

Luke regained control as he said, "I'm not upset with you as much as I'm embarrassed with my own behavior. I never should have said the things I said."

Shivering, she replied, "Wait here, I need to get my coat."

As she ran back to the apartment, Luke yelled, "Get some shoes also."

A few minutes later she reappeared, wearing a coat, shoes, and a knitted wool hat. She looked at Luke and smiled. "Can we agree to forget the last ten minutes?"

"That sounds good to me."

Jami motioned to the building and said, "Can we walk? Many of the people who live here are strict Muslims, so it's probably better if they don't see me with a man in the apartment."

In an attempt to lighten the mood, Luke smiled and commented, "Nice hat."

She laughed. "Are you making fun of me?"

He looked at her. "No, I'm being serious."

It was hard to ignore just how beautiful she was. Her long thick hair, clear expressive eyes, and gorgeous smile made it hard for Luke to look away. Her feisty personality seemed unusual for someone who grew up in a country where women are suppressed as second-class citizens. As they walked, she said, "Please tell me what you know about the bombing."

Luke relayed what he had heard from Blade without using his name. She processed the information quickly, asking, "Have you been able to verify any of this?"

"No. I thought you might be able to help."

"Did you look up the dates for the baseball games he told you about?"

Luke laughed. "You're kidding me, right?"

She looked at him sincerely. "Why is that funny?"

"Jami, there is no bigger rivalry in professional sports than the Yankees and Red Sox. I played baseball in high school, and for much of my life I dreamed of playing in Boston. I didn't have to look up the dates; they are etched in my memory forever. Baseball is a religion in Boston."

She smiled and asked, "How can I help?"

"Can you ask some of the people you trust at the mosque about the construction company?" Then he had another idea. "Maybe we can find mosques that were built around 2004 and see who did the construction. There have to be records for building permits."

She looked at him and said, "I'll do anything to find the people who killed my sister."

Then she stopped walking, turned to face Luke, and asked, "How did you decide that my sister was innocent?"

"When I started thinking about everything that happened, nothing made sense. She wouldn't have been on that stage if the bombs were planted years ago. And then I read a note that my brother wrote about Ablaa."

"What did it say?"

He smiled at her. "It said that she was the kindest and most loving person he'd ever met and that she was an inspiration to him."

She grabbed his arm. "Luke, she really was a very special person. As you can see, I have a temper. Ablaa was always calm, always peaceful and kind. I never saw her raise her voice in anger."

"I wish I could have met her."

Smiling, she replied, "Me too."

As they passed a small coffee shop, Luke asked, "How about I buy us a couple of cups of coffee to go?"

She agreed, and he entered the shop for a few minutes. When he came out, he handed a cup to Jami and said, "I think one of the workers in there recognized me."

"I'm not surprised. You're in the newspaper almost every day."

Luke grew serious. "Jami, you need to be very careful. It's more important that you're safe than it is to get information. Only talk to people that you would trust with your life. Whoever killed Ablaa and Aaron would kill us in a heartbeat if they knew what we are doing."

"Don't worry, I'm going to pretend that a friend is looking for a building company and wants a recommendation. Then I will ask if there are any local companies that employ Muslims. I don't think my friends will suspect anything."

"OK, just be cautious. I'll research the mosques that were built around 2004, and I may even go visit a few to see what I can find out. Maybe someone will talk to me."

"Why don't you call me in the morning and we will compare notes?"

Being cautious, Luke replied, "Let's not talk about this on the phone. How about we meet in front of the coffee shop tomorrow morning at ten?"

She agreed. They said good-bye, and Luke headed for his car.

# 34

LUKE TOOK OUT HIS cell phone and made a call before starting the car. John answered, "Good morning."

Relieved, Luke asked, "How did you make out last night?"

"Great. I stayed in the office, and got up early to start work. I've already fixed the sink in the doctor's office, and now I'm organizing Aaron's office. Someone named Jim Hathaway called. Says he's going to meet me here this afternoon."

"He's a really nice guy. I'm sure you'll like him."

In a soft voice John said, "I can't thank you enough for everything you've done."

"I'm happy to help."

Luke told John that he was heading back to the house to work and asked him if he would join them for dinner later. John accepted.

Luke then received a call that was disappointing; Sal couldn't find anyone who knew anything about a construction company with crescent symbols on their trucks. He promised to keep looking, but

Luke could tell by the sound of his voice that he had already given up. Maybe he had asked Sal for too many favors.

Once home, he went into the library and logged on to the computer. Bringing up an Internet search engine, he typed in the words "mosques built in Boston 2004." When the results filled the screen, he found a newspaper article describing the construction of a new mosque in Roxbury. Searching the prior and subsequent years, he found four that met his criteria.

He ran out to the car, entered the first address into the navigation system, and immediately headed to Roxbury. Pulling up in front of the mosque, he was amazed at the enormity of the structure. Aware of the fact that Muslims prayed five times throughout the day, he approached the building cautiously, not wanting to disturb anyone.

Luke opened the massive door to peer inside. Seeing and hearing no one, he stepped in. As he looked around he was awed by the architecture. Arched columns led the way to the prayer area, which rivaled that of any Roman cathedral.

Based on his research, Luke knew that this particular mosque also contained a religious school for children and a community room. He walked down a long hallway that led away from the prayer area in hopes of finding someone to talk to. Seeing a young boy walking toward him, he asked, "Can you please tell me where the imam is?" The child smiled and pointed to a doorway just a few steps away.

Luke gently knocked, and a second later the door opened. A peaceful-looking man appeared, dressed in loose-fitting white clothing and a turban. Luke asked, "Are you the imam?"

He shook his head affirmatively, but he warily asked, "Yes, how can I help you?"

Not wanting to reveal his identity, Luke didn't introduce himself but said, "I have a question for you." Again the man smiled, but he didn't speak, so Luke continued. "Can you tell me the name of the construction company that built this beautiful mosque?"

Staring at him, the imam said, "Why?"

Why? Luke thought to himself. Not knowing what to say, he replied, "I'm doing research on mosques that have been built in the area and wanted to talk to the companies who constructed them."

The man said softly, "There were many people involved in the construction. We don't share that information. Please look elsewhere. Now if you will excuse me, our afternoon prayers are about to start."

Frustrated at the lack of information he was receiving, Luke turned to walk out the door. As he began walking down the hallway, he heard the imam say, "Father Miller, when you decide to tell me the real reason you need the information, perhaps we can talk again."

Startled, Luke turned around and began walking back toward the office. Before he reached the doorway, it closed. He knocked several times to no avail. With people entering the mosque for prayers, he had no other choice but to turn back and leave through the same door he had entered just minutes ago. Once in his car, he entered the next address and sped away.

The other three imams had a similar reaction to his questions, although they were friendlier. As Luke entered each mosque, he had a sense that they were expecting him. It was almost as if the first imam he had met called every other mosque in the area and told them not to talk. Two imams said they had no idea who built the structures. The last one told Luke that he had only been at his mosque for a few years and that the construction was completed before he arrived.

While driving home, Luke realized that he already knew the best person to provide the information he needed. If anyone could get the name of the company that requested the building permits for these mosques, it was Lori Simpson. The governor's office certainly had access to this data. Luke wondered if Lieutenant Governor Dick would question why someone would need this information. He also needed to figure out how he was going to ask Lori without giving her the full story.

As he pulled up to the house, he was glad to see that Lori's car was still there. Hearing him enter, the children ran to the front door to greet him, and he lifted each one up in his arms. He carried them into the family room, where Deborah and Lori were talking. Deborah smiled and said, "Well, where have you been all day?"

Luke put Abel and Alessa down. "I had a few errands to run." Changing the subject, he asked, "Were you two up all night?"

Lori answered, "No, why?"

"Well, when I saw your car here this morning, I figured you were probably up all night chatting about your new boyfriend from the restaurant."

Lori looked at Deborah and said, "I think he's jealous!"

They all laughed, and Deborah filled him in. "Richard is out of town at the annual governors' meeting for the next few days, so I asked Lori to stay the night."

Luke smiled and answered sarcastically, "Yeah, sure."

Deborah playfully picked up a pillow from the couch and threw it at Luke. Not wanting to engage with her, he caught it and gently placed it on a chair before excusing himself.

# 35

LUKE LOGGED ON TO the computer again and printed out a new list of the mosques built around 2004. While it printed, he formulated a plan. He decided that the best way to give the information to Lori was to be nonchalant about it. He was happy that her husband was out of town, hoping that one of his assistants could handle the request without Richard's knowledge.

Walking back into the family room, Luke asked, "Going shopping again today?"

Lori smiled and said, "Not sure, but we are definitely going back to that restaurant for lunch!"

Deborah replied, "We are not!"

With everyone laughing, Luke walked over and handed the mosque listing to Lori. "What's this?" she asked.

"Nothing important. I've just been doing some research on mosques in the area. I was hoping you could ask Richard to find out the names of the construction companies that built them by looking up their building permits."

Lori glanced at the list. "But he's out of town for a few days."

This was the opportunity Luke was looking for. "Maybe his assistant could help?"

She laughed. "That's a good idea; she seems to be the only one in his office who works. When do you need it?"

Not wanting to appear overanxious but hoping to get the information as soon as possible, he joked, "Well, it can wait until after you visit your boyfriend at the restaurant."

When they finished laughing, Luke was relieved when Lori said, "How about I just call her now?"

She went to make the call while Luke sat and talked with Deborah. Returning a few minutes later, she handed Luke his list and asked, "Can you fax or e-mail this information to her?"

Not wanting it to print on a fax machine where someone else might see it, Luke said, "I'll e-mail it to her right now."

Hoping to get a quick response, Luke typed a polite note to the assistant, ending it with the words: "Thank you very much for your help; your work ethic is inspiring! Lori." After reviewing it with Lori, he sent it.

Luke decided to take a ride instead of remaining at the house, anxiously waiting for the reply to come. Pulling up to Aaron's building, he saw his truck parked in the back. He smiled. John must have washed and waxed it. Luke couldn't recall it ever looking so good.

He entered Aaron's office, where he found Margaret and John in a storage room, trying to organize several large file cabinets. Luke helped them for a few minutes, until the phone rang and Margaret hurried to answer it. Putting down a box, John said, "Can I talk to you alone for a minute?"

"Sure, let's go into Aaron's office."

Luke sat behind the desk and John pulled up a chair. "Father, I just finished talking with Jim Hathaway. He told me that he was going to add me to Deborah's payroll."

When he didn't continue, Luke asked, "Is that a problem? I thought you already knew that."

"Yes, but there must be a mistake."

"Why is that?"

"He told me that I'm going to be paid sixty grand a year."

Smiling to ease the tension, Luke asked, "What? It's not enough?"

John laughed. "Are you crazy? I didn't want to embarrass Jim, so I didn't say anything. I wanted to talk to you first."

"John, I've discussed this with Deb and she approved your salary. Did Jim talk to you about your house?"

"Yes. He asked me questions about the bank lien. I hope you don't mind that I used the phone to call my wife to get some of the information he needed. When I asked him why he wanted the specifics, he said I should talk to you."

"I want to see if there's any way we can get your house back."

John's eyes filled with tears as he struggled to hide his emotions. When he started to speak, he couldn't, so he looked down while trying to regain his composure. Luke saw a tear hit his shoe. With John still looking down, Luke said, "I can't promise you anything, but if there's a way to work with the bank, we will."

Unable to control himself, John finally looked up with tears streaming down his face and said, "I can never thank you enough for what you've already done for me, but you have to promise me something. You need to promise me that whatever happens, you will let me repay you. I don't want any charity."

Luke stood and shook his hand. "You have my word."

"OK. Now, let me get back to work!" Still emotional, he hurried out of the office.

After John left the room, Luke sat at the computer and signed into his e-mail account. He was excited to see a note with the subject line that read "Info requested by Lori." Quickly clicking on it, he saw three construction company names and addresses. After sending a quick thank-you note to Richard's assistant, he printed the list. Saying good-bye to Margaret and John, he headed to his car.

# 36

**LUKE SPENT THE NEXT** two hours driving by each construction company. He stopped in front of the buildings, watched, and waited, looking for trucks with crescent symbols or anything else that looked out of the ordinary. At the first two locations he saw nothing unusual. The employees all appeared to be normal, hardworking men, and the trucks looked as expected. The third company, which was the farthest away, had built two of the mosques.

Pulling up to this last location, Luke stopped the car and looked around. Seeing no sign of a construction company, he parked and verified the address with the car's navigation system. Either the address was wrong or the company was no longer in business. Since this wasn't in the best part of town, he waited in the car and thought about what he should do next. When he saw an elderly man walking a dog, he got out of the car and asked, "Excuse me, sir, was there a construction company somewhere around here?" The man moved closer, and Luke bent down to pet his friendly dog.

"Did you say a construction company?"

Luke smiled. "Yes, sir."

"There was one here years ago. I've lived in this neighborhood for over sixty years. Seems to me that they've been out of business for at least five or six years. Corner Stone Builders, I think?"

Looking up from his list, Luke extended his hand. "That's right, Corner Stone. You have a great memory, Mr.—"

The man switched the dog's leash to his left hand and said, "Flanagan," while shaking hands.

"Well, Mr. Flanagan, it's a pleasure to meet you." Before the man could ask Luke his name, he purposely continued talking. "Do you remember anything about their trucks or sign?"

The man looked puzzled. "What do you mean?"

"I'm just trying to verify that this was the company that worked on a building I'm researching."

"Are you some kind of bill collector or something?"

Luke laughed. "No, not at all. I heard from a friend that this company's trucks had a green moon on the side. Do you remember anything like that?"

The man thought for a few seconds and replied, "I'm sorry, but I can't recall."

Luke thanked him and got back into the car. Thinking that he may have missed something when he looked at the Yellow Pages, he dialed his mother's number and, after a few pleasantries, asked, "Can you look something up in the 2004 phone book for me? In the Yellow Pages under construction companies, can you find the ad for Corner Stone Builders?"

She happily agreed. As he waited, he could hear her flipping pages. Finally, she said, "It's not here."

Disappointed, Luke replied, "Thanks for looking."

She continued. "No, Luke, the page is not here."

"What do you mean?"

"Someone tore the page out of the book that would have had that listing on it."

Luke smiled and explained to his mom that he tore out the page.

Not understanding, she asked, "Then why did you have me look it up?"

He laughed. "Because I forgot that I had that page!"

He reached into his pocket and pulled out the pages. Looking through them, he found the one that contained the listing and ad for Corner Stone. He examined it closely but didn't notice anything unusual. It looked like any other ad.

While he was still parked, his cell phone rang. Picking it up, Luke was happy to hear the voice of Jim Hathaway, the financial adviser. He told Luke about his conversation with John, adding, "When I told him the salary, he cried."

"Did you find out anything about his house?"

"Not yet. Remember Mr. McMahon from the bank?"

"How could I forget?"

"Well, unfortunately, John's loan is owned by another bank, but McMahon is friends with the president. I gave him the information, and he promised to see what he could do. I made sure to let him know that you and Deb were involved and have given John a job."

"Did he say when he would get back to you?"

"He said he would give me an update sometime tomorrow. I'll call you right after I talk to him."

As Luke headed home, he drove past the Common. Thinking of Blade, he said a few prayers. He worried that the homeless man had used the money to drink himself to death. Luke made a mental note to ask John to try to find Blade and make sure he was OK.

In retrospect, he wondered if visiting the mosques was a good idea. He wasn't completely surprised that the first imam he met recognized him; the entire country had seen his face by now. But he questioned why the man didn't acknowledge that he knew who he was until after he found out what Luke wanted. Was it a coincidence that he was greeted almost immediately by the imams of every other mosque he visited?

He had a sobering thought. If Blade's story was true and if the imams were somehow connected, whoever was responsible for the bombing probably now knew that Luke was onto them. Could his anger about Aaron's death and his unrelenting need to find out who was responsible be putting his family in danger? Luke had seen what these extremists were capable of during his time in Africa: beheadings, amputations, whippings, and electrocution. These tortures that most Westerners in America couldn't even comprehend were not only commonplace in many Islamic states; they were accepted as part of Sharia law.

# 37

AS LUKE PULLED INTO the driveway, he was surprised to see a black Town Car parked next to Lori's Caddy. Worried, he hurried into the house to see what was going on. Hearing voices coming from the family room, he entered and saw a man in a dark suit sitting across from Deb and Lori. When he saw Luke, the man stood, and Deborah introduced him. "This is Mike Dempsey. He's the lead investigator from the FBI."

Luke warily shook his hand and asked bluntly, "Why are you here?"

The man laughed. "Deborah just asked me the same question right before you walked in. I'm visiting all the families that lost relatives in the bombing. I want to assure everyone that we are working night and day to find the people responsible."

Distrustful as to why the FBI was showing up now, weeks after the bombing, Luke asked, "Who else have you met with?"

Again, the man smiled. "You're the first family."

Now suspicious, Luke continued his questioning. "I've met with some of the families; who's next on your list?"

Mike's smile abruptly disappeared as he stumbled. "Um, ah, well, it's getting late and my list is in the office. This was the only meeting I had scheduled for today."

Judging by the looks on their faces, Luke could tell that Deb and Lori were wondering why he was questioning the man so harshly. After reiterating his commitment to finding the bombers, Mike stood and lifted the newspaper off the coffee table. Looking at the Thanksgiving Day picture that Lori's husband had leaked to the press, he said, "Great article. It's nice to see that you think about the homeless." When awkward silence filled the room, he sensed it was time to go. He shook everyone's hands, then Luke led him to the front door.

Before leaving, he handed his business card to Luke and said, "Do me a favor. If you see or hear anything regarding this investigation, please call me."

Luke wondered if the FBI already knew what he knew about the case. As Dempsey walked toward his car, Luke asked, "What would I know about the investigation?"

Turning, he stared at Luke and replied, "Only you can answer that question." A few seconds later, the electric gates opened, and the Town Car pulled into the street.

Still standing in the doorway, Luke wondered why the FBI had really showed up. Why today? Could it have anything to do with the fact the he had visited the mosques? He hadn't talked to anyone at the construction companies, so it couldn't have anything to do with that. And why did he comment on the homeless? Did someone from the governor's office call the feds? Jami?

Deep in thought, Luke was startled when the security gates opened again. Seeing his old pickup truck enter the property, he smiled and greeted John.

At dinner, Luke had a hard time concentrating on anything but the bombing, prompting Deborah to ask several times, "Are you all right?" Sensing that Luke had a lot on his mind, John excused himself shortly after eating. Before he could leave, Luke asked him if he could go to the Common the next day and check on Blade. John agreed and headed back to Aaron's office building to sleep.

On the computer again, Luke decided to find out exactly who Mike Dempsey was. Searching his name, he was surprised to find that he had a distinguished background. Dempsey had gone from being a Navy SEAL to a CIA agent to the FBI, or, like the article said, "from spook to suit." It was interesting that he had spent a good part of his CIA career in the Middle East. There were pictures of him with the king of Saudi Arabia as well as the president of the United States. Whoever he was, he was no ordinary agent.

Next, he typed in the name Corner Stone Builders, hit Enter, and waited. There were several results but nothing really interesting. Not one word about who had owned the company.

Tired, confused, and worried, Luke said good night to Deb and Lori and then headed to bed.

# 38

LUKE WAS ANXIOUS TO see Jami and find out if she had any information. He parked his car, and as he approached the coffee shop, he saw her sitting on a bench outside, wearing sunglasses and holding two cups of coffee. Seeing him, she flashed her beautiful smile and said, "Good morning," as she handed him a cup.

"Good morning to you, too, and thank you very much!" He sat down next to her and took a sip. "Have you been waiting long?"

"No, I just got here a few minutes ago."

Getting right to the point, Luke told her what he'd been up to for the past twenty-four hours. When she heard about his visits to the mosques, she said, "You should have let me go. Maybe the imams would have talked to me."

Concerned that she didn't fully appreciate the seriousness of what they were doing, he stated, "I would never put you in a position like that. You have to remember that whoever is responsible for this bombing has tremendous resources. They killed a presidential nominee." He went on to admit that he thought he made a mistake by visiting the mosques. After telling her about FBI agent Mike Dempsey's impromptu visit and questioning, she began to realize the potential danger of their investigation.

"Maybe we should contact the police."

Luke had thought about this also. But what would he tell them? And he wondered if this Dempsey guy already knew everything he knew. He made a mental note to get in touch with Detective Romo, then asked, "Did you find anything out from your friends?"

"I'm sorry, but none of them knew anything about construction companies run by Muslims. I didn't want to ask too many questions."

"That's a good idea. Don't ask anyone else about it. I think we have enough information."

"What are we going to do next?" she asked.

"Well, let's see if the FBI visits you. I'm going to find out who owned Corner Stone Builders."

"How are you going to do that?"

Not wanting to tell her about Lori, he answered obscurely, "From the same person who told me about the building permits."

They finished their coffees and stood to leave, when Jami reminded Luke, "Please call me if I can help you in any way. Remember, I'll do anything to find the people who killed my sister." Luke promised to stay in touch, and they said their good-byes.

When Luke arrived back home, he hurried into the house to find Deb and Lori. Not seeing anyone, he went downstairs to the gym. They were both jogging on treadmills, and Lori's hair was now brown, like Deborah's. "Nice hair," Luke commented as he walked into the room. Lori fluffed it and smiled, saying, "Thank you." Deb waved, not wanting to talk because she was conserving her breath. Thinking this was a good time to ask for a favor, Luke spoke above the noise. "Hey, Lori, would you mind if I sent another e-mail to Richard's assistant? I need one more piece of information." She nodded and gave a thumbs-up.

After composing and sending the e-mail, Luke sat and thought about what to do next. When his cell phone rang, he looked at the display and saw that it was John. It was almost noon, and he wondered why John hadn't called earlier. "Well good afternoon," he said in a jovial tone. John ignored his remark and said, "Luke, I hate to have to tell you this, but Blade is dead."

Luke was horrified. He immediately headed out the door toward his car. "Where are you right now?"

"Still at the Common."

When Luke began asking questions, John said, "Can we talk when you get here? I don't want to say too much on the phone."

Luke sped to the Common, parked on the street, and ran at full speed toward the fountain. Seeing John forlornly sitting on a bench, he squatted in front of him and cried, "What happened? Was it alcohol?" John was still in shock as he stared straight ahead. Ignoring Luke's questions, he said, "It's my fault. I'm the one who set this whole thing up, and he would still be alive if it wasn't for me."

Luke thought for a minute and said, "If anyone is to blame, it's me. I gave him the money."

"It wasn't alcohol."

Puzzled, Luke asked, "What was it, then?"

John turned to face Luke. "Drugs."

Not believing what he was hearing, Luke asked, "Drugs? Are you sure?"

"One of the guys who saw him said that the needle was still sticking out of his arm when they found him."

"I thought you said he didn't do drugs."

"He didn't."

Luke thought back to the day when they had found Blade drunk.

He had searched his entire body for needle marks but had seen none. He also remembered John's insistence that he wasn't a druggie.

"Where did they take the body?"

"I would assume he's at the morgue."

Luke took the prepaid cell phone from John and called Detective Romo, who agreed to meet them.

# 39

**THE RECEPTIONIST AT THE** morgue recognized Luke and said, "Go right in. The detective is already waiting." Noticing that John wasn't following, Luke turned, and John said, "I'll just wait here, if that's OK." As he followed the receptionist into the big concrete room, he felt the temperature plunge and saw Detective Romo standing next to a rolling table that held Blade's lifeless body. He was talking to a man in a white coat, but Luke couldn't hear what he was saying.

When they noticed Luke, the detective turned and shook his hand. Then he introduced Adam Owen, the medical examiner. Luke stared at the bluish color of the body. It was hard to believe that he had just had dinner with this man a few days ago; now he was dead. Detective Romo said, "Luke, when we spoke on the phone, I didn't know that we were talking about Franklyn Hennessey."

Astonished, Luke asked, "You know him?"

"Yes, but I didn't know they called him Blade."

"How do you know him?"

The detective placed his hand on Luke's shoulder. "I've arrested him at least half a dozen times."

"For what?"

"Disorderly conduct, identity theft, possession of stolen goods, selling drugs, and probably a few other things I can't remember right now. He was a great con man who could make you believe almost anything. One time he tried to convince me that the stolen television he was trying to sell on the street was his mother's. And I almost believed him until we figured out that his mother had died over twenty years ago, long before they began making flat screens. Once, I sent him to jail for a year."

Luke was shocked at what he was hearing and asked, "So you wouldn't believe anything he said?"

Romo laughed. "I wouldn't believe a word he said."

Turning to the medical examiner, Luke asked, "How did he die?"

The man looked at Detective Romo, who nodded, giving him permission to answer. "It was a drug overdose. The needle was still stuck in his left arm when he was brought here. From what I can tell it contained almost pure heroin, sometimes referred to as black tar because of its color and purity, usually imported from Mexico or Asia. It's not uncommon to find victims with the needles still in them because it kills so quickly. He also smelled like alcohol."

Based on Romo's predetermined opinion of Blade, Luke decided to keep his mouth shut. He listened for several minutes as the detective and medical examiner talked about Blade as if he never existed. Their minds were made up: A homeless guy kills himself with drugs in the Common; just another day in the city of Boston.

As Luke walked to the door and said good-bye to the detective, John pulled Luke aside and whispered, "I would like to go see Blade to tell him I'm sorry."

Luke put his arm around the heartbroken man and asked, "Are you sure?"

"I'm sure. It's the least I can do."

Walking back into the room, Luke explained to the examiner that John was a friend of Blade's. Understanding, the doctor said, "Take as much time as you want."

John approached the body slowly. After looking at Blade for several seconds, he fell to his knees and prayed. Luke extended his arms out to his sides and said a prayer. Before they walked out, Luke asked the doctor one last question. "Did you find anything else when you examined the body?"

Curious, the man asked, "Like what?"

"Bruises or any signs that he was beaten up or restrained."

"Restrained? From what I can tell he was so drunk that I doubt he could have stood on his own. There was a mark on his head, probably from when he hit the ground."

When they reached the door, the examiner said, "Well, now that you mention it, there was one thing I couldn't figure out."

Luke and John walked back to the table. "What was that?"

He pulled the sheet off, exposing Blade's naked body. Moving to the other side of the table, he said, "Take a look at this."

They followed him and were speechless.

The examiner continued, "I don't know what the hell this is, but it seems to be self-inflicted. There was a hole in his pants pocket, and his own skin was under his fingernails."

Luke looked meaningfully at John and shook his head slightly to indicate that he shouldn't say anything.

Again, they thanked the examiner and walked out the door.

Reaching the street, Luke told John, "Not here. Meet me at the house."

✝

# 40

**LUKE RACED TO THE** house with John following closely. After passing through the gates, they jumped out of their vehicles and Luke said, "This way." Side by side, they walked around the house to the backyard. Luke slowed his pace, and John said, "Did you see that mark on his leg?"

Luke looked at him, wanting to confirm what he was thinking, and said, "What do you think it was from?"

John answered abruptly. "You know damn well what it was. It was a sign, a clue. I told you he didn't do drugs. He was trying to tell us something."

Quickly, piecing everything together, Luke said, "OK, here's what I'm thinking. Someone from one of the mosques or the governor's office is worried that I'm getting close to figuring out who was responsible for the bombing. Trying to determine how I've gotten this far, they remembered the Thanksgiving picture in the newspaper and its mention of the homeless people from the Common, and they saw Blade's face in the background. It was easy to identify him because of his scar. They sent someone to the park to find him. He was probably drunk when they held him down and put the needle in his left arm, not knowing that he was left-handed. Realizing what was happening, Blade poked a hole in his pants pocket with his right hand and carved the crescent in his leg with his fingernail to leave us a clue."

Luke added, "Unless maybe all of this is just a coincidence and, like the detective said, Blade was a really good liar."

Ignoring Luke's last statement, John moved his arms and mimicked shooting up with a needle. "How do you know he was left-handed?"

Luke replied, "Don't you remember what Deb said to him at the dinner table? She said, 'You're left-handed like me.'"

Now understanding, John said, "Yeah, he would have shot himself in the right arm, not the left."

Luke nodded.

John asked nervously, "What do we do now?"

"Well, the first thing we do is convince Deborah that she and the children need to go out of town for a few weeks, without telling them too many details."

"How?"

"Every year around Christmas, Aaron would take the family skiing for a few weeks in the Berkshires. I think he owns another house in the mountains up there. We need to persuade Deborah that she should go; maybe she can take Lori with her." He continued, "Next, we need to make sure you're safe. Unless you've been followed over the past few days, no one would ever suspect that you've been sleeping in the office building. Thankfully, your picture wasn't in the paper with Blade's, and with the way you're currently dressed, no one would ever suspect that you also had lived in the park. But from now on, you need to be extra careful."

Concerned, John asked, "And what about you? You're probably in more danger than anyone."

Luke had also thought about his own safety. He wondered if the bombers would risk killing him, too. The amount of publicity associated with murdering Aaron's brother, and a priest at that, would be enormous. But they'd already killed a presidential nominee, so obviously they weren't concerned about publicity.

"I think that once Deb goes to the mountain house, I'll go live on Aaron's boat."

"He has a boat?"

Trying to ease the tension a bit, Luke smiled halfheartedly and said, "No, he has a yacht."

The two men continued to finalize their plans going forward, including Luke's desire to pay for Blade's funeral. Realizing that he needed to check his e-mail to see if Dick's assistant had sent the name of the owner of the construction company that built the mosques, Luke told John that he would see him at dinner. As John walked toward his truck, Luke had another idea. "Hey, John, hold on a second." He caught up to John in the driveway. "What about Star?"

John thought for a minute and replied, "Do you think she saw something?"

"I guess we'll never know unless we find her. Do you think she would talk to you?"

"I really don't know. Either she'll think I had something to do with Blade's murder, or she'll consider me a friend. I guess it wouldn't hurt to try."

Worried that John might be putting himself in danger if he went back to the park, Luke questioned, "Do you think it's worth the risk?"

"I'm going to stop by the Common on my way to Aaron's office. I'm not going to talk to anyone unless I see her. I promise to be careful."

"Are you sure?"

"I think I owe it to Blade, and I'd like to make sure that Star is safe."

Luke made him promise to call as soon as he left the park. As the truck pulled out of the driveway, Luke hurried inside and logged on to the computer.

# 41

**THE E-MAIL FROM LT.** Governor Simpson's assistant was short and sweet, with only two words: "Vincent Russo." Clearing the e-mail screen, Luke began typing frantically. The name search showed that there were more than two million matches. Using quotation marks to find an exact match, he added, "Corner Stone Builders." Now there were only eleven results returned.

Clicking on the first listing displayed, he noticed that all of the articles were from newspapers. The first headline was chilling: "Local Businessman and Wife Killed in Hit and Run." The details of the tragic accident saddened him. Vincent Russo was a well-respected member of his community who did a lot of charity work. His wife volunteered at the local hospital and neighborhood Catholic church. The last paragraph said that they were survived by three children: Vincent, Trinity, and Faith. Looking for the date, he saw that the accident had occurred years ago, in 2001.

Already knowing that Vincent didn't bring up many results, Luke decided to look up Trinity, since it was an unusual name. The results for "Trinity Russo" displayed only one exact match. It was a local newspaper article about a beautification project in the town of Greenwich,

Connecticut. She was listed as one of a group of wealthy locals who banded together in an attempt to spruce up Greenwich Avenue by replacing the light poles and planting trees and flowers.

Next, Luke searched for "Faith Russo," and although he found a few pages of results, none of them appeared to be related to Vincent. At this point, Luke began to question Blade's story even more. How could a successful Italian immigrant who donated a tremendous amount of time to charity with a wife who volunteered at the local hospital and church be connected to the bombing in Boston? He was obviously a Christian and not a Muslim; his girls were named Trinity and Faith.

Luke decided that he would drive to Greenwich in the morning and ask around. While he thought about what to do next, his cell phone rang.

"Hi, Jim, how are you?"

After a few pleasantries, Hathaway got to the point. "Regarding John Daly's foreclosed house, I have the numbers from the bank of what it would take to reclaim it."

"Great, what are they?"

"Well, they want twenty-three thousand dollars in back payments and interest. And because he hasn't had a job in such a long time, they also want a cosigner for the loan."

Luke asked, "What's the total amount that he owes?"

After shuffling papers for a second, Jim answered, "About a hundred fifty thousand."

Realizing that he could easily pay off the entire amount himself, if anything happened to John, Luke said, "Let's do it."

Jim agreed to move forward with the bank and keep Luke informed. After thanking Jim, he joined the others in the family room.

When the nanny led the children out of the room for their afternoon nap, Luke took the opportunity to talk to Deb and Lori about going to the mountain house. He told them he was worried about their safety and that he would feel better if they were out of town for a few weeks. They finally agreed, and Deb said, "It might be fun to get away, after all." They decided to give all of the employees time off with pay, while leaving a single security guard stationed at the front gate.

When Luke realized that he hadn't heard from John for over an hour, he dialed his number.

"Hi, Luke, I was just about to call you."

"Are you OK?"

"Yes, I'm fine. Just finished my second lap around the park. No sign of Star."

Disappointed, Luke thanked him. Before hanging up, he asked for another favor. "John, when you get to Aaron's office, can you please ask Margaret to call a local funeral home so we can get Blade buried as soon as possible? Just make sure it's not tomorrow. I'll be out of town for the day."

When John questioned where Luke was going, he told him that he would explain everything after dinner that night.

Back on the computer, Luke carefully planned his trip to Greenwich. Mapping it out, he realized that the drive would take him a little over three hours. Thinking about the best way to find Trinity Russo, he found the addresses of all the local Catholic churches, the Greenwich Historical Society, and the Greenwich Architectural Review Committee. He thought about calling ahead of time, but he knew that people were suspicious of giving out information over the phone. He also knew that if they saw he was a priest, he might be able to get more information.

At dinner, there was an undeniable tension in the air. Deborah had already told the staff that they would be on a paid vacation until after Christmas, so they were excited, but everyone else had one thing on their minds: Was Luke going to figure out who killed Aaron? And in doing so, was he putting himself and his family at risk?

While the table was being cleared, Luke motioned to John to follow him outside. As they walked around the house in the bone-chilling air, Luke explained why he was traveling to Greenwich in the morning. He told John that he would be leaving at five in the morning and planned on being home by dark. They agreed to call each other throughout the day.

After John drove away, Luke walked back into the house and saw Deb and Lori carrying suitcases up from the basement. Hastening to help them, he patiently waited until they were packed, and then he made several trips to load the luggage into Deb's SUV.

# 42

THE NEXT MORNING, IT was still dark outside when Luke walked into the kitchen to grab a bottle of water before getting in the car. When he closed the refrigerator and turned, he was startled to see Deborah standing in the hallway. He asked, "Is everything all right?"

She answered in her gravelly early-morning voice while rubbing her tired eyes. "Yes, everything is fine."

"What are you doing up this early?"

"I just wanted to say good-bye and remind you to be careful."

Luke smiled. "Thank you. You be careful also. I've already loaded the address to the Berkshires home in your GPS. I'll call you later, but call me if you need anything."

Anxious to get on the road, Luke walked toward the front door with Deb following. When he turned to say good-bye one last time, she hugged him without saying a word.

The sun had been out for an hour when Luke reached the Greenwich Historical Society office. Not expecting anyone to be there this early in the morning, he nevertheless climbed out of the car, stretched, and walked to the door to see if the hours were posted. A sign read, "See you after the holidays." Disappointed, he walked back to the car and headed to the second address on his list.

Before entering the office building, he already knew that this attempt to find Trinity was a long shot at best. On the directory next to the elevator, he saw the name for Design View Architects, the office where the review committee met. Knocking, he was surprised when a young girl opened the door. "Can I help you, Father?"

Luke smiled. "Well, I hope so. I'm looking for a lady named Trinity Russo; she's on the Greenwich Architectural Review Committee."

The girl went to her desk and began flipping pages. Looking up, she said, "I'm sorry, but they don't meet again until next month."

Not wanting to give up, Luke asked, "Do you happen to know if Trinity Russo is on the committee?"

She looked up and thought for a second. "I'm really not sure. Mr. Reilly would know, but he won't be in until after ten."

Luke thanked her and let her know that he might return in a few hours. She smiled.

He had only been in Greenwich for a half hour and was already down to his last lead—the one lead he hoped he didn't have to use. He parked his car on the street and hurried up the stone steps into Saint Mary's Church, realizing that the eight o'clock mass was probably almost over. He entered the beautiful building and quietly sat in a pew in the back and joined the mass in process. When he went up to receive Communion, the priest smiled, seeing his collar.

After almost everyone had left, Luke approached the presiding priest and introduced himself. He wasn't surprised when the priest replied, "I know who you are, and I'm so sorry for your loss." He introduced himself as Father Leo and motioned for Luke to follow him. His warm smile and caring eyes gave Luke optimism that he would help if he could. Entering the small sacristy in the back of the church, they sat down to talk. "So what brings you all the way to Greenwich, Father Luke?"

Even though Luke knew this question was coming, he was unwilling to divulge all the details. "I was hoping that you could help me find someone named Trinity Russo, who may be a parishioner."

Leo smiled. "Is she a friend of yours?"

"No, I've never met her."

Realizing that Luke wasn't telling him everything, but still willing to help, Leo asked, "What makes you think she's a parishioner?"

"It's a long shot, but I thought I would give it a try."

Leo picked up the phone receiver from the table, but before dialing, said, "I can have the secretary check our records, but I feel obligated to ask you why you want to talk to her."

Luke replied without divulging the real reason he was there. "I need to ask her a few questions about some work that her family's company did in Boston." Downplaying it, he continued, "No big deal, just a few simple questions."

Leo dialed and asked, "Can you tell me if we have a parishioner named Trinity Russo?"

A few seconds later, he thanked the secretary and put down the phone. "I'm sorry, Luke, but we don't have anyone by that name in our files."

Luke thanked him and opened the door to leave, stopping when Leo said, "We do have a Trinity Lombardi, though."

Realizing that she might have been married, Luke asked warily, "Can you give me her address?"

Reluctantly, Leo redialed the secretary and jotted down the information for Luke. After thanking him, Luke quickly walked out the door and headed toward his car, and Coachlamp Lane.

Turning onto the block, he wasn't surprised to see the grandeur of the houses. If Trinity was working on beautification projects in Greenwich, she certainly might live in a neighborhood like this. Checking the address one last time, Luke pulled into the long, curved driveway and parked.

The stately stone house was impressive. He counted four chimneys and three garage doors. He took a deep breath, checked his watch, and decided that she would probably be awake by now. After he rang the bell a few times, the door opened. A young girl, who must have been about eight, smiled and asked, "Can I help you?"

"I'm Father Luke from Boston. Is your mother home?"

She left the door ajar and walked away. Luke waited patiently until the door opened again and Trinity appeared. Seeing Luke, she started to cry and asked, "Is Vincent dead?"

Confused, Luke answered quickly, "No, I'm not here for anything like that."

She wiped her eyes and quickly composed herself, asking, "Then how can I help you, Father?"

"I'm very sorry to bother you at home. I just wanted to know if you are Trinity Russo."

She hesitated and answered, "Yes, Russo is my maiden name."

"I have a few simple questions about your father's building company. I was hoping you could help."

"No problem, I'm happy to help, but I'm in the middle of cooking breakfast for my daughter. Would you mind coming in and waiting until I'm done?"

Luke followed her inside to a room that faced the backyard and was adjacent to the kitchen. While Luke sat and waited, Trinity finished making breakfast. Luke didn't care if he had to wait all day; he was just happy he had found her.

# 43

TRINITY EXPLAINED THAT HER daughter, Grace, was going to school late that morning because the class had a field trip. "If you wouldn't mind, we're running late, so if you take a ride with me, we can talk after I drop Grace at school." She led the way toward a white Range Rover and unlocked the doors. Grace jumped in the back and Luke sat in the front. As they drove toward the school at a reckless pace, Luke felt like he was a passenger in an off-road car race, and he said a few silent prayers.

Based on the way Grace was dressed, Luke wasn't surprised when they sped into the parking lot of Greenwich Catholic School. After saying good-bye, they were back in the zone, speeding down the road again. With her eyes fixated on the traffic in front of her, Trinity said, "I was really sorry to hear about your brother."

Luke thanked her. As he started to ask her about her father's company, her cell rang. "I'm sorry, but I really need to get this."

Luke smiled. Not wanting to listen to her conversation but having no choice, he heard her say, "I'm going to have to cancel lunch." She looked at him while continuing to talk to the person on the phone. "Something has come up. I'll call you later to explain."

She turned onto Greenwich Avenue and parked in front of Michaelangelo, which looked to be some kind of exclusive gift store. Thinking that she had an errand to run, Luke waited in the car until she said, "Aren't you coming?"

He followed her across the street and into a restaurant called Mediterraneo that had just opened its doors. The hostess recognized Trinity, smiled, and said, "Right this way, Mrs. Lombardi." They were led to a table in the contemporary dining room near a window. After ordering coffee, Trinity looked at Luke and said, "OK, Father, how can I help you?"

Easing into the conversation, Luke responded, "First of all, let me just say how sorry I was to read about the accident involving your parents. They seemed like wonderful people."

Trinity's eyes filled with tears. "They were the best people I've ever known, and I miss them so much."

Luke smiled. "I'm sure God has blessed them."

She nodded and he continued. "Were you involved with your father's construction company?"

Concerned, she replied, "What do you mean?"

"Did you work there, help out, or anything like that?"

"No, I'm the oldest in the family and was in college when the company became successful. Why do you ask?"

Studying her face for a reaction, Luke replied, "I visited several mosques in Boston last week that were built by Corner Stone, and I had a few questions about the construction."

Not flinching, she responded, "I'm sorry, Father, I wouldn't know anything about that. My brother ran the company for a few years after my parents died, so he could probably tell you everything that you want to know."

Encouraged, Luke asked, "Does he live around here?"

She took a deep breath and frowned. "No, he still lives in Massachusetts. Cape Cod, to be precise."

"Do you talk to him often?"

Another deep breath. "No, we haven't talked in several years. After my parents died, he changed. Vincent hurt his back unloading a truck at the shop one day and became dependent on painkillers. To make things even worse, while he was home recovering, he began drinking. I spent a fortune checking him into several different rehab facilities, and I thought he was finally cured. When he showed up for Gracie's fifth birthday party inebriated, and vomited in the yard in front of my friends and family, I told him he wasn't welcome here anymore. That's why I was so upset when I saw you at my door today. I recognized you immediately, and knowing that you are from Boston, well, I thought he'd finally killed himself."

"I'm sorry that I frightened you. That wasn't my intention."

Changing the topic, she asked, "How have you been since the bombing?"

"As you know, it feels terrible. It's like a really bad dream. Sometimes when I wake up in the morning, I forget for a few seconds that he's gone, and I feel good until reality sets in. I wish I could go back in time and tell him all the things I should have told him before he was gone."

Teary-eyed, she asked, "He had two young children, right?"

Luke smiled. "Yes, two angels, Abel and Alessa."

Her motherly instincts were in high gear when she asked, "How old are they?"

"Three and four."

Innocently, she stated, "Well, thank God that you're there to help your brother's wife."

Hoping to get more information on Vincent, Luke asked, "Do you think your brother would talk to me?"

"I don't see why not, that is, if he's not drunk or high. Before the drugs, he was a great person and someone that everyone admired, but now, only God knows."

"Do you have his phone number?"

"No, but I think I have his address at the house."

After their food was served, the restaurant began filling up. When several customers recognized Luke, he quickly paid the bill, and they headed back to Trinity's house. She went inside to find Vincent's address while Luke waited in the driveway. Returning, she handed him a piece of paper with the information. He thanked her, and she walked back toward her car. As she opened the door to the SUV, Luke asked, "Can I get your cell phone number in case I have any other questions?"

She smiled and said her number slowly so Luke could enter it in his phone. When she was finished, Luke gave her his. Before she left, Luke innocently asked, "Are you in contact with your sister?"

She furrowed her brow and said, "My sister?"

Confused, Luke replied, "Don't you have a sister named Faith?"

"No."

"But the newspaper article said your parents were survived by three children: Vincent, Trinity, and Faith."

She laughed. "Not Faith. My adopted brother, Fatih."

Hearing the name, Luke's heart raced, "Where is he from?"

"Saudi Arabia. Why?"

Despite the unsettling feeling he had just gotten in his stomach, he calmly replied, "I was wondering if he would know about the construction of the mosques."

"I'm sure he would. His parents moved in next door to us, and his father helped my dad get a lot of new business."

Confused, Luke asked, "But I thought you said he was your adopted brother?"

She moved closer to Luke. "It's another really sad story. Fatih's family moved into our neighborhood when I was away at college. His father would always stop by our house to see my dad. At first, my father was wary of the Abu family, but they turned out to be such great people. I don't know the details, but as I mentioned, Mr. Abu really helped my dad with his business, and eventually they became very close friends. About a year later, something happened with Mr. Abu's job that required him to travel back and forth to the Middle East for work. When his parents began traveling together, Fatih stayed at our house for weeks at a time while attending high school. During a trip to the Middle East, while Fatih was living at our house, both of his parents were killed in a plane crash. It was so sad. That same day, my parents decided that they would adopt him."

"Do you still see Fatih?"

She smiled. "No, after staying in Boston for a few years, he decided that he wanted to return to the Middle East. He wanted to go home."

"Have you talked to him recently?"

"No, I haven't talked to him in many years. Vincent might still be in touch. I'm just not sure."

# PART 3

*"Deep faith eliminates fear."*
—Lech Walesa

# 44

LUKE ENTERED VINCENT'S CAPE Cod address into his GPS and saw that it was about five hours away. Since it was still early afternoon, he decided to drive there directly, hoping to get a chance to talk to him that night.

While on the road, Luke made a few calls. First, he checked in on Deborah. She was already driving to the mountain house, and he could hear Lori chatting in the background. As Lori's voice became louder, he heard her say several times, "Ask him." Finally, Deborah said, "Hold on," and she handed the phone to Lori.

Lori got right to the point. "We saw your picture in the paper this morning and were wondering who that was with you."

Luke had no idea what she was talking about. "My picture was in the paper?"

"Yes, you were sitting on a bench drinking coffee with a lady in dark sunglasses."

Now he knew. "That's Jami. Her sister was killed in the bombing with Aaron."

There was silence for a few seconds and then Lori replied, "Oh, we never saw her before and couldn't imagine who she was."

"Her sister was a special adviser to Aaron, and we've spoken a few times since the bombing," he said.

Once they finished talking, he called John, who was working at Aaron's office. John told him that Blade's funeral was scheduled to be held in two days. The authorities had already checked, and Blade had no known relatives. John added, "We thought it would be best if he was cremated. Is that all right with you?"

Luke knew that the Catholic Church had changed its views on cremation in the early 1960s, but he realized that many people still didn't know it. "That's fine, John. Do they know that I want to have a small service and say some prayers?"

"Yes, I already told them. Blade's body will be on display, and after your prayer service is finished, he will be cremated. We can pick up the ashes the next day."

"John, thanks very much for taking care of this. You've been a big help."

Pulling onto I-95 northbound, Luke knew he would be on this road for almost two hundred miles. He set the cruise control, adjusted his seat, and relaxed, letting his mind wander. He kept asking himself if someone could be so devious that they would plant a bomb years in advance of an event taking place. If Blade's dates were correct, many famous people had given speeches in the Common after the bomb was buried. Were they waiting for a certain time, or a particular person, before blowing up the stage? It had been rumored that the pope was going to visit Boston again. Based on the previous papal visit, he probably would have been at the Common. In fact, even the president had spoken there; why didn't they explode the bomb then? Was it because he was a Democrat? Was being a Republican the link?

Tired of overanalyzing, Luke turned on the radio just in time to hear a special bulletin being broadcast. "Another bombing has taken place, this time in New York City." Stunned, Luke jerked forward and listened intently. "A car bomb has just exploded in front of the Stock Exchange on Wall Street. At least fifteen people have been killed and many more injured. Police and antiterrorism units are on site." Luke said a prayer.

Still driving, he listened to the same report over and over again. No one had claimed responsibility for the bombing, and lower Manhattan was closed to cars and trains. He knew it was a selfish thought, but now the FBI focus would be diverted from Boston to New York. Obviously there was little chance that he would have any help figuring out who killed his brother.

He merged onto I-195, which signaled that he would soon be on the Cape. When the GPS finally announced, "Your destination is on the right," he pulled into the narrow driveway. The houses were modest compared to Trinity's neighborhood, but even though they were only a few feet apart, they had the advantage of being situated directly on the beach. Noticing a bright orange Jeep in the driveway, he hoped that Vincent was home. He walked toward the wooden front step and saw old newspapers along the walkway and shoes on the front porch. The old boards squeaked as he approached the door.

Luke knocked a few times, but there was no answer. Peering around toward the back of the house, he thought he heard music, and he headed for it. The backyard contained a small brick paver patio littered with beer cans, but no sign of anyone. Returning to the front door, he turned the knob and it opened. He stuck his head inside and yelled, "Is anyone home?" When there was no reply, he yelled again. He heard a noise, and a few seconds later a tall young man, probably in his early thirties, walked into the living room. Seeing Luke, he was obviously annoyed when he said sternly, "Can I help you?"

Luke smiled and replied, "I'm Father Luke Miller from Saint Leonard's Parish in Boston. Your sister gave me your address."

"You're not going to save me, Father; I know my sister has bought into all this God stuff, but I haven't."

"I'm not here to convert you. I've been doing some research on buildings in Boston and had a few questions about Corner Stone Builders." Daring to be pushy, Luke continued, "Can I come in?"

Vincent waved his hand indifferently, and Luke entered the modest house. Sarcastically, Vincent asked, "Can I get you a beer, Father?" as he walked barefooted toward the kitchen.

Luke surprised him when he said, "That sounds great."

"You're kidding me, right?"

Luke smiled. "I'm serious. Do you think priests only drink wine?"

Vincent returned and handed Luke a Corona.

"Thank you."

Vincent said, "You wanna sit?"

Luke sat in a canvas sofa while Vincent flopped into a white bean-bag chair. After taking a slug of beer, he asked, "Well, Father Luke, how's my perfect sister?"

Luke looked at him and replied, "She's perfect."

That made him smile. "Are you sure that you're a priest?"

They both laughed.

"I think she misses you, and I know that she's concerned about you."

Vincent became serious. "I miss her, too. How well do you know her?"

"I only met her and your niece a few hours ago."

Sitting up as best he could in the unstructured chair, Vincent asked, "How is Grace?"

Luke smiled. "She's perfect, just like her mom." He added, "She's a beautiful, happy young girl."

As Luke was talking, Vincent's expression changed as he recognized him. "Hey, you're the priest from TV. The one whose brother was killed."

"Yeah, unfortunately, that's me."

"That sucks. Take it from someone who knows what it's like to have someone in your family killed suddenly." Luke agreed. They spent the next half hour bonding over their mutual sorrow. Luke found that he truly liked Vincent. He was smart, articulate, and interesting. Looking at his watch, Vincent asked, "Hey, why don't we go get some dinner? There's a place right down the street that has awesome food." Luke gratefully agreed. He was starving.

# 45

**VINCENT INSISTED ON DRIVING,** so Luke backed his Mercedes out of the narrow driveway and waited until the Jeep pulled out before pulling back in. As they entered the Bee-Hive Tavern, Luke was amazed at the greeting Vincent received. Men at the bar stood and came over to shake his hand. Women kissed and hugged him. Even the owner appeared and welcomed him. He introduced Luke to everyone, not only to be polite, but also because he was showing off that he was hanging out with a celebrity. Luke could tell that many people recognized him, but they were all courteous and friendly.

During the next hour, Luke decided one thing—that Vincent was no killer. Now he had to determine how much information he was going to tell him. After they ordered, Vincent noticed a small crowd of people standing around a television at the bar. He asked Luke, "Do you know what's going on?"

"There's been another bombing."

Shocked, Vincent asked, "Where? Was anyone hurt?"

"At the Stock Exchange in New York City. The news said at least fifteen dead."

"That sucks." He looked directly at Luke. "I guess you're one of the lucky ones, Father."

Confused, Luke asked, "What do you mean?"

"When your time comes, you'll be prepared. People like me will never be prepared."

"Prepared for what?"

Vincent smiled. "You know, prepared to meet God."

Engaged, Luke said, "Are you worried about not being perfect?"

"Well, yeah, I've had some issues in my life. I'm nowhere near perfect."

"Only one person on earth was perfect," Luke assured him. "His name was Jesus. Do you think that I haven't sinned?" To make him understand, Luke asked, "Do you have any children?" Vincent shook his head no and Luke continued. "Well, let's pretend that you have a son who is seven years old and he loves baseball. But unfortunately, he's not the most coordinated child on the team. As a matter of fact, he's really not a very good ballplayer. Would you be disappointed in him?"

Vincent thought for a few seconds. "Not if he was doing his best."

"Exactly." Luke smiled. "Well, how do you think God feels? He doesn't expect you to be perfect—you never will be. But He wants to know that you are giving it your best. So, when we strike out, we must try hard to do better the next time. Don't look back, look forward. Remember, He's on your side no matter what. And remember one more thing—even your perfect sister Trinity isn't perfect."

Vincent considered this. He raised his wineglass, and Luke did the same. As their glasses touched, Vincent said, "Amen, Father."

Luke was actually enjoying Vincent's company and could tell that Vincent felt the same. Unfortunately, during dinner, they were constantly interrupted by Vincent's friends, all wanting to talk to Luke about the bombing. The lack of privacy meant that Luke would have to wait until they returned to the beach house before asking his questions.

After Luke paid the check, the restaurant owner stopped by again and asked to take a picture with them. Before Luke could protest, Vincent said, "Sounds great! Let's get everyone in the shot." Luke cringed but didn't want to disappoint the crowd. After several photos were taken, however, Luke said, "That's enough already! I'd really appreciate if these pictures didn't end up in the newspaper. OK?"

On the drive home, Vincent asked, "What else did Trinity tell you about me?"

Luke answered honestly. "She said that you were a great person. She also said that you had some issues with painkillers and alcohol."

"Anything else?"

Luke, not wanting to embarrass him with the details, said, "She told me about the last time she saw you, at Grace's birthday party."

Vincent frowned. "Well, Father, if you see her again, please let her know that I've been off the drugs for over two years. As you know, I still drink, but not in excess anymore."

"Why don't you call her? I have her number."

Vincent laughed. "I don't even have a phone. My entire life takes place within a fifteen-mile radius of my house. I have great friends and an easy life."

"But," Luke said, "no family."

"Yeah, I know. You have a point."

Entering the house, they relaxed in the family room. He had Vincent's full attention now, so Luke related everything Trinity had told him about Corner Stone Builders. Luke asked, "Is there anything you can add?"

"I'll tell you anything. Just tell me what you want to know."

Luke knew that Vincent's parents were gone before Blade said the bombs were buried in the park, so he asked, "Why don't you start with when you took over the company?"

Vincent thought for a few seconds. "Well, once my parents were gone, it was frightening. I really didn't know what to do. But the guys who worked for my dad for many years helped me through it. And Fatih was a big help."

This was the opening Luke was waiting for. "How involved was Fatih?"

"To be honest with you, if it wasn't for Fatih and his family, the company probably would have gone out of business. His father had a lot of connections with the Muslim community, and we started building all of the new mosques in the Boston area. Not only was the work interesting, it was extremely profitable."

"Tell me more about Fatih. When was the last time you talked to him?"

Now getting suspicious, Vincent countered, "Why don't you just tell me why you're really here?"

# 46

**LUKE GAMBLED THAT HE** could trust Vincent and decided to go for broke. "Are you a baseball fan?"

Vincent looked at Luke like he was crazy. "Isn't everyone? I love the Sox. What does this have to do with anything?"

"Where were you in October of 2004?"

"I'll never forget. I had my back operation the week before the playoffs and watched the games from my hospital bed. That's when I got hooked on the pain pills. Why?"

"And Fatih was running Corner Stone?"

"Yes."

"Did he also make the decision to have green crescents painted on your trucks?"

"Yes, Fatih thought it would be a good idea, being that almost all of our business was coming from building mosques. I didn't care."

"When was the last time you talked to Fatih?" Luke asked again, hoping to get an answer before telling him more.

"It's been several years. Why, what are you getting at?"

Luke took a deep breath and said, "What if I told you that I have a witness who says that Corner Stone trucks worked in the Common every night during the 2004 Sox and Yankees playoff games. The odd thing is that they only worked at night, and only during home games, while all of the cops that normally patrolled the park were at Fenway. My witness says that they dug several deep holes and made sure that they were covered up each night before they left."

Vincent looked at Luke skeptically and said, "You expect me to believe that Fatih buried bombs in the ground and let them sit there for years? You're crazy. I don't think he's capable of something like that. He went to our church, played on the high school football team, and even dated one of my friend's sisters. He became an American when he lived with us. Luke, if it wasn't for Fatih's family and the contracts they brought to Corner Stone, Trinity and I wouldn't be living the lifestyle we do today."

Luke asked, "Don't you find it strange that as close as you were to Fatih, you never heard from him again?"

"I did at first, but I figured he got married or something and went on to live his own life."

"Did you ever question anything he did while he was running the construction company?"

"Well, now that you mention it, when I returned to work after rehabilitation for my back, I was surprised that he had fired a few of our long-term employees and hired several other foreigners in their place. Supposedly, they were friends of his."

Wanting to confirm his suspicion, Luke asked, "Middle Eastern men?"

Vincent nodded his head yes and said, "It's still hard to believe that Fatih had anything to with the bombing."

"But there are too many coincidences to ignore."

Thinking about everything he had learned in the past several minutes, Vincent asked, "Who is this witness? Where is he now?"

Luke frowned. "His name was Franklyn Hennessey."

"What do you mean, was?"

"He's dead."

Vincent rubbed his eyes with his hands. Luke could tell that he was afraid to ask the next question. "How did he die?"

"I think he was murdered." Luke explained everything to Vincent, who was captivated. When he found out that Blade had carved a crescent in his leg with his fingernail, he put his head in his hands.

Eventually, Vincent looked up. "Did you go to the police?"

Luke described Detective Romo's unconcerned reaction when he found out that Blade was dead, adding, "Until today, I didn't know that you had an adopted brother from the Middle East. I thought you had another sister named Faith, not a brother named Fatih."

"What's your next move?"

Luke hesitated. "Do you have any idea where Fatih is or how we can contact him?"

"I haven't heard from him since he moved back to Saudi Arabia."

"Do you have any contact information for him? A phone number or e-mail address?"

Still holding his head, Vincent answered, "I have a storage unit in Dorchester. It contains all of the files from Corner Stone: tax returns, accounting ledgers, and some furniture from the company office. There could be some information in the files, but I'm not sure. I haven't opened it in years, but I still pay the bill every month."

Luke asked, "Would you mind if I went there and looked through the files? I promise not to disturb anything. I'll call you as soon as I'm finished, and either mail you the key or bring it back."

"That won't be necessary."

Luke was puzzled. "Why?"

"Because I'm going with you."

# 47

**THE NEXT MORNING, LUKE** opened his eyes and heard the sound of waves crashing in the distance. From the couch, he looked out the window and saw that it was still dark. He sat up, stretching, and saw that Vincent's bedroom light was already on, and he heard the shower running. After Luke folded his blanket and rearranged the couch pillows, Vincent appeared, and they were ready to go.

Wanting to talk with Vincent during the hour-and-a-half ride to the Dorchester storage unit, Luke suggested that they drive together. As they walked out into the dark, salt-filled air, Vincent noticed that his Jeep was blocking Luke's car and said, "Let's just take my truck." They sat in silence for the first half of the trip as they listened to reports on the radio about the bombing in New York City. The Stock Exchange would open with increased security. According to the news reports, there were as many police officers in the area as pedestrians. The surrounding streets were still closed to cars, and the subways were running on limited schedules. All riders were being searched.

Luke's cell phone buzzed, and he looked at the display before answering. "Good morning, John."

"Did I wake you?" John asked.

"No. Is everything all right?"

"Yes. I'm sorry to bother you so early, but I wanted to let you know that Detective Romo called the cell phone you gave me."

"What did he say?"

"Well, he was surprised that you didn't answer and asked me what I was doing with his phone. Not knowing what to say, I told him that you left the phone at home and I heard it ringing, so I decided to answer it for you. Then he said to tell you that based on the recent events in New York, he's been reassigned outside of Boston to an undisclosed location. He said that he'd try to stay in touch."

Not wanting John to worry, Luke said, "OK, I'll call him when I get back. Let's make sure we go to Verizon and get you a phone." Looking at Vincent, he added, "Maybe we should get two."

Vincent smiled and John asked, "Two? Why?"

"I'll explain everything when I see you."

As they drove, Luke asked more questions about Fatih. Although Vincent still couldn't accept that Fatih might have been involved in the bombing, Luke could tell that he was beginning to have concerns about his adopted brother. Luke had a difficult question to ask, but he decided to wait, hoping that Vincent would bring it up first.

A few miles before they reached Dorchester, Luke's cell phone rang again. Vincent looked at him and said, "Now you know why I don't have a phone." Luke smiled and looked at the display. Seeing that it was Jim Hathaway, he quickly answered. Jim got to the point and told him that all of the paperwork for John to get his house back had been completed by the bank. Mr. McMahon, the bank president, had expedited the approval process as a personal favor to Jim. Concerned, Luke asked, "Does Deborah have to sign the loan agreement?"

"Yes, she has to cosign." Luke thanked Jim and let him know that she was away for the next couple of weeks. They agreed to touch base when she returned.

In Dorchester, Vincent turned off Washington Street and into a large brick storage facility. He parked his Jeep, saying, "I'll be right back," and he walked into the office. He returned a few minutes later and said, "I just wanted to let them know we're here." Pulling his Jeep around a bend in the driveway, Vincent stopped at a red garage door with the number sixteen written in large white numerals. Luke watched as Vincent struggled with the padlock before finally getting it open and rolling up the large door.

When the outside light illuminated the dark room, Luke was pleasantly surprised to see that the storage unit was set up like an office, with a large wooden desk in the center and file cabinets lining the walls. Vincent looked at Luke and grinned. "Just the way I left it." He walked inside and sat behind the desk. "This was my dad's desk. One of these days, I'm going to bring it back to the beach house."

"It's a beautiful piece of furniture."

After looking around, Vincent took charge and directed Luke to search one file cabinet while he started on another one. Luke began by carefully removing handfuls of folders and reviewing their contents. After reading several files containing accounting information, Luke was amazed at the cost associated with the building of the mosques and the profit Corner Stone had made on these buildings. Getting back on track, he scanned every piece of paper for one word: Fatih.

An hour later, Luke was getting tired and wanted to take a break. As he returned a stack of files to the cabinet, he turned to see Vincent looking directly at him, holding a frayed yellow folder in his hands. "You need to see this."

Luke hurried over, and Vincent laid out several pieces of paper on the desk. The first one was the article from an Arab-American newspaper detailing the events of the plane crash that killed Fatih's parents. There weren't many specifics, other than the fact that the private plane crashed shortly after takeoff from Riyadh.

Next, Vincent pushed another newspaper article toward Luke. Recognizing the picture of Vincent's parents from his research, Luke read it carefully before looking up and saying, "I'm so sorry; they seemed like such great people." Vincent smiled with tears in his eyes. Next he handed Luke a picture of himself dressed in a football uniform with his arm around a teammate. Looking at it closely, Luke asked, "Is that Fatih?"

Vincent nodded. "Yes. Because he was so short and thin, he never played in a game, but he came to every practice, and his enthusiasm was an inspiration to everyone on the team. The entire school admired him."

The last piece of paper was an e-mail that Fatih had sent to Vincent's father on his birthday. As Luke read the words, he felt like he could have been reading a note from any American teenager to their dad. Luke understood why Vincent doubted Fatih's involvement in the bombings, because even with everything he knew, Luke was starting to have some doubts himself.

Then, out of nowhere, Vincent asked the question that had been on Luke's mind ever since he had met Trinity. "If Fatih is really responsible for the bombings, do you think that he had anything to do with my parents' deaths?"

# 48

**LUKE AND VINCENT SPENT** the next three hours searching the remaining folders. By early afternoon they conceded defeat, having scanned every document in the unit. Disappointed, Vincent said, "I'm sorry, I thought we would find more information."

Trying to be positive, Luke answered, "Hey, we found a few good things: the picture and the note to your dad."

Skeptical, Vincent asked, "What good is the note?"

"Maybe he still has the same e-mail address." Luke took out his cell phone and called his friend Carlos Sanchez, the archdiocese's computer expert. Hoping he'd be able to help trace the e-mail address, Luke arranged to meet him for dinner at a local Mexican restaurant.

Luke and Vincent rolled down the storage-unit door and locked it before heading back to the Jeep. Not knowing where to go, Vincent asked, "Are we going back to the Cape?" Luke thought for a second and said, "Do you know anything about boats?"

Vincent had been sailing since he was very young. He explained that his father loved the water, and even though they couldn't afford it at the time, he bought Vincent a small skiff for his tenth birthday. This prompted Luke to ask, "Do you have time to take a look at my brother's boat with me? I know nothing about boats and can really use some help."

Vincent smiled. "No problem. Just tell me where to go."

When they got to the marina, Vincent parked the Jeep on the street and followed Luke to the dock. As they walked, Luke took out his key ring and located the one for the boat. He knew exactly which one it was because it had a fish etched on it. Once Luke stopped, Vincent saw the name *Blood Brothers* and realized which boat it was. "Luke, that's not a boat; it's a freaking yacht. Not only that, it's a Hatteras!"

Luke had no idea what he was talking about. "Is that something good?"

Vincent laughed. "It's better than good. It's one of the finest yachts made." Looking at the name again, Vincent said, "I can't believe he registered it in Massachusetts."

"Why?"

Vincent went on to explain that most people who buy expensive boats usually register them in Rhode Island or a handful of other states that have no sales tax. For a boat this size, the amount of money saved would be enormous.

Anxious to get on board, Vincent jumped from the dock to the back of the boat and extended his hand to help Luke. Seeing bubbles coming up from around the boat, Luke asked, "What's that?"

Vincent laughed again. "You really don't know anything about boats, do you?" Luke shook his head. "That's a bubble system to keep the water from freezing around the boat and causing damage." It had been extremely cold lately, and Luke noticed a layer of ice in the harbor.

Luke handed Vincent the key, and he quickly opened the door that led to the boat's interior. He rushed in, eager to see the inside. They were both amazed. The salon looked more like a five-star hotel than a boat. There were luxurious couches, walls with large windows, and a huge flat-screen TV. Vincent sat down on the couch and said, "This is unbelievable."

Walking through the main room, Luke peered into the kitchen. Again, he was in awe. Custom mahogany cabinetry lined the walls, and granite counters and stainless steel appliances completed the look. There was even a dining table with six chairs.

He moved down the hallway and entered the master bedroom, where he saw a king-size bed, a flat-screen TV, and a private bath with a tub and shower. As they continued exploring, they found that the yacht had two more good-sized bedrooms and another full bath. This boat was truly something special. Wanting to take advantage of Vincent's boating experience, Luke asked, "Is there any reason that I couldn't live here for a few weeks?"

Vincent looked around. "The electricity is on and I'm sure there's heat and water, so I don't see why not." Envious, he continued, "Are you really going to stay here?"

"I think so. No one would ever think to look for me here, so I don't have to worry about the press."

Luke glanced at his watch and saw that he had just over an hour before he was scheduled to meet Carlos Sanchez. Looking at Vincent, he asked, "When did you plan on going back home?"

Vincent shrugged. "It doesn't matter to me. What do you have in mind?"

"Why don't you come to dinner? My friend Carlos is an interesting guy. I'm sure you'll like him. Then, if you want to stay on the boat tonight, you could teach me how this thing works."

Luke could tell that Vincent liked the prospect of staying on the boat. However, living in luxury wasn't the main reason, since Vincent replied quietly, "If Fatih had anything to do with my parents' deaths, I want to be there when you catch him."

Hoping that they would have an answer regarding Fatih's involvement within a few days, Luke responded, "If you want, you can stay here until we figure this out."

"Let's take it one day at a time."

As they prepared to leave, Luke's cell phone rang.

"Hello."

Trinity said, "I'm sorry to bother you, Father, but I wanted to know if you saw Vincent and if he's all right."

Luke smiled. "Hold on. He's right here." Before they could protest, Luke handed the phone to Vincent. At first Luke could tell that the conversation was uncomfortable, but after Vincent let his sister know that he was off the painkillers and living a drug-free life, they started talking like long-lost friends. When they began discussing Gracie, Luke knew that he had made the right decision by handing Vincent the phone. They were still deep in conversation when Vincent reached the Jeep, and he said to his sister, "I'm going to get a cell phone tomorrow. I'll call and give you my number."

He hung up and looked at Luke. "Hey, I owe you. I can't tell you how much this means to me. You've just changed my life."

# 49

**THEY PARKED ON BEACON** Street, and Luke led the way into Sol Azteca, a traditional Mexican restaurant. Luke spotted Carlos sitting at a table in the back. As they approached, Carlos stood and introduced himself to Vincent. Everyone sat down, and the waitress appeared. Carlos took charge and ordered a carafe of the homemade sangria, saying, "Trust me, you'll love it."

Luke got down to business by handing Carlos the e-mail from Fatih to Vincent's dad. Carlos glanced at it and said, "What's this for?"

Luke looked at Vincent and answered, "We wanted to know if there's any way to trace that e-mail address and link it to a street address."

Carlos took a sip of wine and asked, "What are you up to now?"

Luke took the time to explain everything to Carlos, leaving out the fact that Blade was dead. Vincent confirmed the parts of the story that involved his family and Corner Stone Builders. Once they had finished, Carlos asked incredulously, "Please tell me that you've gone to the police, right?"

Luke said, "Well, kind of," and explained the problem with Blade's credibility. He assured Carlos that he had been in contact with

Detective Romo and promised that as soon as he had some real proof, he would turn the investigation over to the authorities.

After taking a long sip of wine, Carlos explained, "If this e-mail still exists electronically, there's a chance that I can examine the header information and find the IP address. Once I have that, there are online services that can be used to determine where the e-mail server is located. They can even provide latitude and longitude information, which will narrow it down to a city."

"And what if we only have a hard copy of the message?" Luke asked sullenly.

"Then there's nothing I can do."

Frustrated, Luke pressed Carlos. "If you were in my position and you really needed to find out where this person was located, what would you do?"

Carlos thought for a second, finished his glass of sangria, and blessed himself. He took out a piece of paper from his pocket and scribbled down a name and phone number. "Call Arnold and tell him what you want. I'm sure he can help you."

Luke looked at the number. "Who is he?"

"He's a professional hacker. Many companies, including the diocese, use him to assess the security risk of their networks. Believe it or not, there are many attempts to break into the diocesan network every day. Arnold uses his hacking skills to evaluate how secure our systems are. You can tell him that I gave you his name, but I don't want to know anything about what you decide to do." Carlos looked at his watch. "You might want to call him now. He only works at night."

Luke stood and walked outside. Arnold answered on the first ring, demanding, "Who is this?"

"Father Luke Miller. Father Carlos Sanchez gave me your name."

"And what can I do for you, Father?"

"I want to hire you to do a job."

"When?"

Boldly, Luke pressed. "How about right now?"

There was silence on the line. Eventually Arnold said, "I get five hundred dollars an hour."

"No problem."

"It has to be cash."

"OK."

Luke agreed to meet him at a nearby Starbucks in an hour. Before hanging up, Luke asked, "How will I know who you are?"

"You won't, but I know who you are."

Luke returned to the table and gave Carlos and Vincent an update. They finished eating, and he thanked Carlos again and paid the bill. As they were leaving, Carlos looked at Vincent and said, "Please make sure he doesn't do anything crazy."

Vincent laughed. "How could he? He's a priest!"

Recalling the incident at the abortion protest, Carlos answered softly, "Being a priest doesn't guarantee anything."

---

At Starbucks, Vincent got in line to order a coffee while Luke stood to the side, waiting. A man wearing a black baseball cap walked into the store and directly toward Luke saying, "Follow me."

They headed to the back of the room and sat down. Arnold placed his laptop on the table and opened it. "What can I do for you?"

As Luke started to answer, Vincent approached. Seeing him, Arnold shut his laptop and stood. "It's OK, he's with me," Luke said.

Arnold sat back down and Vincent joined them. Luke pulled out the e-mail and said, "We'd like to know if this e-mail address is still valid and where the person using it is located."

Arnold immediately asked, "Do you have it online?"

Luke frowned. "No, just that piece of paper."

"How much information do you want?"

Before Luke could answer, Vincent interjected, "As much as we can get."

Arnold thought about this, then he looked up, and Luke saw his dark eyes for the first time.

"How well do you know this person?"

Vincent jumped in. "He was like a brother to me."

Looking directly at Luke, Arnold said, "How devious do you want to be?"

When Luke didn't answer, Vincent did. "I don't care how you do it. I want to know as much as I can about him."

Arnold smirked. "Then here's what I suggest we do. You tell me everything you know about this guy: his hobbies, interests, and especially his vices. I'll develop a few web pages and attempt to entice him to sign up for a service that's advertised by sending him e-mail. When he bites, we'll know where he is. If he's like eighty percent of Internet users, we'll know a whole lot more."

"What do you mean?" asked Luke.

"The pages I'll develop will be offered free of charge but will require the user to enter an ID and password. Once he enters the password, my code will trap it. If he's like most online users who use the same password for everything, we can then use that password to access his e-mail account or any other online service that he subscribes to."

"That's great!" said Vincent.

Arnold reopened his laptop and said, "This job will take me about five hours." Looking at Luke again, he asked, "Are you good with that?"

Luke nodded. Directing his attention back toward Vincent, Arnold said, "Tell me his vices."

"Well, after we graduated high school, I was looking for something in his room one day and found a magazine containing"—embarrassed, he looked at Luke—"nude pictures of young Asian girls. Even when we were in school, he always seemed to be fascinated with very young girls."

Not wanting to hear any of this, Luke stood and asked, "Vincent, can you finish taking care of this?"

"No problem," Vincent replied, and he handed over his keys. Luke walked out, wondering what in the world he was getting himself into.

# 50

LUKE STARTED THE JEEP and turned on the heat. He realized that he hadn't spoken to Deborah in a while, so he dialed her number. She answered, "I thought you forgot about us!"

"You know better than that. How have you been?"

"Great. We've been sledding, skating, and skiing. The children are in their glory, and Lori is a big help."

"Have you been recognized?"

"No, I've been wearing my wig." She quickly changed the subject. "The children have been asking for you. They're sleeping now, but can you call back in the morning to talk to them?"

"Yes, of course I will. I miss them too."

"Maybe you could come here and spend a few days with us."

"Well, there are a few things that I need to take care of, but maybe next week."

Her voice softened. "Are you being careful?"

Luke deliberated the question and wondered if he was really being honest when he replied, "Yes, of course."

Before hanging up, Deb said, "Just so you know, I miss you too."

Luke closed his eyes and tried to relax. It wasn't long before he heard the car door open as Vincent jumped in and said, "That guy is awesome." When Luke didn't respond, he continued, "I can't wait to see what happens."

Luke asked, "Do we need to call him? When will we know something?"

Vincent turned to look at Luke. "He said not to worry, and he would get in touch with us."

They pulled up to the marina and boarded the yacht. Vincent insisted that Luke sleep in the master bedroom while he took one of the others. Since they were both tired, they quickly said good night and headed to their rooms.

Luke lay on the soft bed and looked up at the ceiling, which contained a skylight. Pressing several buttons on the nightstand, he finally found the switch that opened the shade. The crystal-clear sky was full of stars. Looking up, he wondered if he was getting too involved in the investigation, but he told himself that Aaron would be doing the same thing if Luke had been the one killed on that stage. He asked God for protection before falling asleep.

He woke to the vibration of his phone in his shirt pocket. Startled, he looked at the display and saw that it was 11:52 p.m. He answered the phone quickly. "Is everything all right?"

"I'm sorry it's so late, but I thought you'd want to know that I found her."

Confused, Luke asked, "Found who?"

John answered, "Star."

Luke sat up in bed. "You're kidding me."

"No, I'm serious. She didn't really want to talk to me, but I told her about Blade's funeral tomorrow."

"And what did she say?"

"She said that she would be there."

"That's great. Did she say anything else?"

"Not really. She seemed more frightened than usual, but I think she might talk to you."

"What makes you think that?"

"Because she specifically asked if you were going to be at the funeral."

# 51

**LUKE OPENED HIS EYES** and saw rays of sun entering through the skylight over his bed; it was a beautiful morning. Glancing at the clock on the nightstand, he saw that it was 7:15. He hadn't slept this late in years. He walked into the salon, where he sat on the couch and looked out the sliding glass doors toward the back of the boat.

He was making a mental list of everything he had to do that day when he heard Vincent stirring in his room. Soon after, he appeared and sat down across from Luke. They were both disheveled, having slept in their clothes.

"Good morning, Vincent."

"What time is it?"

Luke laughed. "It's about 7:30, why?"

"It's way too early to be awake."

"Well, why did you get up?"

"I'm a very light sleeper. Been that way my entire life."

"Well, I'm sorry if I woke you."

Vincent stood and walked toward the kitchen. "I don't think it was you, I think it was the movement of the boat."

A few minutes later, Vincent returned with two cups. They sat in silence, sipping coffee and thinking about Fatih. Noticing the time, Luke asked, "Why don't you come to the funeral with me?"

"Who's going to be there?"

"Only two, maybe three people."

Not having anything else to do, Vincent agreed. They took their showers then headed out, to make their way to the crematory in Forest Hills. Before they pulled out of the marina, Luke asked, "Can you reset the trip counter so I know how far away we are?" Vincent pressed a button on the Jeep's dash.

As they pulled out of the lot, Luke asked, "How about we stop at my brother's house for a few minutes so we can get some clean clothes?"

"Just tell me the way."

Vincent was astonished when they turned into Aaron's neighborhood. "Luke, these houses are almost as big as some of the mosques we built."

Knowing that his brother had built one of the most impressive homes in the area, Luke smiled, but he didn't respond. When they reached the driveway, the only guard that was left to watch the empty house stepped out of his car and approached the Jeep. Seeing Luke, he waved and quickly opened the gates.

Speechless, Vincent followed Luke through the front door. Once they entered the foyer, he said, "This is incredible. Do you mind if I look around?"

"Not at all, but we don't have much time."

Luke went to his room to get some clean clerical clothes for himself and an outfit for Vincent. He opened his closet and pulled a few items from the top shelf, including his Bible. Wanting to make sure that Aaron's gun was still there, he placed his hand under a stack of sweaters and moved it around until he felt the cold steel barrel. As Luke walked into the hallway, Vincent emerged from the basement and said, "This house is awesome." Before Luke could respond, he continued, "Do you know your brother had a Lamborghini?"

Luke smiled. "Is that what that is?"

Vincent shook his head. "How many bedrooms are there?"

"I think there are seven bedrooms and ten bathrooms."

As they walked toward the front door, Vincent felt compelled to say, "I've built and been inside some really nice houses, but I've never seen anything like this."

After waving to the guard, they were on their way to see Blade for the last time. Turning into the crematory parking lot, Luke asked, "How many miles have we gone?"

Looking at the odometer, Vincent replied, "Almost seven."

The stone-and-brick building looked like a small church. On top of each roof peak was a metal cross, and the sides were lined with elaborate stained glass windows. Luke pointed toward John's truck and said, "Park over there."

As they walked inside, Luke noticed Blade's bicycle propped up against the building. John was waiting in the hallway. "Hi, John," Luke said, extending his hand. As they shook, he could see that most of John's attention was focused on Vincent. Releasing his grip, John immediately turned and introduced himself. When Vincent said his last name, "Russo," Luke could see the concern in John's eyes. In an attempt to put him at ease, Luke said, "John, Vincent is trying to help us find his adopted brother Fatih. I'll explain everything after the service."

An older, white-haired man wearing a dark suit approached. Recognizing Luke, he said, "Right this way, Father." He led them to a quiet room that contained Blade's casket with two candles burning on either side. As Luke's eyes adjusted to the dimly lit room, he saw

Margaret sitting in the front row. He hugged her and thanked her for coming. In the back of the room, he saw a woman who he assumed was Star. She looked younger than he expected, and she was dressed in dark clothing. He walked back and squatted down in front of her while she sat. "I'm Luke Miller. I'm truly sorry for your loss." She didn't speak, but she nodded, acknowledging his presence. When she looked directly at him, he realized where she had gotten her nickname from: She had a blue star tattooed under her left eye.

Luke went back to the front of the room and knelt in front of Blade's casket. After saying a few silent prayers, he turned and began the service. Knowing that Blade had lived a difficult and tortured life, he focused on the forgiving nature of God. Luke paged through his Bible until he found the parable of the prodigal son. After reading it, he explained how it related to each part of Blade's life. He concluded by saying, "Franklyn Hennessey has found his way home, and Jesus has welcomed him with open arms."

Everyone present paid their final respects by kneeling and saying a silent prayer at the casket. Luke asked John and Vincent to go outside, as he waited for Star to exit. After about fifteen minutes, she walked out. Seeing Luke, she nervously looked up and down the hallway as he approached.

Truly concerned, Luke asked, "Do you need a place to stay?"

She didn't speak but shook her head no.

Luke quickly reached into his pocket and took out a piece of paper. He jotted down his cell phone number and said, "Please call me if you need anything."

When he tried to hand her some cash, she finally spoke. "I don't need any money, but thank you anyway."

Respecting her wishes, Luke put the money back and asked, "Did you see what happened to Blade?"

Her bloodshot eyes filled with tears. Again, she didn't speak, but this time she shook her head yes.

"Please, can you tell me what happened? I want to help."

No response.

Luke decided that he would ask her yes and no questions, so she didn't have to say too much.

"How many men were there? One?" He paused. "Two?"

She nodded.

"Did you see their faces?"

She shook her head no.

Painting the full picture, Luke said, "The two men held Blade down, rolled up his sleeve, and put a needle in his arm."

A tear fell from her eye as she nodded yes.

"Did they see you?"

She shook her head no, and she began to cry harder.

With his heart breaking, Luke walked close and hugged her. She didn't return his embrace but stood with her arms at her side.

Exiting the building, Luke asked Star, "Did you ride that bicycle all the way here?"

Again, she nodded affirmatively.

Realizing that Star had traveled several miles, Luke asked, "Can I give you a ride home?"

She shook her head no. Before leaving, Star said very softly, "Can you wait here for a minute?"

"Of course."

She walked toward the back of the building and returned carrying a small puppy. As she reached Luke, John and Vincent walked over to see what was happening.

"After Blade got the money, he bought the dog. He always wanted one but knew that he couldn't afford to feed it. Can you bring him to the pound? I can't take care of him."

Abruptly, she handed the dog to Luke and got on the bicycle. As she rode away, Luke raised his voice and said, "Star, please call me if you need anything."

She didn't respond.

# 52

VINCENT TOOK THE PUPPY from Luke and placed him in the back of the Jeep. Luke asked John to meet him at the local Verizon store so everyone could get their own phones. The dog, who looked like a baby German shepherd, whined while lying on the backseat. Trying to comfort him, Luke reached back and rubbed his belly. Before they had reached the store, the puppy was sleeping on Luke's lap in the front.

Vincent parked and rushed around to the passenger door to help Luke get out. Picking up the sleeping puppy, he held him in his arms as they entered the store. When a pretty girl rushed out from behind the counter to pet the snoozing pooch, Vincent looked at Luke and said, "Maybe I should keep him." They both laughed.

John was already inside, checking out the phones with a salesperson. When Luke approached, he heard John asking about the least expensive phone and plan that he could purchase. "John, pick any phone you want. I'm going to add you to my plan; it's a requirement of your new job." John smiled, but not wanting to waste money, he continued questioning the clerk.

Once John and Vincent had selected their phones, Luke asked the clerk to add them to his plan. Vincent protested, but Luke insisted. "It's really inexpensive to add a phone when you already have an account." When Luke requested that another phone be added, John asked, "Who's that for?"

Luke looked at him and replied, "Star. Tomorrow after we pick up Blade's ashes, we're going to try to find her."

John agreed to follow them to the boat so that Luke could tell him all that he had learned while he was away. When they settled down on the yacht, Luke and Vincent explained everything to John. He was amazed at their story, and all three of them were convinced that Blade had been telling the truth.

"So what do we do now?" asked John.

"We wait to hear from Arnold," answered Luke.

They ordered pizza, played cards, and watched television on the boat for the rest of the afternoon. During one of the card games, they made a bet that whoever won the game could name the pup, who was now sleeping on Luke's bed. When Vincent won, he announced that the dog's name would be Justice. Luke and John nodded in agreement.

Growing bored, they decided to take a ride to the local pet store to get a collar and food for Justice. As they pulled into a parking space, Luke said from the backseat, "I'll stay here with the dog. I really don't want to be recognized." While he waited, his phone rang. Answering it, he was elated to hear Arnold's voice. "Father Luke, can you talk?"

"Yes."

"I just got a hit on the website." At that moment, Vincent and John returned and opened the car doors. Luke hushed them and put his phone on speaker. They sat in the Jeep with the engine off, waiting to hear what Arnold had to say.

"He just signed on a few minutes ago."

"Hi, Arnold, this is Vincent. Which site did he access?"

"The porn site."

Vincent cursed and said, "I knew it!"

"Where is he?" Luke asked.

"Riyadh."

Luke looked at Vincent and said out loud, "Saudi Arabia." He glanced at his watch. "It's close to midnight there." Thinking quickly, he continued, "Did you get an address?"

"Not yet. That's the next step in the sign-on process. But I do have a password."

"What is it?"

"Ismail."

"That was his father's name," Vincent exclaimed.

Arnold explained, "OK, here's what you need to do. Wait until you are fairly sure that your friend in Saudi Arabia is sleeping. Go to the website for his e-mail hosting service and sign on to his ID using the screen name from the e-mail you showed me and the password I just gave you. But remember, if you read any of his unread e-mail, there's a chance that he will know. Some e-mail services change the status of an e-mail once it's been read. If this happens, I'd suggest that you delete the e-mail so he can't tell. Also, if you log on while he is logged on to the system, some providers send notifications that multiple users are on the same ID. As you already know, I work nights, so call me and let me know how it goes."

Luke thanked him, and they headed back to Aaron's house so they could use the computer. They decided to wait until seven that evening to log in, knowing that Riyadh was eight hours ahead. Even if Fatih was a night owl, he would most likely be sleeping by 3:00 a.m. But that meant waiting for hours, so they settled in and tried to watch

TV. Luke found himself looking at his watch every five minutes. The anticipation of finally confirming his worst fears was killing him.

Ten minutes before seven, he decided that they had waited long enough. Signing on, he pulled up the main e-mail screen and typed in Fatih's user name and password. When a small box appeared at the center of the screen, he knew it wasn't good news. He read out loud, "Invalid password, try again." Luke carefully retyped the password again. When he pressed enter, the same message appeared. Vincent cursed. Knowing that if he entered the wrong password too many times the system would lock him out, Luke cleared the screen.

Dejected, he quickly dialed Arnold's number and told him what happened, concluding, "It's over. We've hit a dead end."

"Don't be so sure," Arnold replied.

# 53

LUKE WAS ROUSED FROM a deep sleep by his ringing cell phone. He looked at the clock and saw that it was 3:16 a.m. He mumbled, "Hello?"

Arnold said quickly, "OK, he just signed on to the website again. Do you have a pen and paper?"

Luke fumbled through the nightstand drawer. "Go ahead."

"Try this password: infidel66."

"Why did he create another password?" Luke asked.

"He didn't. A lot of people automatically type their most-used password when they are prompted to enter one online. Knowing this, I had the application capture all passwords that had been typed. A few minutes ago, your friend in Saudi Arabia typed infidel66 and received a message that it was invalid. Remembering, he immediately entered the old one, Ismail."

Before ending the call, Luke promised to let Arnold know what happened. He wanted to sign on now, but since it was already late morning in Saudi Arabia, he restrained himself, wanting to ensure that Fatih wasn't signed on to his e-mail account. As much as he tried, Luke couldn't sleep. He wanted to figure this out now. Lying in bed, he had a startling thought. The time zone difference between Boston and Saudi Arabia made it almost noon in Riyadh. Fatih would be on his way to midday prayers. He rushed to wake Vincent.

He peered into Vincent's room and saw him sitting up in bed with Justice at his side. "What are you doing up?" asked Luke.

"I told you, I'm a very light sleeper. Why? What's going on?"

Luke excitedly recounted his conversation with Arnold, and they agreed that now was the time to sign on to Fatih's account.

They sat side by side as Luke entered the password. Before he could press Enter, Vincent asked, "What does infidel mean?"

"It means one without faith," Luke replied soberly. He pressed Enter, and they held their breath as the screen returned and displayed a list of e-mail messages. Vincent yelled, "Oh my God, I can't believe it."

Luke's heart was pounding as he quickly scanned the list of e-mail. To be cautious, he decided to start with the ones that had already been read. After reading the first twenty, he grew disappointed and saw that this was leading nowhere. Fatih's e-mail were mundane—notes from friends, comments on the local camel and horse races, and so on. Admittedly, a thirty-year-old man's social life was different in Riyadh than it was in the United States. There was no nightlife to speak of, alcohol was forbidden, and there was no dating before marriage. The big nightly activity was walking the main streets after prayer services.

After continuing to search for an hour, Luke said, "It doesn't look like we're going to find anything here, but I have another idea."

"What's that?"

"In the morning, I'll find out if my friend Jami knows someone in Riyadh who can look up where Fatih is living."

Not willing to give up, Vincent took control of the keyboard, insisting, "Let's try a few more."

Luke watched as Vincent navigated to the "sent" items list. He paged down and started reading e-mail after e-mail. Luke had closed his eyes and was dozing off in surrender when he heard the typing stop. Opening his eyes, he was surprised to see Vincent staring at him. Vincent didn't say a word but pointed to the screen. Luke scanned the note and didn't see anything interesting until the bottom, where it said, "Give my regards to Ismail."

Vincent looked at Luke in disbelief of what he was seeing and said, "That bastard!"

Luke didn't know what to say. After rereading the e-mail, he reassured Vincent, "Ismail is a very common Arab name; I wouldn't jump to any conclusions. For all we know, he could have a son named after his dead father."

Vincent thought for a few minutes and then began typing again. They scanned every e-mail folder but found no other clues. Noticing that Vincent was visibly upset, Luke said, "Let's go back to bed. I promise I'll call my friend first thing in the morning. We know a lot more than we did yesterday, and we'll know more tomorrow. You should know by now that I'm not giving up until I figure out who killed my brother, and if Fatih had anything to do with your parents' deaths, he'll pay for both."

"You're damn right, and I'll make sure of it," Vincent said through clenched teeth.

Vincent again brought up getting the police involved. Luke was adamantly against it, since they still had no real evidence. He added, "And I don't think the police would be too happy to hear that we hacked into Fatih's e-mail account." To prove his point, Luke took the keyboard and typed into the search engine, "What's the penalty for hacking into an e-mail account?" When the screen refreshed, there were thousands of hits. Luke scanned down the list, and it didn't take long to confirm that this was a serious offense, with huge fines and jail time measured in years.

Both men returned to their rooms, but neither slept. Luke again was tortured with the thought that someone was evil enough to plan a vicious attack years in advance. If his worst fears were confirmed, he would be uncovering one of the most devious terror plots ever. One thing was sure. He was going to catch Aaron's killer even if he had to go to Riyadh to do it.

## 54

LUKE AND VINCENT WERE still awake as the sun began to rise. Knowing that it was too early to call Jami, Luke suggested that they go downstairs to the gym for a workout. Luke ran on a treadmill for several miles. Watching in the mirrored walls, Luke saw Vincent pick up a few weights, hit the heavy bag a few times, and ride the exercise bike for a few minutes. Eventually he sat on a bench and stared out the windows. Understandably, Vincent was traumatized at the realization that his adopted brother might also be his parents' killer.

After showering, Luke dialed Jami's number. She answered, "Hi, Luke."

"Good morning, Jami. I hope I didn't wake you."

She laughed. "No, I have my last class before the holiday break this morning."

"I really need to talk to you. When will you be free?"

"Class ends at ten thirty. What did you find out?"

"Can you meet me in front of your apartment complex at eleven?"

"Yes."

"I'll be in a bright orange Jeep. Since I don't want our picture to be in the newspaper again, I'll be sitting in the back, and a friend of mine will be driving."

Jami said, "OK, I'll look for you."

Luke knew what he wanted to do before meeting Jami, and he asked Vincent to take a ride. Once on the road, he called John to see if he could go to the Common and try to find Star. John agreed, and Luke and Vincent drove back to the crematory in Forest Hills with Justice in the backseat. They parked in the lot, and Luke said, "Wait here. I'll just be a minute." Walking inside, he was greeted by a man in a dark suit who went into the back office and returned holding a black wooden box. When Luke asked about the bill, he was told that Margaret had sent a check in advance.

He had another idea during the drive back. He directed Vincent to drive to Beacon Hill, where he managed to find a parking spot on the crowded street. Again, Vincent waited in the car with the dog, and Luke rushed across the street and rang the bell at Mark Aldridge's house. The same young girl he had met previously answered the door. "Come this way, Mr. Miller. He's in the library having tea. Can I get you anything?"

Luke smiled. "No, thank you, I'm good."

When Luke appeared in the doorway, Mr. Aldridge's face lit up, and from his wheelchair he enthusiastically waved Luke in. "Come in! It's so nice to see you again, Luke!"

Luke understood once again why Aaron liked the old man so much. "It's so nice to see you, Mr. Aldridge."

"Please, sit down, and call me Mark."

Luke sat on a small sofa directly across from him. "I'm sorry that I haven't been to visit sooner. I've been very busy."

Mark smiled. "You sure have. I read about you in the newspaper almost every day. I can't believe that you had that good-for-nothing

Lieutenant Governor Richard Simpson at your house for Thanksgiving. Don't you know that he's a Democrat?"

Luke laughed. "Really? But his wife was working with Aaron."

"Lori is a very special person. Why she's married to that jerk, I'll never know."

Not wanting to keep Vincent waiting in the truck, he got right to the point of his visit. "Mr. Aldridge, in all of your time as a political consultant, did you ever hear of someone named Mike Dempsey? He worked for the CIA and now says he's the lead investigator in charge of the bombing incident for the FBI."

The old man looked up but was deep in thought. "I know that name; just give me a few seconds to think." He gently tapped his index finger against his forehead. "Tall, with dark gray hair around his sideburns?"

"Yes."

"I know who he is. Before Dempsey left the CIA, the president had submitted his name as a candidate for director of operations. Then about a week later, his name was abruptly withdrawn without any explanation."

"What does that mean?"

"It means that he probably had something in his background that would embarrass the administration. Why do you ask?"

"He unexpectedly showed up at Aaron's house with the pretext of being on the case, but I am suspicious."

Aldridge was visibly concerned and pushed himself up in his wheelchair. "What do you mean?"

"Well, he said that he was visiting all of the families that had lost loved ones in the bombing. When I asked him who else he had visited, he stumbled and didn't answer. He couldn't tell me the name of one other family on the list. It just seemed strange. Then he picked up the newspaper and commented on the article from Thanksgiving Day about the homeless."

The old man seemed shaken. "Well, I can tell you this. He and the lieutenant governor know each other. Both of them have friends in very high positions, including the oval office. Those people must be very concerned about something you're doing, and Dempsey was sent to your house to find out."

Luke was worried as Mark cautioned, "You better be careful. Luke, what exactly have you found out about the bombing?"

Now, not wanting to expose another person to danger, he replied, "I have a few ideas, but nothing I want to tell you yet. As soon as I have proof, you'll know."

"Luke, you don't realize the type of people you're dealing with," Mark replied emphatically. "They'll go to any length to protect themselves and won't care who gets in their way."

# 55

VINCENT DROVE THEM THE short distance to the Common. As they pulled up to the curb, Luke took out his cell phone and called John's number.

"Luke, I've found her."

"Where are you?"

"At Frog Pond."

Luke ran into the park, carrying Blade's ashes. Reaching the pond, Luke wasn't surprised to see that children were ice-skating, since the weather had been cold enough to freeze the six-inch-deep water. When he looked around, he saw Star sitting on a bench and John standing nearby. Seeing Luke, John began walking in his direction. When they met, John said, "She won't talk to me. She thinks that I had something to do with Blade's death."

"That's ridiculous."

Luke hurried over and sat down next to her. She never looked at him, so he began speaking. "This box contains Blade's ashes. I want you to have them." Luke tried to hand the box to her, but she didn't move. He placed it on the bench next to her. Then he reached into his pocket and took out the cell phone. "Please take this and call me if you need anything. You can use it to call anyone you want. Mine and John's numbers are stored on the contact list. You can call me anytime for anything." Again she didn't move. Luke stood and looked at John. As they began to walk away, Star said, "Take his ashes."

Luke stopped and turned to look at her. "I think Blade would want you to have them," he said.

"I can't do anything with them. He worked on fishing boats when he was younger. Maybe you could spread them in the ocean."

Luke reluctantly picked up the box. As he walked away, he looked back and saw her examining the cell phone.

When he got back to the Jeep, Vincent said, "I thought you were giving her the ashes." Luke explained that she wouldn't take them and wanted them spread in the ocean. Vincent smiled. "Looks like we're going to have to take that yacht of yours for a ride after all."

"Yeah, but we'll have to wait till the ice melts."

Vincent knowledgeably replied, "Just because the pond in the park is frozen doesn't mean the harbor is. Salt water freezes at about six degrees Fahrenheit compared to thirty-two degrees for freshwater."

"But there's ice around the boat right now," Luke pointed out, skeptically.

Wanting to educate him, Vincent continued. "That's because there's a mixture of fresh and salt water in the harbor, sometimes called brackish. As you get closer to the ocean, the water turns to all salt and doesn't readily freeze. We could ease the boat out of the marina and not have to worry."

They headed for Jami's apartment building as Luke directed the way. Pulling up, they saw Jami already pacing outside. "There's a spot over there," Luke said, pointing. Vincent parallel parked and waited. As Jami approached, Luke opened the door. He introduced her to Vincent, and she climbed into the backseat.

Luke quickly told her everything about Corner Stone Builders while letting Vincent fill in the parts of the story concerning Fatih. She was neither skeptical nor surprised at what she was hearing. When they finished, she thought for a few minutes before asking, "What is his last name?"

"Abu," Vincent answered.

"Unfortunately, that's a very common name in the Middle East. Do you know his middle name?"

"I think it was Mohammad," Vincent said.

"That's little help. That's the most common name in Saudi Arabia." Jami reached into her purse and took out a pen and a used envelope to write on. "What were his parents' names?"

"Ismail and Kamilah."

"Do you know their middle names?"

Vincent shook his head no, but he reached into his folder and retrieved the newspaper article about the plane crash. Then he handed her the football picture with Fatih standing by his side.

"Anything else?" she asked.

"We have an e-mail address and know that he's in Riyadh, but that's about it," Luke said.

"How do you know where he is?" she questioned.

Not wanting to divulge all the details about their connection with the computer hacker, Luke answered, "Trust me. He's in Riyadh."

Jami was deep in thought, and Luke could see that she was troubled. She sat and stared at the picture of Fatih. When Vincent said, "Please be careful with the picture. It's the only one we have," she ignored his statement and said, vehemently, "If this man had anything to do with my sister's death, I'm going to find him. No matter what it takes." Luke knew exactly how she was feeling. He felt the same way.

Conscious of the time difference in Saudi Arabia, Luke asked Jami, "Do you think you can make some phone calls now?"

"Yes, I know someone connected to the government there. I'm going to call him immediately."

Luke thought for a minute and asked, "Would your contact in Riyadh talk to me?"

Confused, she asked, "When?"

"The day after tomorrow."

"Probably, why do you ask?"

"Because I'm going to book the next flight to Riyadh."

Vincent spoke up. "Then I'm going with you."

"Do you have a passport?" Luke asked.

Vincent frowned. "No."

"Well, that leaves you out."

Jami suggested that he use British Airways, and they finished discussing the matter. Luke could tell that something else was bothering her as she got out of the Jeep, and as she walked away, he said, "Please be careful."

As they drove back to the boat, Luke suddenly blurted out, "Do you still remember the office phone number to Corner Stone?"

Without hesitation, Vincent recited the number but said, "Luke, the company has been closed for years." Unhearing, Luke quickly punched it into his cell and put it on speaker. After three rings, they were both stunned when an answering machine picked up. "Hi, you have reached Corner Stone Builders. Please leave a message and we'll return your call."

✝

# 56

*Riyadh, Saudi Arabia. 7:15 p.m.*

FATIH ABU'S CELL PHONE rang in his pocket as he walked down Olaya Street. Figuring that it was one of the friends he was meeting at a nearby coffee shop, he nonchalantly pulled out the phone. It was a text message. He opened it and froze in his tracks. His black eyes blinked several times as he read and reread the message.

He placed the phone back in his pocket, turned, and began walking quickly in the opposite direction. It was a warm night, and Fatih began sweating as he started jogging down the crowded street toward his car, which was parked several blocks away. Approaching, he stopped to catch his breath before getting inside. Within minutes, he pulled up to a huge concrete compound containing several buildings. The security gate opened, and he drove inside the walled complex.

Running from his car, he entered the largest house on the property. As he walked into the main room, he yelled, "Where's father?"

The older lady sitting on the sofa said nothing but pointed toward a room in the back. He quickly traversed the marble floor and knocked before entering.

"Who is it?"

"Father, it's me, Fatih. Can I come in?"

"Yes."

Fatih hurried to his father, who was sitting behind a large, ornate desk. Unable to speak, Fatih opened his phone and showed Ismail the text message.

"When did you get this message?"

Out of breath, Fatih responded, "Just a few minutes ago. I hurried home as soon as I saw it."

His father calmly clasped his hands and placed them under his chin. "Maybe it was just a wrong number."

"No one has called that number in many years," Fatih said.

After contemplating that thought, Ismail said, "Let's see if anyone calls again. It's probably nothing to be concerned about."

Fatih was shaken. "And what if it does ring again?"

His father paused. "It depends."

Ismail stopped talking and put his finger to his lips to indicate silence, as he stood. Seeing his father staring at the crack of light under the closed door, Fatih looked and saw a shadow moving. Ismail reached out and slowly turned the knob before flinging the door open. Catching his wife standing there, he grabbed her by the hair with one strong hand and said in a deep voice, "What do you think you're doing?" She grunted in pain but didn't speak. Still holding Kamilah, he dragged her into the other room and threw her on the couch. "Mind your own business." Fatih watched but didn't say a word.

Walking back into the office, Ismail slammed the door and sat down. Fatih spoke. "What if it's that priest, the one who was asking questions at the mosques?"

His father looked up, expressionless. "I think you already know the answer to your question. Give me the phone number from the text message, and I will have someone find out who it belongs to. Just in case, make sure you are packed and ready to go."

Fatih walked out of the office and passed his mother without saying a word or acknowledging her presence. He hurried out of the house and across the concrete courtyard, passing several large palm trees before entering a small white stone dwelling. A young girl sat up as he entered. Ignoring her, he looked at his phone to see if a new Corner Stone message appeared. Instead, several of his friends had sent messages asking why he didn't show up at the coffee shop. Responding to them was unimportant now. He hurried into his bedroom and began feverishly packing a bag.

# 57

WHEN LUKE ARRIVED BACK at the boat, he had another idea. Since it was daytime, he assumed that Arnold, the hacker, would be sleeping when he dialed his number. But to his surprise, it was answered on the second ring.

"Hi, Father."

"I thought you would be sleeping. I was going to leave you a message."

Arnold yawned. "Normally, I would be, but there's a hackers' conference on the web today, and I wanted to attend."

"You're kidding, right?"

Laughing, Arnold replied, "I'm serious. What can I do for you?"

"If I give you a phone number, can you figure out the physical address of the phone?"

"As long as it's not a cell phone."

Knowing the routine, Luke asked, "How much will it cost me and how long will it take?"

"You catch on quick, Father. It'll cost two hundred fifty dollars and will take anywhere from five minutes to an hour."

Luke gave Arnold the number, thanked him, and waited. After about ten minutes, his phone rang. "OK, here's the address."

Luke wrote down the information and said, "I owe you a lot of money. When can I pay you?"

Again, Arnold laughed. "No rush. I'm sure you're good for it."

Vincent stood and picked up Justice. Luke asked, "Where are you going?"

Vincent looked at Luke quizzically and pointed at the piece of paper. "Aren't we going to that address?"

Thinking, Luke said, "Yes, but we need to go to Aaron's house first."

---

Recognizing the Jeep this time, the guard opened the gate and waved them in. Luke hurried into the house. Reaching his room, he opened the closet and put his hand under the stack of sweaters to retrieve Aaron's gun. He placed it on the bed and removed his jacket. He took Aaron's long coat out of the closet and put it on. At that moment, Vincent unexpectedly entered the room. Seeing the semiautomatic lying on the bed, he said nervously, "I'm getting a whole new opinion of the priesthood."

Luke picked up the gun awkwardly. "This was Aaron's. I don't even know if it's loaded."

Vincent put his hand out, and Luke carefully gave it to him. Pulling the clip out of the bottom of the handgrip, he said, "It's loaded, all right; nine millimeter with fifteen rounds." After Vincent checked the safety, he attempted to hand it back to Luke, who refused and said, "Maybe you should hold it."

Vincent put it in his pocket.

Leaving Justice in the backyard, they sped to Boston's South End.

Without a GPS in the Jeep, they got lost a few times before finding the address. The dilapidated office building was in a bad area. After parking, Vincent motioned to his Jeep and said shakily, "I hope it's still here when we get back." As they walked to the entrance, Luke saw a drug deal going down on the street corner.

There was no sign of anyone inside the building. Luke looked at the makeshift directory pinned to the wall and saw that there was a check-cashing service on the second floor. They walked up the filthy stairs to the next floor and found a few people standing in line waiting to get cash. Seeing a metal detector in the doorway, Luke motioned for Vincent to stay outside. A huge armed security guard stood in the corner. Luke walked over to him and asked, "Would you happen to know where the superintendent of the building is?"

The big man yelled, "Hey Traynesha, where's the super?"

"I saw her earlier in 3B."

Luke and Vincent climbed another flight, and when they came out of the stairwell, office 3B was directly in front of them. Luke approached and knocked on the half-open door. A voice yelled, "Yeah?" Luke entered and saw an elderly lady on her hands and knees scrubbing the tacky vinyl floor. Looking up, she said, "What can I do for ya?"

Luke explained that Vincent's family owned Corner Stone Builders. He told her that they had dialed the old office number and were surprised when an answering machine picked up, since the company had been closed for a number of years.

Still scrubbing, she looked up and repeated herself, saying, "What can I do for ya?"

Luke struggled with his words. "Well, the answering machine is located somewhere in this building."

"How do you know that?"

Luke didn't know what to say, so he said nothing, prompting Vincent to chime in. "One of our friends works for the phone company."

When she didn't respond, Vincent reached into his pocket and pulled out a twenty. Grabbing it, she stood and asked, "What did you say the name of the company was?"

"Corner Stone Builders."

She looked puzzled. "Most of this building is empty. I don't know any company named Corner Stone who has ever rented here."

Vincent pulled out another twenty and asked, "What are the names of the companies that are renting here?"

She pulled the bill from his hand. "There's a tattoo parlor, a check-cashing agency, and some sort of export business."

"Anything else?"

"Well, there's another office that's rented, but I've never seen anyone go there."

Vincent pressed, "Then how do you get the rent?"

"It's wired directly to the landlord's bank."

This time Luke pulled out two twenties, handed them to her, and said, "Can you let us into that office?"

She hesitated and looked at the money in her hand a few times. Before she could answer, Luke added another twenty.

"Right this way."

# 58

THE SUPER OPENED THE office door for them, saying, "Make sure you lock up before you leave," and then she left them alone.

Vincent and Luke entered and looked around. There wasn't anything to see. It was an empty room with dust lining the windowsills and cobwebs hanging from the ceiling. "This doesn't look promising," Vincent finally admitted. Luke shrugged his shoulders in defeat as he crossed the room. "Maybe it's the import-export place?"

Disappointed, Vincent said, "Or maybe Arnold doesn't know what he's talking about."

Luke stopped in front of a narrow door and opened it. "Or maybe he does."

Vincent hurried over to see what Luke was looking at. Inside the small, dark closet was some sort of sophisticated machine sitting on a stack of boxes. Looking in, Vincent exclaimed, "Holy shit!"

Luke bit his lower lip nervously. "That's no ordinary answering machine, and I'm not sure what it is, but we probably know someone who does."

They both said at the same time, "Arnold."

Hoping he was still awake, Luke quickly dialed his number again.

"Father, I'm going to be able to buy a new car if you keep calling," Arnold said when he answered.

"I have another question. Just add it to my bill." Arnold didn't respond. "Vincent and I are at the address you gave us. There's some kind of answering machine here that looks like a computer and we have no idea how it works. We thought you might be able to help."

"I can't come over there now, but can you take a few pictures of it with your phone? Be sure to get the model numbers and any serial numbers in the pictures. But be careful not to jar the machine. Send me a few text messages with the pictures attached."

Luke hung up and looked toward the closet. "Vincent, can you open the blinds so we can get some light in here?" With the room illuminated in bright sunlight, Luke took his first picture. It took him a few minutes to figure out how to attach it to a text, but soon he was snapping picture after picture and sending them to Arnold. After his seventh message, the phone buzzed. It was a text from Arnold that said two words: "ENOUGH ALREADY!"

Not wanting to annoy him any more than he already had, Luke paced back and forth until Vincent said, "Why don't we call the number and see what happens. It would let us know that we are definitely in the right place." He searched his pockets and said, "Luke, I must have left my phone in the Jeep; let me borrow yours."

Luke handed him the phone. Vincent quickly entered the number. A few seconds later, two green lights began blinking on the front of the machine. "Yes!" Vincent yelled as he walked over and gave Luke a high five.

As he handed the phone back, Vincent became serious. "Luke, I don't know how you figured all of this out, but I'm beginning to worry that we're in over our heads. I don't want to aggravate you, but do you think we should go to the feds?"

Luke paced, thinking. "I would, but I honestly believe that they would laugh at us. Right now, we have the word of a homeless man who has no credibility and has spent time in jail. The only witness to his death is his schizophrenic girlfriend who would never testify or talk to anyone. And we've located an answering machine in an empty office. And to tell you the truth, I don't trust the FBI guy Dempsey. Let's see what Jami comes up with. By the time I get back from Riyadh, we'll know if we can prove our case."

Vincent stepped closer. "What do you think you're going to find over there?"

"I'm not really sure, but I'm hoping to get the proof that will solve Aaron's murder."

After several minutes of silence, Luke's cell buzzed, and he put it on speaker so Vincent could hear. "Thanks for calling back so quickly. What did you find out?"

Arnold replied, "OK, that machine is what's called an intelligent remote caller ID system. It's a fairly complex unit. I'm assuming that it's been configured so that the office you are in is most likely set up as the service control point. This machine could be networked to several others at any location."

Trying to simplify his explanation, Arnold slowed his pace, softened his tone, and took a deep breath.

"To make a long story short, here's what it does in layman's terms. Once a call is received, it's programmed to send that message or phone number to as many as a dozen other devices. So if someone wanted to make it seem like they had an office in Boston, but he really lived in, well, let's just say Saudi Arabia, they could route messages through this machine. So a call or voice message sent to the machine could trigger an alert on a phone, computer, or networked system anywhere in the world. And if the recipient responded, you would see a phone number that looked like they were located in Boston."

Thinking quickly, Luke asked, "Is there any way to figure out what number or device this machine is linked to?"

"Good question, but there's no easy way. I've scanned through the owner's manual, and that particular machine requires that you create a unique PIN and password. It also has a triggering device that alerts everyone linked to the system if it's logged into or any type of change is made to the unit. These systems are often used by outsourced customer-service firms to mask the fact that they are located in India. The security is built into the systems so they can't be tampered with."

Luke and Vincent suddenly came to the same realization as Luke deliberately asked, "So, if I called this number from my cell phone, there's a chance that my phone number was transmitted to somewhere else in the world, like Riyadh?"

"Definitely yes."

# 59

**BACK AT THE HOUSE,** Luke logged on to the computer to check flights to Riyadh. Scanning the British Airways site, he reviewed his options. The next flight that still had availability took off from Boston's Logan airport at 8:15 a.m. and landed in Riyadh at 6:00 a.m. the following day, a total flight time of almost fifteen hours, including a stopover in London. Before confirming his reservation, Luke called Jami's number to see if she had located an investigator who could help find Fatih once he landed. Hearing the extra-long ring, he realized that she was still on the phone.

While anxiously waiting for Jami to return his call, Luke continued reading the British Airways website. He was surprised to see that the airline's food was Sharia compliant. Not understanding what that meant, he started surfing the net and discovered that a halal certification for a Muslim was similar to a kosher accreditation for a Jew. As he read further he learned that there were specific guidelines regarding the type of food served and the way it was prepared. Understandably, it meant no pork, no animals that were dead prior to slaughtering, and no alcohol. But what really surprised Luke was the last requirement: The animals that were eaten had to be slaughtered in the name of Allah. Who would have thought that British Airways was worried about Sharia compliance?

Disturbed at Sharia's encroachment into everyday life, Luke continued searching. He was surprised that there were mutual funds that were specified as Sharia compliant, including the Dow Jones Islamic Index that targeted Muslim investors. He also discovered a court case from New Jersey where a trial judge found a Muslim man innocent of raping and beating his wife over a period of several months because his actions were based on his "religious belief" in Sharia law. The article quoted the man as saying that in his religion, it was his "right" to rape her.

Hearing something buzzing, he looked over and noticed his cell phone vibrating on the desk. He glanced at the display before answering and saw that it was Jami.

"Have you been on the phone since this morning?" Luke asked.

"Yes," she softly replied.

"Is everything all right?"

She sighed. "Yes, just extremely complicated."

Confused, Luke asked, "Why?"

Jami ignored his question and said, "I found a private investigator who's willing to help us. Are you still considering going to Riyadh?"

"Yes, I'm about to book the flight. Will the investigator meet with me?"

"He said he would. He wants to know your flight number so he can pick you up at the airport."

"That's great," Luke said. "Just give me a second." He pressed Enter on the keyboard and confirmed his reservation. After giving her his itinerary, he asked, "Are you sure you're OK?"

He thought he heard her voice quiver, but she finally answered, "Yes, I'm fine."

"You don't seem like yourself today."

She said softly, "I'm fine, just tired. Before it gets too late in Riyadh, let me call the investigator and give him your flight information."

Worried, Luke said, "Is there anything I can do to help?"

"No, I'll talk to you tomorrow."

"Probably not, since I'll be at the airport early."

After hanging up, Luke printed his boarding pass, logged off, and thought about what to do next. First, he called John and asked him to come over so that he could fill him in on his plans. Next he called Deborah.

She answered on the second ring. "Hi, Luke!"

"How have you been?"

"Great. The kids are having a wonderful time. They miss you, though."

"I miss them, too."

He could hear her walking and shutting a door. She whispered, "I just wanted to let you know that Lori may be returning to Boston in a few days."

Concerned, Luke asked, "Is everything OK?"

"Not really. She's going to meet with her lawyer and file for divorce. I'm sure she wouldn't mind me telling you, but I don't want to talk about it in front of the children."

Luke thought about suggesting counseling or having them talk to a priest, but as much as he prayed for understanding, he disdained her husband, Dick, with a vengeance.

"I'm sorry to hear that," he said insincerely.

Deb snapped back, "I'm not. If you knew half the things I know about that jerk husband of hers, you would understand." Changing the topic, she continued, "Can you come up and stay with us? Maybe next week?"

He decided not to tell her that he was going to be on his way to

Saudi Arabia in the morning, not only so that she wouldn't worry but also at this point, the less she knew, the better. "I'd really like to, but let's see how things go."

Before hanging up, Deborah added, "I told Lori that she could stay at our house if she wants. Her mother-in-law lives at their house, and she doesn't want her to know that she is home. I've already alerted our security guards." She added, "We really miss you. Please come to see us."

"I'll call in a few days."

Luke found Vincent in the family room watching a football game with Justice lying on his lap. Seeing Luke, the dog began wagging his tail. "Vincent, don't get up. I'm going to pack some things for my trip."

"You decided to go?"

"Yes, I'm leaving in the morning. When John gets here, I'll tell you both the details."

While Luke was packing, John arrived with pizzas. They ate, and Luke told them about his travel plans.

They finished their meal, and Luke left John and Vincent watching the game while he drove to visit his parents before his trip. En route in Vincent's Jeep, he called his mom to let her know that he was coming. She was waiting at the front door when he arrived.

"I'm so glad you're here," she said. "You have to talk to your father. Since we moved back home, reality has set in, and all he does is sit in his chair and stare into space. He still can't accept Aaron's death. The fact that whoever murdered your brother is still out there is eating him alive."

Luke entered the house and went directly to the living room. He sat down next to his father and said softly, "Dad, don't worry, I'm going to figure it out."

Not understanding what he was talking about, his father blankly responded, "Figure what out?"

"Who killed Aaron."

Turning to face him, his expression changed, and he asked, "How? The police don't have a clue."

"I'm not working with the police. I'm working this myself, and I think I'm getting close."

His father's eyes widened in shock. "Luke, even though nothing would make me happier than finding the people who killed Aaron, I couldn't bear to lose another son. Please be careful."

"OK, I will. I'm going to be away for a few days."

"Where are you going?"

"I can't tell you, but hopefully by the time I return, this will all be over."

# 60

JOHN PULLED INTO THE departure area of Logan International Airport and dropped Luke at the curb. Waving good-bye, Luke walked into the terminal and glanced at the monitor to find his gate. As he looked at his reflection in the glass windows, he hoped that his dark clothes and unshaven face would help him to fit in when he arrived in Riyadh. After waiting for over an hour in the security line, he sat at the gate with his head down, trying not to be recognized.

Once boarded, Luke reclined his seat and attempted to relax. He noticed that many of the female passengers were dressed in hijabs or head scarfs, and a few had on full burqas. Most of the men wore dark, loose-fitting clothing, similar to what he was wearing. One thought kept crossing his mind: Was he really about to meet his brother's killer?

When the plane's wheels touched down in London, he opened his eyes. As additional passengers began boarding, a woman with a head scarf that hid everything but her eyes quickly sat in the empty seat across from him. After taking off, he closed his eyes again and prayed for guidance once he landed in Riyadh. When he felt a nudge the first time, he thought it was an accident. When it happened again, he opened his eyes to see who was poking him. The woman across the aisle was staring at him. Unsure of what she wanted, he made eye contact, and as she uncovered her face, he exclaimed, "Jami, I can't believe you're here!"

Her eyes crinkled as she smiled. "I was sitting up front, but when we landed in London, I asked the flight attendant if I could change my seat. Since the plane wasn't full, she said I could sit anywhere."

Luke smiled. "Were you in first class?"

"Yes, I thought you would be sitting there, so I decided to spend the extra money."

Luke realized that Jami must have read the newspaper accounts regarding his inheritance. "I know it probably doesn't seem like it, but I normally live a very simple lifestyle. You should go back to your comfortable seat. We can talk once we land."

"No, this is fine."

Once the plane took off, Luke was glad to see that it was more than half empty. With no one sitting nearby, he could discuss the details of the trip with Jami and not have to worry about anyone overhearing their conversation.

"So, who is this private investigator and what's his name?

"His name is Masud, and he's supposed to be very good."

"How did you find him? Are you sure he can be trusted?"

"He works for a friend's company and I'm told he can help."

Luke sensed that she was holding back information and began to wonder if he had done the right thing by telling her everything he knew. "That's it? He works for a friend's company?"

Jami's eyes darkened. "It's not just any company; it's the largest company in Saudi Arabia, and he's the head of security."

"I don't know what arrangements you made, but I want to be the one to pay his fees."

"That won't be necessary."

Frustrated at her short answers, Luke asked, "Why not?"

"He's doing it for free."

Luke was astounded. "Who exactly is your friend?" he asked.

She took a deep breath, and Luke could tell that she was agitated. "Two years ago when I was still living in Cairo, I went to visit a girlfriend who was away at college. She was attending King Saud University in Saudi Arabia, one of the best schools in the Middle East. When she was showing me around the campus, my head scarf blew off in the wind and a young man picked it up for me." She took another deep breath. "He never said a word to me. Three days later, I returned to Cairo. A few weeks after that, I returned home from school one day, and the man, Layth, was sitting in my house with my father. He had asked to marry me. My parents were so happy. His family owned one of the most successful companies in Saudi Arabia and they were very rich."

Seeing that the more she talked, the more upset she became, Luke said softly, "But you didn't get married?"

"At first, I went along with it, but I didn't even know him. When I told my family that I wanted to call off the wedding, they were furious. As you know, this is not something a woman can do in that part of the world."

Luke knew all too well the horror stories of Muslim women who turned down marriage proposals. There were documented cases of attacks where humiliated men had doused their brides-not-to-be with sulfuric acid, disfiguring their faces by burning the skin until their bones were exposed, often causing them to go blind. The underlying rationale seemed to be that if the man who was turned down couldn't have his chosen bride, he would make sure that no one else would want her. These attacks had a catastrophic effect on the victims' lives, not only physically, but psychologically, socially, and financially.

She continued, "My entire family turned against me, except for Ablaa. Have you ever heard of Chop Chop Square?" Luke shook his head. "My father sat me down and explained that there is a public square in Saudi Arabia where executions take place. Crowds gather to see criminals killed by beheadings or mutilated by amputations. This is not uncommon; it happens on a weekly basis. I think my father told me about this for two reasons: He wanted me to marry Layth, and he wanted to warn me about the dangers of not marrying him. Ablaa understood and insisted that I come to Boston, where she was attending school."

Luke interrupted her story. "Did you think the man who proposed to you was going to try to hurt you?"

She didn't answer the question but said, "His family was very powerful, and I disgraced them. Ablaa and I agreed that I should leave without anyone's knowledge. So I did and have never returned until now."

Concerned for her safety, Luke asked, "Why did you decide to come back?"

"I already told you. I'll do anything to see that the people who killed my sister pay for what they've done." She looked at him, and he saw tears in her eyes. "I'm here for the same reason you are. We're not so different, Luke."

He was upset that she might be putting herself in danger. "Does Layth know you're coming?"

"Yes, I called and begged for his help. The private investigator who will be meeting us at the airport works exclusively for his father's company. He has connections with government officials in Saudi Arabia."

Not wanting to discuss her past anymore, Jami said, "We should get some rest. Once we get to Riyadh we're going to have a full day ahead of us."

She closed her eyes and Luke did the same, both with the hope that the nightmare would soon be over. But Luke wondered if it was just beginning.

# 61

**WHEN THE PILOT ANNOUNCED** that they would soon be landing, Luke opened his eyes and saw that Jami had moved from the aisle seat to the one near the window. He saw her staring at the ground below and wondered how she was feeling. Being a priest, he felt uneasy, knowing that Saudi Arabia was an oppressive country when it came to religious freedom. In Egypt, Christians were tolerated, even though they were a minority and were often persecuted. In Saudi Arabia, there were Christians, albeit most of them foreign workers, but they were forced to practice their faith in secret. Churches were outlawed, as were Bibles and all other religious items, including statues, necklaces, and anything else that indicated a faith other than Islam. The Saudi holy cities of Mecca, where Muhammad is buried under a green dome, and Medina, which contains the mosque of Muhammad, are forbidden to anyone except Muslims. Luke often wondered why the United States considered the Saudis such close allies when their government was as repressive as it was.

Moving back to the aisle seat, Jami turned to look at Luke but didn't speak, prompting him to say, "It's going to be all right, I promise.

I'm not leaving your side." A look of concern filled her expressive eyes. Luke gazed out the window and saw exactly what he had expected: sand. Saudi Arabia, the largest country in the Middle East, is 95 percent desert.

Before landing, Jami said, "We can't be seen together. I'll contact you. When you leave the plane, don't look for me. Masud will be waiting for you at the baggage claim." Before Luke could protest, she stood abruptly and quickly walked back to her original first-class seat.

Luke walked off the plane, and after a few questions at customs he headed toward the baggage claim. The airport was an architectural masterpiece, with fountains, columns, and soaring arched ceilings. As soon as he entered the baggage area, Luke saw a man with a dark complexion heading his way. The man smiled and unexpectedly shook Luke's hand. "Nice to meet you, Mr. Miller. I'm Masud."

Luke smiled back. Hearing the man's perfect English, he asked, "Where are you from?"

He laughed. "I was born about ten miles from where we are standing, but I went to school in California."

"What school?"

"Stanford."

Luke knew that many foreign Muslims attended school in the United States. He had even read of a puzzling trend taking place where Muslim students had begun attending Christian universities. Some universities had installed footbaths so Muslim students could wash their feet before prayers instead of making do by using bathroom sinks.

"That's a great school," Luke responded.

"Yes, it is."

Walking out of the airport and into the warm air, Masud stopped at the curb and looked in both directions. Within seconds, a black sedan arrived, and a young man jumped out to open the back door. Luke and Masud climbed in back, and they drove out of the airport. Not much was said during the half-hour ride to central Riyadh. When they finally turned into a parking lot, Luke looked up and saw the sign for the Four Seasons at Kingdom Centre.

Masud exited the car first and Luke followed. As they walked into the impressive building, Masud said, "Mr. Miller, you have an open-ended reservation here. Just let the desk clerk know when you will be leaving."

He motioned to a group of chairs in the lobby. "Please, sit down." Luke sat, and Masud pulled his chair close. "Do you know who Layth Abbar is?"

"Only that Jami knows him."

"Jami?" Masud questioned. "Oh, you mean Jamilah."

"Yes."

"I work for the Abbar family. They are very powerful and have great influence in Saudi Arabia. Layth met with me personally to let me know that it was important that you receive all the information you need. It is his desire that you leave here satisfied, and it is imperative to me that he is satisfied." Luke smiled and Masud continued, "Since yesterday, I've had a team of men investigating Fatih Abu and his family. We have much to discuss, but I think you should go to your room and rest while I meet with my men. I will be back to pick you up in three hours."

Luke innocently asked, "What about Jami, I mean Jamilah? Will she be with you?"

Masud frowned. "Mr. Miller, there are vast differences between Saudi Arabia and the U.S. In this county, a single woman cannot be seen alone with a man in public unless they are married. Women who ignore this law are put on trial for prostitution and can be sentenced to death. I understand and appreciate your country and its traditions, but most people here do not. Women cannot drive and must adhere to a strict dress code that ensures their entire body is covered in public." Trying to further educate Luke, he said strongly, "You should also know that alcohol is prohibited, and there are no theaters, bars, or nightclubs." Looking directly at Luke, he added, "And absolutely no churches. If you go to a restaurant while you are here, make sure you sit in the single men's section."

Luke looked up and said, "Are you serious?"

"Yes, Mr. Miller, I am. This is not Cairo; it's much stricter. Even the shopping malls contain separate floors that are restricted to women only."

Luke tried to suppress a yawn, and Masud said, "Go, get some rest. I will come back soon."

Masud followed Luke to the desk to check in and let him know that all of his expenses had been taken care of by Layth. They walked to the elevator together. After shaking his hand again, Masud said, "I will see you in a few hours."

Luke entered his room and was astonished at its opulence. It was nicer than his bedroom at Aaron's house, and it wasn't just one room, it was an entire apartment. After exploring for a few minutes, he collapsed on the bed. Completely exhausted, he tried to rest, but Jami's safety continued to preoccupy him. He wondered what she was doing right now. Was she with Layth, and if so, was she safe?

# 62

LUKE'S DEEP SLEEP WAS violently disturbed by a ringing phone. Not knowing where he was initially, his heart raced. On the fourth ring, he regained his bearings and answered, "Hello?"

"Mr. Miller, I'm in the lobby."

Luke rushed into the bathroom to quickly freshen up and then hurried onto the elevator. When the door opened at the lobby level, Masud was standing directly in front of him. "Did you get some rest?"

"Yes, thank you."

As they walked outside, Masud said, "I'm going to be driving this time, but you can sit in the back if you feel more comfortable."

Luke declined and got into the passenger seat. They pulled out of the parking lot and onto the busy street. Luke asked, "Have you seen Jamilah?"

"No, I haven't."

"Do you know where she is?"

"I don't, Mr. Miller."

Getting frustrated, Luke said, "Please, call me Luke. And if you talk to Layth, let him know that I'm not leaving until I know she's safe."

Masud pulled the car to the side of the road and turned to face him. "Luke, my job is to help you find Fatih Abu. I don't know anything about Jamilah. I didn't even know she existed until yesterday. But I do know that she is very important to Layth. Please know that I'm going to do whatever I can to help you, but I can't assist you with Jamilah."

"I apologize if I offended you, but you can understand that I'm concerned for her safety."

"I understand. Let me tell you about Layth. He is the youngest of his three brothers and is one of the most gentle people I have ever met. He is very educated and has traveled the world. But the most important thing you need to know about him is that he has a kind heart. I cannot imagine him hurting anyone. When he told me about Jamilah, his eyes filled with tears. He said that she was the most beautiful woman he had ever seen."

"Thank you for telling me that."

When they pulled up to a small office building and parked, Luke asked, "Where are we going?"

"This is one of my offices. We are going to meet with three of my men so they can tell you what they have found."

"Can they be trusted?" Luke asked.

Masud answered seriously, "Yes, with their lives."

They gathered in a small room containing a conference table and several chairs, and each one of Masud's team introduced themselves in English.

Masud pointed to a young, dark-haired man who appeared to be in his early twenties, who spoke slowly and with purpose: "I've talked to a few of his friends. All of them have told me the same thing, that he hasn't been seen since yesterday."

He pointed to the next man, who said, "I've had his father's compound under surveillance for the past twenty-four hours."

Luke interrupted. "His father's compound?"

The young man looked confused. Masud said, "What's wrong, Luke?"

"I thought his parents were killed in a plane crash."

Masud looked around the table. "I can assure you that they are alive and well."

Luke's heart raced. Masud nodded, and the young man who had been talking continued, "His father hasn't left the compound, but he is there. His mother walks a young girl to the local school in the morning and goes to get her in the afternoon. I think she's Fatih's wife."

Luke bluntly asked, "How old is she?"

The young man hesitated and Masud said, "Answer the question."

"Based on the school she is attending, I would guess that she is between eleven and twelve."

Luke shook his head in disgust.

Masud pointed to the last man, who said, "I've also been trying to find Fatih."

Masud glared at him. "Well, keep trying!"

Looking at Luke, Masud asked, "What would you like to do?"

"I want to talk to his mother."

Masud agreed. "That is probably a good place to start. We can try to detain her when she returns to school this afternoon."

Before dismissing his men, Masud said, "Let me know immediately if you find out anything else."

Luke thanked each of them. Masud looked at his watch and said, "We have a few hours. Is there anything else you would like to see while you are here?"

Luke thought for a minute. "How about Chop Chop Square?"

Masud looked surprised. "You mean As-Sufaat square?"

Unsure, Luke replied, "The place where the beheadings take place."

"Are you sure? You might see more than you wished for."

"Yes, I'm sure."

✝

# 63

**AFTER DRIVING FOR TWENTY** minutes, Masud parked the car and said, "Follow me." As they walked to As-Sufaat, Luke noticed that the perimeter was lined with palm trees and occupied benches. Once inside the square, he looked down and saw huge granite slabs intermingled with decorative tiles. The center of the busy square was crowded with people, including many families with laughing children, giving the whole scene a festive atmosphere. Surprised, Luke asked, "This is where the executions take place?"

"Yes. Come this way, I'll show you."

Luke was flabbergasted. These people where acting like nothing bad ever happened here. Walking toward the middle, Masud pointed to a large drain. Luke commented, "What's that?"

"It's for the blood."

Masud explained that decapitation was reserved for crimes such as murder, adultery, drug trafficking, and renouncing Islam. Mere thieves would only have their hands or feet amputated.

Horrified, Luke asked, "When do these atrocities take place?"

Thinking that Luke was truly interested, Masud continued. "Here's what happens on an execution day. A van surrounded by police cars arrives unannounced. The criminal, shrouded in white linen, is drugged so that he can't fight back. He is forced to kneel, and the executioner takes his place. To use your baseball pastime as a metaphor, the executioner takes one check swing with our traditional curved sword, which the condemned man feels as the cold steel touches his neck. Then the slaughterer pulls back and, as you would say in the States, swings for the fences. The head rolls away from the body, which stays upright for a few seconds with blood spurting before falling to the ground. Local merchants often bet on which way the body will fall. You would be surprised at how much blood there is. That's why the drain is required. The executioner wipes his sword, and the body and head are thrown into the van. Minutes later, after the granite is washed down, it is as if nothing ever happened."

Luke looked at him with revulsion and asked, "Does compassion have any meaning in this country?"

Stone-faced, Masud looked at him. "Compassion is considered a weakness. If you want, I'm sure that I can find out if there's going to be a beheading tomorrow."

"That won't be necessary."

As they walked, Luke became more convinced that anyone raised in this environment had no choice but to place little value on life. In a perverse way, he could now understand how Fatih and his father were capable of plotting the intricacies of a long-term plan that involved killing Vincent's parents, taking over a construction company, and planting a bomb in Boston. He was staggered to realize that Fatih had the ability to unfeelingly murder his adoptive parents, who had cared for him as a natural son.

He wondered if two religious cultures that were so dramatically different could coexist in America. How could Christians who believed in religious freedom and forgiveness coexist with Muslims who beheaded nonbelievers and used torture for minor infractions of religious laws?

They stopped to eat lunch, but Luke was in no mood for food. Looking at his watch, Masud finally said, "We'd better get going."

During the drive toward Fatih's parents' compound, Masud conferred with his men by phone. As they got close, he parked on a street a few blocks away. When Luke prepared to exit the car, Masud said, "I will be going with you."

Confused, Luke asked, "Why?"

"For two reasons: in case Kamilah speaks only Arabic or in case she won't cooperate." Before Luke could protest, he continued, "We will talk to her before she gets to the school and meets Fatih's wife."

They stood on the side of the desolate street, near a narrow alley. Masud's cell phone rang, and he said to Luke, "She's on her way."

Luke's heart pounded as they waited. Seeing Kamilah in the distance, Masud said, "There she is. I'll make the initial contact. Don't say or do anything until I tell you." Luke was apprehensive about what was going to happen, but it was too late.

When she was just a few feet away, Masud stepped into her path and she stopped. He moved closer and said something in Arabic. She didn't respond. He pulled a badge out of his pocket and grabbed her by the arm. She tried to fight by pulling away, but his grip was too tight. He dragged her into the narrow alley where Luke was standing.

As she saw Luke, he could tell by her eyes that she recognized him. Masud was yelling at her in Arabic, but she still wasn't responding. Unexpectedly, he reached up, grasped her around the neck, and slammed her into the concrete wall. She groaned, and Luke immediately intervened. "Let her go now!" he yelled as he grabbed Masud's arm with brute force. When Luke wrenched Masud's hand away, she fell to the ground, weeping.

Luke helped her to her feet and said strongly, "You need to talk to me. I know what your son did." He was horrified when she opened her mouth and grunted. At that moment, he realized that her tongue was cut out. In shock, he buried his face in his hands. Then instinctively, he reached out to hold her in his arms. Quickly realizing that he shouldn't be touching her, he abruptly stepped back. Unfazed, Masud stepped in and handed her a pen and a piece of paper that he took from his pocket. Again, he began yelling in Arabic. She took the paper and started writing. When she showed the paper to Masud, Luke asked, "What does it say?"

Masud said, "She didn't know what they were planning. When she found out what they were going to do, she threatened to go to the authorities, so they cut out her tongue."

Luke cringed and asked softly, "Where is Fatih now?"

She stared at him but didn't write anything. Luke stared back, unsure of what to do. Unexpectedly, Masud grabbed her by the throat again, this time putting his gun to her head. Before Luke could react, he screamed, "Answer the question."

She nodded and Masud released her. She began writing, this time in English. "He's not here."

Frustrated, Masud pulled back the trigger and aimed. Luke grabbed him by the arm. Seeing this, she began writing as she stared at Luke. "He left for the U.S. this morning."

Suspiciously, Luke asked, "Why is he going back now, after all these years?"

She wrote, filling the page, "TO KILL YOU."

# 64

KAMILAH QUICKLY SCRIBBLED, "I have to go. School will wonder why I'm late. If I ever say anything about what happened in Boston, they will cut off my hands. I've suffered enough."

Luke looked at her and quietly asked, "Were the Russos' deaths an accident?"

She looked down at the ground. Luke had his answer.

Shaken, Luke watched passively as Masud took out his gun again and placed it against Kamilah's head. He yelled in Arabic for a few minutes before finally releasing her. She quickly ran away, looking back at Luke one last time.

Walking back to the car, Luke demanded, "Was that really necessary? And what did you say to her before you let her go?"

"I swore that if she ever told anyone about what just happened, I would have her entire family killed. I know where her sister and brother live. I also promised her that I would kill Fatih's wife and her entire family. And lastly, I threatened that I would cut off her niece's fingers until she bled to death."

Luke looked at him in horror. This prompted Masud to say, "I did it for your benefit."

Luke doubted that it was for his benefit alone. Masud clearly enjoyed playing the torturer.

Before they got into the car, Masud said, "I wouldn't suggest talking to Fatih's father, but if you want me to arrange it, I will."

Luke ignored him and said, "I'm changing plans and leaving for Boston now. I want to see Jamilah before I leave." Masud nodded and picked up his phone.

They stopped at the hotel to check out and rebook Luke's flight, then Masud drove Luke to the airport. When they pulled up to the terminal, Luke asked, "When am I going to see Jami?"

Masud looked in his rearview mirror. "Any second now."

Looking back, Luke saw a black limo approach. Masud got out and talked to the driver for a few minutes. Returning, he told Luke, "She's waiting in the car."

Luke hurried out. The limo driver opened the back door, and Luke climbed in. Jami looked at him and said, "Luke, I will miss you."

"You're not coming back with me, are you?"

She shook her head. "No, it was part of my agreement with Layth. I promised to marry him."

Luke's eyes filled with tears. "Why are you doing this?"

He could see that she was overcome with emotion. "Because Ablaa would have done it for me." Then she asked, "Why are you doing this? You're putting yourself in great danger."

Overcome with sadness, he replied, "Because Aaron would have done it for me."

She removed her head scarf and smiled through her tears. "You see, Luke, we are not that much different after all." Seeing that her driver was preoccupied outside the car, talking with Masud, Luke reached over and hugged her. She returned his embrace.

Before he could leave, Jami said, "Make sure he pays. I will make sure his father pays, even if I have to hire someone myself. Layth will help."

Luke said despairingly, "I can't believe I'll never see you again."

She forced a smile. "Maybe once Layth understands how stubborn and hotheaded I am, he will divorce me. As Luke began to open the car door, she said seriously, "I'm sure we will meet again."

When Luke turned away to head toward the terminal building, the limo driver approached him and introduced himself. "Mr. Miller, I'm Layth Abbar. It's an honor to meet you." Surprised, Luke held out his hand, but Layth bowed. Luke did the same. "I want you to know that if you need anything else, please let me know," Layth said.

Luke stared at him. "Be good to Jami."

Layth smiled. "She already has me driving her around in a limo." Luke smiled back. Becoming serious, Layth continued, "I have loved her since the first time I saw her."

Looking into his eyes, Luke believed him.

## 65

**CONCERNED THAT LUKE WAS** already late for his flight, Layth had Masud follow him into the airport. As they arrived at the security area, they found hundreds of people impatiently waiting in line. Several men were yelling and pushing without any regard for the women and children in the queue. Masud walked over the counter and said something to a young man. Minutes later, another man in a dark suit appeared. Luke watched as the two men talked in Arabic for a few seconds. Looking at Luke, the man waved and led him past the crowds to a separate area where he was searched and his bag was x-rayed. Luke waved to Masud and rushed through the terminal. Arriving at the gate, he was the last passenger to board the plane.

Exhausted, Luke realized that he had hardly eaten anything or slept in the past day. With stops in Dubai and London before arriving in Boston, he knew that it would be another twenty-three hours before he was home. Regardless, his mind raced as he tried to anticipate what Fatih was planning. He hoped Deborah and the children were safe in the mountains. John should be untraceable, since Aaron's office building was titled under a separate LLC, making it almost impossible to connect to the family. And Vincent should be out of danger, since no one knew he was back in Boston. And who would even think to look on a boat in the middle of winter?

Then he had a sobering thought. What about his parents? Could they be a target? He quickly did the math in his head to determine what time Fatih would get to Boston. Even if Fatih had left five hours before and had a flight with only one connection, he wouldn't land in Boston before Luke reached his first stopover in Dubai. Luke would call his parents as soon as he landed and demand that they leave their house and stay away.

Luke couldn't sleep and was consumed with anxiety as the plane made its first landing. He grabbed his small carry-on bag and quickly made his way through the walkway and into the gate area. Since his cell phone was useless here, he rushed to find a phone. Looking around, he realized that he was already a world away from Saudi Arabia. Upscale stores like Chanel, Givenchy, and Dior lined the airport terminal. Western food was readily available at McDonald's or Starbucks. Luke found a business center, where the receptionist helped him place the international call. As the phone began ringing, Luke thanked her and she walked away. Realizing that it was the middle of the night in Boston, Luke rehearsed what he would say when his father answered the phone.

"Hello?"

"Dad, it's Luke, everything is fine and I don't want you to worry, but please listen carefully to what I'm about to say. You need to leave the house within the next hour and go out of town. Don't tell anyone where you're going. Maybe you can go to Uncle Ira's house in Vermont?"

His father responded groggily, "What? Are you sure you're OK?"

"Yes, Dad, I'm fine."

He could hear his mother in the background, questioning what was going on.

"Where are you, son?"

"I'm in Dubai, but I'll be home soon."

"Where the hell is Dubai?"

"I'll explain everything when I see you. But now, please promise me that you will leave the house soon."

"Why?"

"It's just a precaution, but I want to make sure you're safe."

His father hesitated and asked, "Are you safe?"

Luke wasn't really sure himself, but he said, "I'm fine."

Luke's mother got on the phone and started asking more questions. Luke did his best to avoid answering them directly, but he was finally able to convince them to leave. Before he hung up, Luke's dad got back on the phone. "Did you find Aaron's killer?"

"Yes, but now I need to make him pay."

# 66

**FATIH WALKED THROUGH LOGAN** airport in Boston, looking like any other American. With his black Levi's, Abercrombie sweatshirt, and iPod, he confidently made his way to the customs counter. When he was summoned by the agent, he smiled boldly and handed her his U.S. passport. Seeing the stamp from Riyadh, she looked up and said, "Welcome home."

Having only a small carry-on bag, he headed past the baggage claim and out the sliding glass doors to the curb. He took a white linen shawl out of his bag and draped it over his shoulders as a signal. A few minutes later, an empty cab pulled up with its taxi light off. He jumped into the backseat, and they slowly made their way out of the airport. As they drove, he asked the man about his family and his life in the Middle East before he came to the States. Before long, Fatih directed the driver to a deteriorated warehouse by the water. As they pulled into the parking lot, his cell phone rang. "Hello, Father."

"Are you in the car?"

"Yes."

"There's a bag with a gun under the seat. Screw on the silencer and follow the plan we discussed."

The plan had been in place for many years, with several different scenarios mapped out in great detail. Having Blade killed was easily handled from Riyadh, but killing the priest was another story. Fatih's father, Ismail, had determined that this required a hands-on approach. Even though there was no hard evidence linking them to the bombing, the priest was getting close and might soon go to the local police. He had to be dealt with now. Fatih was more than willing to die to protect his father, but the plan was to make Luke's death look like a suicide. They would shoot him in the head and place the gun in his hand. They joked about the newspaper headlines, "Heartbroken Priest Couldn't Wait to See God." Once Luke was dead, Fatih would drive to the outskirts of Boston, pick up another car, and assume a new identity. Then he would make his way to the Canadian border and stay there for a few months before going back to the Middle East.

Ismail said, "Call me when you are finished," and Fatih ended the call.

He exited the cab, saying, "Wait here for me. I'll be right back." But then he looked down at one of the tires and stopped. "Your tire has a nail in it," he said to the driver, pointing at the front of the car. The man hurried to get out and bent down to look. Fatih quietly moved behind him and nonchalantly pulled the trigger. The old man's limp body lay on the freezing asphalt. Fatih whispered, "Allah Akbar," before taking the linen cloth from around his shoulders and wrapping it around what was left of the dead man's blood-soaked head. Following the plan, Fatih took the driver's wallet and cash, so that it appeared he was robbed. Fatih dragged him by his feet until his body was hidden behind a dumpster. He smiled while backing up the car as several seagulls landed and pecked at the last pieces of flesh that lay on the ground.

He took the portable GPS unit out of his bag and scanned the preprogrammed addresses. He selected Saint Leonard's Church. Once there, he parked on the street and studied a picture of Luke that he had retrieved from the Internet. Then he entered the church and sat in a pew in the back, listening to a group of elderly parishioners as they prayed the rosary. When an old woman began walking out, he followed her to the gathering space. "Excuse me, can you tell me if Father Luke Miller is here?"

She smiled. "I'm sorry, but he hasn't been here for weeks. I hope he comes back soon."

"Me too," Fatih said with a smile.

He returned to the cab and selected the next address from the GPS. It was getting dark as he drove past Luke's parents' house and parked as far away as he could while keeping it in sight. Seeing no car in the driveway, he waited. He took a pack of gum from his bag, unwrapped a piece, and tried to relax. When his patience ran short, he left the car and walked down the block. He looked up and down the street before making his way up the narrow driveway and into the backyard. He peered into the windows but didn't see anyone. Walking up the back steps, he put on a pair of gloves, then he leaned against the old wooden door, pushing with all his weight. On the second shove, the door jamb splintered, and he fell into the kitchen.

He cautiously entered every room in the small house and quickly determined that it was empty. Returning to the bedroom that Luke and Aaron had shared as boys, he mockingly took time to study their baseball trophies and pictures. "These infidel Americans cared more about baseball than God. What blasphemy."

Once back in the cab, he thought about where he would go next. Newspaper articles and the Internet had been valuable sources of information on the man he was about to kill. He knew what his old truck and new car looked like, and he even knew the name of the bank where he kept his inheritance. He was especially anxious to meet Luke's friend Jamilah. He had vowed that one day he would return to the States and slit the throat of that little bitch who betrayed her religion by befriending the priest.

He started the cab and drove toward his next stop: Aaron's mansion.

# 67

AFTER A LONG AND unexpected delay in London, Luke's plane finally landed in Boston. It was now the middle of the night, but he turned on his cell phone and frantically called John's number. He apologized for waking him and said, "Can you pick me up at the airport?"

Hearing the panic in Luke's voice, John replied, "I thought you weren't coming home until tomorrow."

"Change of plans. I just landed."

"I'll leave right now."

Luke said, "Before you pick me up, could you swing by Aaron's house and see if Lori's car is in the driveway? If it is, make sure the guard is still at the gate."

"Why?"

"I'll explain when I see you."

Luke rushed through the airport. Before entering the line for customs, he called his mother's cell phone and was relieved to hear that they were staying with Uncle Ira. He felt even better when his father said that they had talked with Deborah earlier and she was concerned that Luke wasn't answering his cell phone. It was too late to call her now. Despite his parents' protest, he refused to get into the details of his trip but promised to explain everything in the morning.

---

Fatih parked the cab a few blocks away from Aaron's house and pulled on a hooded sweatshirt. Now dressed all in black, he walked along the tree line of each house until the mansion was in sight. He slowly approached the security guard's car while pulling the gun out of his belt. The car's window was open; he could smell cigarette smoke and hear music from the radio. The interior light was on, and the man appeared to be reading the newspaper. Not wanting to kill him and ruin his chance to make Luke's murder look like a suicide, he backed away and carefully walked the perimeter of the property to see if there were any other guards. When he reached the back of the lot, he noticed a small clearing in the woods. Entering, he was surprised to see an aluminum ladder glistening in the full moon's light. After checking the rest of the property, he ran back and climbed over the wall. When he reached the other side, he positioned the ladder so he could climb back over, just as Luke had done so many times before.

He crept silently around the house and peered into each ground-level window. Seeing a white Cadillac in the driveway, he hoped the priest was home. He crouched by the front door and looked through one of the etched glass side lights, and he saw a green indicator light on the alarm keypad. Knowing that this typically meant that the system was disengaged, he checked every window and door to see if any were unlocked. Not having any luck with the ground floor, he ran and grabbed the ladder from the back wall to see if he could reach the second-floor windows. After a few tries, he pushed on one and it opened. He listened for an alarm and, not hearing one, he hoisted himself through the window and landed in a large bathroom with a whirlpool tub. He closed the window behind him, then took a penlight from his pocket and began searching for Luke.

He shined the light around the bedroom adjacent to the bathroom. Seeing a Bible on the nightstand, he thought that he had found the priest but was disappointed to find that no one was in the bed.

He proceeded to the hallway, moving quickly with his gun in one hand and the light in the other, and checked each room carefully. There was no sign of anyone until he walked through the open door that led to the biggest bedroom in the house. It was dark, and a woman he assumed was Luke's brother's wife lay in a short, silky nightgown, sleeping facedown on the bed. From the back, Fatih could see her brown hair, long shapely legs, and black thong. He stared at her in disgust, yet found himself becoming uncontrollably aroused. Mad at her for causing him to lose control, he pointed the gun at the back of her head and thought about pulling the trigger, whispering, "I should kill this worthless whore." But regaining his composure, he forced himself to walk out. When he finished looking through every other room in the house, he walked out the gym door, leaving it unlocked in case he had to return.

Once back in the taxi, he sat and thought about what he should do next. If Luke was staying at the house, he should have already been home. When he saw a set of headlights in his rearview mirror, he sank down in his seat. Seeing Luke's old pickup truck pass by, he smiled and thanked Allah.

He followed the truck, making sure to stay far enough behind that he wasn't noticed. When it stopped by the security guard's car, he was happy that he hadn't killed the man. After a few minutes, he was surprised when the truck pulled away. He followed and was confused when the pickup turned toward the airport. Realizing that there were a lot of other cabs on the road, he sped up and followed closer, confident that he wouldn't be noticed. Fatih was now worried that if Luke got on a plane, he would have no chance of killing him.

Surprisingly, the truck turned at the sign for "arriving flights." The pickup pulled over to the curb and parked. Confused, Fatih did the same. When a police officer approached the pickup, he began to panic. Moments later, the truck pulled away and Fatih followed. As expected, the truck circled the airport, and after a few minutes they were back at the arrivals curb. Fatih waited and hoped that the police wouldn't make Luke move the truck again. Hearing a knock on the window, he jumped and looked as a woman in a dark suit asked, "Are you available?" Startled, he didn't understand, but then realized that she wanted a cab. Knowing that his taxi light was off, he pointed silently at the car's roof, and she walked away.

He waited behind the truck for what seemed like an eternity, praying that a police officer would not make him move the cab. Then, suddenly, he saw a man pass through the sliding glass doors and head toward the truck. When the man turned to open the door, Fatih was shocked. It was his target, the priest.

# 68

**AFTER PARKING, LUKE AND** John rushed through the light snowfall toward the boat. Vincent met them at the back and helped each one aboard, anxious to hear what had happened in Saudi Arabia. Hunched around the kitchen table, Luke quickly relayed the events of the last forty-eight hours. Vincent was shocked to learn that Fatih's parents were still alive.

When Luke further explained that Fatih's mother, Kamilah, couldn't talk because they had cut out her tongue, the other men were horrified. Vincent was visibly shaken because he had been so close to Fatih. He had eaten dinner with him, slept in the same house, and had even attended church with him. Once Vincent heard that Kamilah admitted that her husband and son were responsible for the bombing, he stared at Luke with an unspoken question. Luke replied by simply nodding his head. Now Vincent knew for sure that his parents were murdered by Fatih and Ismail. Tears welled in his eyes.

Continuing, Luke sadly explained that Jami wasn't returning. Without her help, his trip would have been a failure. She had sacrificed her freedom to catch the people who had killed her sister, and in doing so had led them to their own families' killers. The final shock came when Luke told them that Fatih had just returned to Boston. When they asked why, Luke reluctantly admitted, "To kill me."

Vincent jumped from his chair and pleaded, "We need to go to the police, and I mean now!"

John whispered, "So that's why you wanted me to check on Aaron's house."

Luke nodded.

Despite what Vincent thought, Luke wasn't sure that he had enough evidence to arrest Fatih, but perhaps he might be able to convince Detective Romo to help. Even though it was the middle of night, Luke picked up his cell phone and dialed the detective's number. When he didn't answer, Luke left a message that he thought he knew who was responsible for the bombing in Boston. He added, "If you want to meet in the morning, I'll be at the harbor on my brother's boat. No one will see you."

They agreed that they should be safe on the boat for the night, and they hoped they would be hearing from Romo in the morning.

When John stood to go, Luke said, "Why don't you stay with us tonight?"

John declined and added, "I'm supposed to meet with someone who might want to lease Aaron's office first thing in the morning. I want to make sure it's clean before they arrive." John bent down to pet Justice, who was sleeping on the floor, then shook hands with Vincent and Luke before leaving.

Walking into his bedroom, Luke noticed that Vincent had placed Blade's ashes on his nightstand. He touched the box and said, "Keep helping me, Blade." After taking a shower and putting on a pair of sweatpants, he heard a knock on his door. It could be only one person. "Come in, Vincent," he said. Vincent entered the room, holding Justice in his arms. "I'm sorry to bother you, Luke, but I wanted to talk to you alone."

Luke smiled. "No problem." Vincent sat and said, "Can you tell me exactly what Kamilah said when you asked her about my parents?"

Luke explained, "It was the last thing I said to her. She was looking directly at me, and after I asked the question, she looked at the ground, ashamed at what her family had done."

"I can't believe it. She was like a second mother to me. She made me dinner, bought me clothes, and took care of me when I was sick."

"I am positive that she had nothing to do with any of this," Luke assured him. "They cut out her tongue and threatened to amputate her hands if she ever mentioned Boston again. She's suffered immensely because of her evil husband and son. She can't be held responsible for anything that happened to your family or mine. I'm sure her feelings for you were genuine. It was obvious that she was brokenhearted. Remember, she didn't have to tell me anything, but she told me everything."

"Where do you think Fatih is now?"

"I'm not sure, probably in some fleabag hotel watching porn and waiting to see if he can find me in the morning."

"And what do you think he's going to do if he finds you?"

"Probably try to run me down with a car or shoot me when no one's around."

"Does that frighten you?"

Luke forced a smile. "Not really. I'm prepared."

"Prepared for what?"

"To meet God."

Vincent smiled back. Luke asked, "What would you do if you saw him again?"

Pulling the gun out of his belt, Vincent aimed it at the wall and said, "No question about it, I would shoot him as soon as I could. I want him to pay and, more important, I want him dead."

✝

## 69

**LUKE COULDN'T SLEEP. HE** stared out the skylight and watched as eerie-looking clouds floated by, alternately obscuring and revealing the bright full moon. Vincent evidently wasn't sleeping either, for Luke could hear him tossing and turning in the next room. How could they sleep, knowing that Fatih was in Boston? The cold reality was that Fatih was probably hunting for Luke at this very minute. Luke was tortured thinking about what he would do when he came face to face with his brother's killer. He thought about what Vincent had said. Did Luke also want Fatih dead, or could he be satisfied with him just being captured? If it came down to a choice, would he kill Fatih to save his own life? Horrified, Luke wondered what kind of priest thought like this.

He glanced at the clock and saw that it was 4:12 a.m. Feeling the boat move, he figured that Vincent was taking Justice for a walk. Looking up at the skylight, he heard a muffled crack and saw something splatter on the glass. Hearing another, he heard Justice yelp. Realizing what was happening, he knew he was trapped. He could hear footsteps approaching, but he didn't have time to lock the door. Petrified, he crouched down next to the bed, feeling helpless. His mind raced, and suddenly he had an idea. He reached up to the top of the nightstand and frantically felt for the skylight control panel. Finding it, he punched each button until it began opening. When it had moved just a few inches, the door crashed open.

Like a trained assassin, Fatih quickly scanned the room, looking for his victim. When his eyes met Luke's, he smirked and slowly raised his gun, confident that this would be an easy kill. Desperate, Luke one-handedly grabbed the box of Blade's ashes from the nightstand and hurled it at Fatih with all his strength, still forcing down the skylight switch with his other hand. All those years of baseball pitching finally paid off; his aim was perfect. The box hit Fatih squarely in the head and unexpectedly popped open, filling the air with ashes. The room went dark. Luke could barely make out the bright moon through the skylight above him. He knew his cell phone was on the bed, and taking advantage of the darkness, he desperately began running his hands over the covers in an attempt to find it. Finally, feeling it but unable to see the display, he fumbled for the send button, knowing that Detective Romo had been the last person he called. He pushed it twice.

Hoping that the skylight had opened enough for him to escape, he jumped on the bed and reached through the opening, pulling his body up with his arms. When he was halfway out, he began hearing shots and saw flashes of light in the dust as Fatih began blasting aimlessly.

Crouching down on the bow of the boat, he saw Vincent's lifeless body. The white deck was covered with deep red blood. Luke could clearly see the bullet hole in Vincent's forehead, and when he moved closer he was horrified to see that the entire back of Vincent's head was gone. In anguish, he stood and ran to the small railing surrounding the bow. Hearing another shot, his heart pounded as he saw Fatih halfway out of the skylight, pointing the gun directly at him. He had no choice but to jump. Looking quickly at the frozen water, he didn't hesitate. He pushed off hard enough to reach the thick ice, away from the boat's aerated perimeter. Landing hard, he felt the wind knocked out of him. As he struggled to recover, he saw Fatih's monstrous eyes looking down at him from the boat. Staggering up, he began running full speed away from the yacht. Suddenly, he felt a burning sensation in his left hamstring; he knew he was hit. He reached down to grab his leg and confirmed what he already knew. His hand was drenched in blood.

He heard a loud grunt behind him as Fatih landed on the ice. Terrified, Luke looked back to see that Fatih was catching up. With his injured leg he was no match, and he knew it wouldn't be long until he was dead. He pleaded to God for help. Knowing that Fatih was just feet behind him, he was puzzled that he hadn't yet shot. Suddenly, he saw Fatih's gun slide past him on the slick ice. Bewildered, he stopped and turned. Fatih had somehow fallen through the same ice that Luke had just run across. Each time Fatih tried to hoist himself out, the ice around him fractured as if it were paper thin. Snatching the gun at his feet, Luke pointed it at Fatih, who was screaming in agony in the freezing water. Thinking about Aaron's death and overcome with anger, Luke aimed at Fatih's head and slowly squeezed the trigger.

Immediately consumed with remorse, Luke flung the gun away, extended his arms, and began to plead for forgiveness both for himself and Fatih. Interrupted by the sound of a nearby helicopter, he took off his belt and pulled it tightly around his upper thigh. Dizzy from fear, the cold air, and loss of blood, Luke staggered toward shore but fell and passed out after taking a few steps.

# 70

**LUKE'S EYES FLUTTERED OPEN.** He was surprised to see Deborah, not God. She was sitting in a chair, bent over, with her head lying on the side of his hospital bed. As his eyes adjusted to the light, he quietly watched her sleep and wondered what had happened. Hearing him stir, she gradually opened her eyes, which immediately filled with tears when she saw him looking back at her. Quickly standing, she shoved her chair aside and leaned over to hug him, carefully making sure that she didn't disturb the needles and tubes in his arms.

When she released her grasp, he mumbled, "Is everyone safe?" Tears fell from her eyes as she said, "Everyone except for Vincent and the cabdriver Fatih killed." Luke was still groggy from anesthesia, but he silently wept as he thought about his friend from the Cape. A nurse walked into the room and excitedly asked, "How long has he been awake?"

"About five minutes," Deb answered.

The nurse bent down and said, "Father Luke, it's a true honor to have you in our hospital."

Confused, he simply said, "Thank you."

As the nurse walked out, Luke was surprised to see a police officer standing by the doorway.

"Deborah, what's going on? How long have I been here?"

She smiled. "You were brought here last night. It's late afternoon now. They had to operate on your leg, but everything is going to be fine."

Tired and groggy, he closed his heavy eyes again.

---

The next time Luke awakened, his parents were in the room. Uncharacteristically, his father came over to the side of his bed and grabbed his hand. No words were spoken, but the expression on his father's face alone was enough to assure Luke that all the past disapprovals and disappointments in him were gone. His mother looked on, crying tears of joy that her husband had finally forgiven her youngest son.

Out of nowhere, Luke asked, "Is he dead?"

They didn't have to ask who he was talking about. Luke's father spoke up. "Your brother's killer is alive, but the cops have him and he will pay."

Still exhausted, Luke closed his eyes again.

---

The next morning, Luke was feeling stronger as he lay in bed and watched the sun rise outside his window. He reached for the television remote and pressed the power button several times, but it wouldn't turn on. When a nurse walked in he said, "Good morning, do you know when I can get out of here?"

"No, but the doctor will be in to see you sometime this morning."

He tried the remote again. "Also, can you please have my television turned on?"

She hesitated and stammered, "I'm sorry. The orders were for no TV."

Before Luke could question her, she quickly hurried out. Again, he noticed a police officer outside his room.

A few hours later, Deborah appeared, and Luke asked, "Deb, what's going on? They won't let me watch TV."

She sighed and leaned over to press the call button by his bed. Immediately, Luke's private nurse, Tasha, arrived, and Deborah asked, "Can you please help me move his bed to the window?"

They carefully positioned his bed so he could see and drew back the drapes. Looking out the window, Luke was amazed.

## 71

**A CROWD HAD GATHERED** on the street in front of the hospital. Police cars lined the entrances. It looked like the last time the pope had visited Boston. Innocently, Luke asked, "What are they doing here?"

Tasha and Deb looked at each other and laughed. Tasha said, "They're all here to see you!"

Confused, he asked, "For catching Fatih?"

Deborah explained, "Luke, you're a national hero."

"What do you mean?"

Ignoring his question, she said, "Monsignor Swiger and the bishop are waiting to see you."

"The bishop? What does he have to do with this?"

Ignoring him again, Deborah opened the door and the two men rushed to Luke's bedside.

Swiger spoke first. "Father Luke, thank God you're safe."

Luke smiled. The bishop added, "I am truly blessed to finally meet you."

Luke was mystified. Why all the fuss? Sensing this, Deborah walked over to the bed and handed him a folder from her tote bag. As he opened it, she said, "These pictures were taken from a medical helicopter that had passed over you after dropping two accident victims at the hospital."

Luke stared in disbelief. The first picture showed Luke running across the ice with Fatih following. The second photo was of Luke's bloody footprints on the snow-covered ice. The next one showed Luke looking at his blood-soaked hand, with Fatih directly behind him. Flipping to the next picture, Luke was stunned. Fatih had fallen through the ice, and Luke was standing over him, praying with his arms outstretched to his sides. The combination of the dark red blood in the pure white snow, along with the full moon, gave the photo an unnerving appearance. But what he saw next was even more shocking.

With his arms outstretched and the moon to his back, a dark shadow in the shape of a cross was cast on the bright snow-covered ice. The way Fatih was positioned made it appear that he was clutching the cross in an attempt to be saved. The blood, the moonlight, the cross, and the gun at Luke's feet created a scene that was unearthly. Hollywood couldn't have done a better job.

Bishop Dunne spoke up. "Luke, these pictures have been in every newspaper. Many people believe that they show the triumph of Christianity over Islam, since the Muslim man is grasping the cross in an attempt to be saved. Of course, the Muslim community denounces this. This is the biggest religious event in the world."

Confused again, Luke said, "But, it's just a few pictures."

Both priests looked at Deborah.

She grabbed his hand and took a deep breath. "There's more to it, Luke. The crime scene investigators have determined that the only explanation is that as you ran on the ice away from the boat, the water changed from a mixture of fresh and salt to all salt. Because of this, the farther you ran, the thinner the ice became." Luke remembered what Vincent had told him. "In the spot where you were standing, the ice was less than half an inch thick. Fatih is much shorter than you and weighs at least twenty-five pounds less." Stating the obvious, she continued, "Don't you see? He fell through the ice and you didn't. When the police helicopter rescued you, they said that every piece of ice they touched was so thin that it shattered, and yet you inexplicably lay on top of it. People around the world are calling it a miracle."

She reached into her bag and handed Luke a newspaper. The front page showed the picture of Luke praying over Fatih and the headline read: "Miracle on Ice!" The bishop interjected. "Luke, even when you passed out, the force of your fall didn't break the ice." Deborah handed him another newspaper. This time the headline read, "He Walks on Water!" The subheading read, "Second Coming?"

Luke scoffed. "This is crazy. It was just luck."

"Don't be so sure," said Deborah. She reached over and pushed the call button. When Tasha opened the door, Deborah said, "Can you please ask the doctor to come in?" A few minutes later the door opened, and a gray-haired man entered and came to Luke's bedside. Deborah took charge. "Doctor Friedman, can you please explain to Luke what you found when you operated on his leg?"

He smiled. "Father, you're a very lucky man. Most people don't understand that getting shot in the leg can be very serious and is often fatal. The femoral artery in the leg is one of the largest arteries in the entire body, second only to the aorta that leads directly to the heart. The pressure in the femoral artery is enormous. There have been reports of blood shooting over six feet when that artery is severed, and in most cases the victim dies in a matter of seconds."

Wanting him to get to the point, Luke asked, "Was my artery hit?"

"Yes, but the bullet actually lodged in it and stopped you from bleeding to death. Because Fatih was so close to you when you were shot, the bullet was still extremely hot when it entered your body. The hot slug actually cauterized your artery. I've never seen or heard of anything like this happening before. Only a few strands of artery tissue held it together. If they had snapped, the artery would have contracted and retracted into your body. Once that had happened, you would have died seconds later. If Fatih was farther away when he pulled the trigger, the bullet probably wouldn't have been hot enough to cauterize the wound."

Now stunned, Luke was convinced that God had been with him on the ice.

Deborah nodded to the doctor, who continued, "When I gave the police the bullet I had extracted from your leg during surgery, they explained that it was a hollow point; it's meant to splinter upon impact. You, Vincent Russo, and the taxi driver were shot with bullets from the same gun. The slugs that killed them splintered, but yours didn't. If it had, you would be dead." He added, "I'm a Jew, Father Luke, but I must say that when I think about everything that's happened to you, there's no rational explanation for you still being alive. It truly is a miracle."

# 72

**TWO DAYS LATER, WHEN** the staff wheeled Luke out of the hospital, there was pandemonium. Crowds lined the streets trying to get a glimpse of him. The Vatican had even sent a special investigation team to Boston. People all over the world were celebrating, with one exception: the followers of Islam.

Many pro-Muslim groups were saying that the police rescued Luke first, even though he wasn't in imminent danger, and by doing this, Fatih stayed in the freezing water longer than he should have. He developed severe frostbite and as a result had to have both of his feet and several fingers amputated. It was insinuated that Detective Romo was the person responsible for making that decision. When Luke found out about the amputations, he reflected on the irony, considering what Fatih had done to his own mother.

Although Dr. Friedman wanted him to rest, Luke insisted that he say the funeral mass for Vincent at Saint Leonard's. On his way to the church, he was amazed to see people lining the streets and cheering as his limousine passed. They held signs, threw flowers at the car, and blessed themselves. When his motorcade pulled onto Hanover Street, it was so crowded that they couldn't move. Ignoring police orders, people surrounded his car and tried to get a glimpse of him through the tinted windows.

It took more than forty-five minutes for Luke to get to the church. Once inside, he sat in his wheelchair in the sacristy. Every prominent church leader was attending the service. Luke asked one of his fellow priests, "Can you please get Vincent's sister, Trinity? I want to see her before the service." A few minutes later, the door opened, and Trinity stepped into the room. She knelt down in front of him and cried while he bent over to embrace her.

"Thank you so much," she said.

Confused, he replied, "For what?"

"For putting Vincent on the phone the other day. If it wasn't for you, I wouldn't have had a chance to talk to him before he died."

She looked at Luke and wiped tears from her eyes. "Do you know the last thing I said to him?"

Luke shook his head.

"I told him that I loved him."

When it was time for the Mass to start, Trinity asked if she could wheel Luke to the altar. Followed by a large procession of priests and altar boys holding candles, they made their way down the crowded aisle. People stood and struggled to get a glimpse of Luke as Trinity pushed the now even more famous priest to the front of the church, with her daughter by her side.

Once on the altar, Luke looked out at the jam-packed church. He thought about the last time he had stood there, for Brad Thompson's funeral. So much had happened since that day. Then, against the doctor's orders and to everyone's amazement, Luke stood, extended his hands out to his sides, and began the service. The image of Luke standing and praying in this position overwhelmed many people in the audience, and they began weeping. Standing for the entire mass, he recounted his last days with Vincent, explaining to everyone that without his help, Luke would have never found Fatih. Luke reiterated that Vincent had helped solve one of the biggest crime mysteries in the history of Boston, and in doing so, had renewed the faith of millions. Luke ended by saying, "Because of this, I'm sure that Vincent was prepared and smiling when God welcomed him home."

After an extremely moving and emotional service, Luke wanted to have a few minutes alone in the church. For security reasons, he couldn't attend the burial service at the cemetery. Once the church had emptied, he slowly wheeled himself to the statue of Mary holding the crucified Christ. Finally having a minute to reflect on the events of the past few days, he started to weep. There was no denying the fact that he had put into motion the events that ultimately caused Blade's and Vincent's deaths. Was finding Aaron's killers worth two innocent lives in return? And what about Fatih? Would his incarceration prevent future attacks and inevitably save the lives of many other innocent people? Knowing what he knew now, would he have made the same choices if he had to do it all over again? Looking at the statue while wiping the tears from his face, Luke knew that he would have to bear the burden of these questions for the rest of his life. After several minutes, he finally composed himself and once again thanked God for his protection and guidance in finding Aaron's killers. Before leaving, he asked for the answer to the one thing that he still hadn't figured out: Who was the target of the bombing and why?

Once he finished praying, Luke turned and began wheeling himself toward the back of the church. Standing near the exit were two men in dark suits. Luke recognized Mike Dempsey, the FBI agent who had questioned him at Aaron's house, but he didn't recognize the man standing next to him. Dempsey flashed an artificial smile and said, "Nice to see you again, Father." Luke stared suspiciously but didn't respond. Looking at the other man, Luke extended his hand and said, "I don't believe we've met."

Shaking hands, the man replied, "Joe Tanner."

"Are you also with the FBI?"

Taken aback with Luke's direct question, the man looked at Dempsey and stammered, "No, I'm with the Justice Department."

Distrusting Dempsey and wanting to get to the point, Luke asked, "How can I help you?"

Dempsey took charge. "Do you know anything about the deaths of Ismail and Kamilah Abu?"

Luke's heart raced. "What? They're dead?"

"Yes. They were found in their compound in Riyadh when it was being searched for evidence."

"How did they die?"

"They were assassinated. Each one had a single shot fired into the back of the head."

Luke looked down and said a silent prayer for Fatih's mother. Dempsey asked, "Do you know where Jamilah Raboud is?"

Ignoring his question, Luke replied, "What does she have to do with this?"

"We want to talk with her."

Luke answered vaguely but honestly, "I haven't seen her in a few days."

Dismissing his answer, Dempsey asked sharply, "Did Fatih say anything to you when he was on the ice?"

Annoyed with his tone and rudeness, Luke sternly replied, "You seem to be fishing for something. What exactly are you looking for?"

"We're trying to figure out why Fatih planted the bombs."

Luke sensed that he was holding back information and sarcastically replied, "That's funny; me too."

Dempsey stared at Luke and shot back, "You don't know what you're getting into. You'd better stay out of this." Composing himself, he toned down his voice and said, "Leave this investigation to us."

Luke fired back, "If I would have done that with the bombing, Fatih would still be having fun in Saudi Arabia."

The door of the church opened, and Detective Romo entered. Seeing Luke with the two feds, he hurried over. When Dempsey extended his hand, the detective ignored it and said, "I know who you are. My men called to tell me that you flashed your badge and ignored their orders to leave the church grounds. In case you didn't get the memo, Father Miller's protection is under my jurisdiction. I would suggest you leave unless you want Luke to contact his lawyer."

Dempsey looked around, smirked, and said, "I thought we were all on the same side."

Romo positioned himself behind Luke's wheelchair and replied, "I doubt that."

Dempsey motioned to his friend from the Justice Department and said, "Detective, just wanted to let you know that Joe will be stopping by the police station to talk to you about the way Fatih was handled the night Father Miller was rescued."

Romo stopped, turned, and threatened, "If you want to prosecute me for saving a man of God before a mass murderer, I look forward to it. But please, make sure the trial takes place in Boston."

Tanner spoke up. "All people are equal under the law."

"Not everyone," Romo retorted, watching them leave.

When Romo backed out of the church door with Luke, hundreds of cameras snapped and thousands of people screamed. Police officers on horseback now lined the congested street. Surrounded by cops, Luke was ushered into a waiting limo. Once away from the crowds and back on the main road toward Aaron's house, he tried to relax.

He felt his phone vibrating and looked at the display. Despite the fact that it was a private number, he decided to answer it anyway.

She was in a panic. "Luke, are you all right?"

He immediately knew who it was. "Yes, Jami, what's wrong?"

"I only have a few seconds. Fatih's mother and father have been killed."

"I know; two FBI agents just told me. I can't believe that Layth had them executed. I thought they would get a fair trial. Fatih's mother was innocent."

She broke in. "Luke, that's why I'm calling. Layth didn't have them killed. He thinks it was someone in the government."

"Why would your Saudi government want them dead?"

"Not *my* government. Yours!"

# EPILOGUE

*"The United States is not, and never will be, at war with Islam."*
—Barack Obama

*"The question that needs to be asked is if radical Islam*
*is at war with the United States."*
—Dale Allan

**LUKE LOOKED THROUGH THE** etched glass windows and watched the falling snow. He could see the security guards at the front gate and knew that others surrounded the entire property. Although he realized that it was for his own good, he felt like a prisoner. For the past week, police had set up roadblocks, only allowing residents who owned homes in Aaron's neighborhood to enter the area.

This time, living at Aaron's house was different. There was closure. Luke's parents had moved back, and his mother babied him like an injured child. He walked with a slight limp, but his doctors assured him that over time he would walk normally again. The combination of no rigorous exercise and his mother's home cooking had caused him to gain a little weight.

Almost overnight, Luke had become one of the most recognizable religious figures in the world. Hordes of terminally ill people traveled long distances in hopes of seeing him and being miraculously healed by the immortal priest who was anointed by God himself. This legendary status was a blessing and a curse. While it brought multitudes of people to churches all over the world, there were many Muslim extremists who wanted to see Luke dead, or better yet, kill him themselves. Trying to protect their star priest, the Vatican assigned two undercover guards to shadow him when he was in public.

The pope's assistant had traveled to Boston to meet with Luke personally. Luke agreed to go to Rome for Christmas as long as his parents, Deborah, and the children could come along. Luke was scheduled to be introduced by the pope to the crowd in Vatican Square during the celebratory blessing. They would be the honorary guests of the pope himself and stay within the confines of the Vatican, where he and his family could be protected. Fearing for his safety, the Church had offered sanctuary to Luke and his family for as long as they wanted.

Luke had promised Detective Romo that he would meet with him before leaving for Rome. He now waited for a police car to pick him up. Seeing the gates open, he told Deb, "I'll see you in an hour."

She hugged him. "Be careful."

This was the first time Luke had been out of the house since Vincent's funeral. The crisp winter air felt good as he took several deep breaths, then walked deliberately with a cane toward the unmarked police car in the driveway, the snow crunching under his boots.

A young officer jumped out of the car, bowed in respect, and said, "Right this way, Father."

He opened the door and Luke got inside. There was another, older police officer sitting in the front. After introducing himself, he said, "Detective Romo is going to meet you at the cemetery—the same place you met before."

Luke wondered why they needed to be secretive again, but he only nodded.

Once they passed several impromptu police roadblocks, Luke was convinced that no one could have followed them. Arriving at the cemetery gate, Luke pulled up his hood and got out of the car, along with the two plainclothes officers, who remained in the street. The two Vatican guards that had followed in another car flanked Luke as he proceeded up the path. Approaching the bench, he saw Romo waiting. Luke asked the guards to stay in the distance as the detective wiped the snow away so he could sit down.

Looking straight ahead, Romo chuckled and said, "Father Luke, you're amazing. You're the only one who would have believed that Franklyn Hennessey had the answer to the bombing in Boston."

Luke smiled ruefully. The detective reached under his coat and pulled out a folder. He handed it to Luke without saying a word. Opening it, Luke saw more pictures of himself on the ice with Fatih, but he hadn't seen these particular photos before, and he wondered why not. In the first photo, Luke was standing on the thin ice pointing the gun at Fatih's head. In the second one, he could see the smoke at the end of the barrel after he had shot, and the petrified look on Fatih's face. The next one showed Luke passed out on the snow-covered ice in a puddle of his own crimson blood.

The detective broke his silence. "I thought you might want these. The medical photographer who took the pictures from the helicopter is a friend of mine. No one else has copies, and the chip has been destroyed."

Luke thanked him.

Romo smiled. "I can't believe you missed him when you were standing so close."

Luke looked up. "I didn't miss. I couldn't kill him. I wanted to, but at the last minute, I moved the gun and shot into the water. How could I ever expect to be forgiven for my sins if I didn't forgive him?"

Surprised, Romo replied, "So you've forgiven him?"

Luke sighed. "Let's just say I'm working on it."

Then Romo reached into his outside coat pocket and handed him Aaron's gun. "This was found on the boat. I thought you might want it."

"No thanks, you keep it."

Turning to look at him, the detective reminded Luke of the danger he was in. "There are more death threats against you than almost anyone in the world. I think you should keep it."

Luke thought for a few seconds and reluctantly put the gun in his coat pocket. "Thanks, I'll hide it in the closet."

Romo added, "But that's not the reason I wanted to see you."

"There's something else?"

"Yes, I have a confession to make."

"What's that?"

"Luke I'm going to tell you something, but you can't say you heard it from me." Luke agreed, and Romo continued. "When that Muslim guy, Fatih, was brought to the police station after being pulled from the water, but before he went to the hospital, he was read his Miranda rights and he immediately refused to talk. He knew the law very well and demanded his one phone call. Well, after he made his call, let's just say, we got the number."

"What do you mean, you got the number?"

Romo hesitated. "Well, it's not exactly legal, but we had a trace on the phone he used. Sometimes we use the phone numbers that criminals call to help us solve cases. We don't record their conversations or anything like that, but we trap the numbers." He handed Luke a piece of paper. Luke looked at it, not understanding.

Detective Romo asked, "Don't you recognize that number?"

Puzzled, Luke read it again and replied, "No, should I?"

"Look again," the Detective demanded.

Luke said out loud, "202-456-"

Romo interrupted. "Luke, 202 is the area code, and all of the numbers to the White House start with 456."

Luke looked at him in disbelief. "He called the White House?"

Detective Romo nodded.